Leaping Man Hill

By Carol Emshwiller

Leaping Man Hill

by

Carol Emshwiller

MERCURY HOUSE ● SAN FRANCISCO

Published in the United States by Mercury House, San Francisco,
California, a nonprofit publishing company devoted to the free exchange
of ideas and guided by a dedication to literary values.

United States Constitution, First Amendment: Congress shall make no law
respecting an establishment of religion, or prohibiting the free exercise
thereof; or abridging the freedom of speech, or of the press; or the right of
the people peaceably to assemble, and to petition the Government
for a redress of grievances.

Cover design by Thomas Christensen.
Cover art, "Paradise Valley," 1987, by Russell Chatham.

Mercury House and colophon are registered trademarks of
Mercury House, Incorporated.
www.wenet.net/~mercury

Printed on acid-free paper
Manufactured in the United States of America.

This book has been made possible in part by
generous support from the Lannan Foundation.

Library of Congress Cataloging in Publication Data
Emshwiller, Carol.
Leaping Man Hill / by Carol Emshwiller.
p.   cm.
ISBN 1-56279-111-7 (paperback : acid-free paper)
I. Title.
PS3555.M54L38   1999
813'.54—DC21   99-33522
CIP

To David Prokash Mutch,
who, like my Abel, is small for his age, and
who was nine when I began this book.

Mary Catherine

I SING-SONG OUT, "Abel, Abel, under the table." That's where he is, all hunched up in a little ball, scared of me I hope, except he looks calm. "Abel isn't able. Abel isn't able … to do anything. He can hum, though. I heard you. You can't pretend you didn't."

That boy's been treated much too kind. Maybe he'll talk pretty soon just so he can tell on me. But probably nobody would listen, especially not his mother. Maybe not much use in talking around here. Maybe that's how it all began.

They say he never did talk. Not ever. Not one single word. With his big brother it's different. He talked just like anybody else and then he got badly beat up and his daddy died and all of a sudden he didn't anymore. With his big brother it makes some sense, but Abel is nine years old and never did know his father and never got beat up as far as I know. He's just copycatting. But a child needs talk around, good or bad, it doesn't matter which. At least *I* expect to do a lot of it.

They live far out. I had to hitch a ride with somebody going that way, but they wouldn't take me all the way on in so I had to walk from their front pasture. The ditches were overflowing and the pasture was too wet. Odd for the desert, but I'd heard about too much water coming down from the mountains this year because of too much snow up there. I thought I'd have to walk through mud, but the road was pretty clear. I could see the house and barns not so far off. You couldn't miss them with those Lombardy poplars around.

I didn't have a lot to carry, but my books are heavy. I had to stop and rest a couple of times. The road is a desert sort of road, perfectly straight and no trees, so I kept hoping somebody would look out the window and see me and come and help me. Of course now that I've been here a day or so, I know better. I'm surprised the mother got out of bed to greet me at all. (Abel must have been hiding. I didn't meet him till supper. Stuck out here all by himself—I mean with just these three people, he can't have seen many strangers. It was the big sister, Charlotte, who hired me. I didn't see her again till the next morning.

She's the one who takes care of everything. She spent the night out with the cows.) The mom was all mussed up from having just got out of bed. She looked embarrassed. She said she didn't remember I was coming today, but now that I know her a little bit, I know she never knows what day it is anyway.

She had stains all down the front of her dress.

Those two brothers look alike except the big one is dark and Abel is a redhead. Well, a pink head like their mom, except she's getting gray. (Just try to get *her* to say something. She will if she has to, but she doesn't have to very often.) When the big one was Abel's age, they thought school would make him talk again, but they say he ran out the back door every time they put him in the front until they gave up. That's why they got me for Abel. They didn't even try school. Besides, they weren't sure Abel could speak at all. With the big one, at least they knew he could. He can read and write. The mom taught him that much. I'm only two years older than he is. If I hadn't already said, I could pretend I was the same age as him.

If he fell in love, maybe that big one would open his mouth and not just to eat; maybe say "I love you," and "Marry me." Nice if it was a teacher who could teach him something. Nice if it was me. I'm supposed to work on Abel, but I think I'll work on the big one in a different way.

I do like the big one. Mainly I like that he's quiet. And there's things I like about this place, too, though it's all tumbledown. You can see how nice it could be with just a little doing. I thought to get a can of paint myself and find a hammer and nails. They wouldn't notice if something got fixed anyway. The big sister and brother only do what's necessary for the stock, and the mom does even less than necessary. She's supposed to do the house stuff. The chickens don't die and the Jersey gets milked.

I thought that grown-up sister was a man when I first came. She seems a lot more like a man than the big brother. Her clothes are all loose so she looks thick. She stamps around in men's boots. I heard her swearing. Her mother doesn't care. The big sister gave me her room. I don't know where she sleeps now. (I wouldn't be surprised if she wasn't sleeping out in the cow barn.) Her cot's small and looks as if she made it herself. There's a good strong lock on the door. That's homemade, too. She laughed when she showed it to me and the secret way it worked. She said she made it when she was, maybe, ten years old. She said she doesn't know anymore what she was trying to lock out back then. "Everything, I guess. Everything and everybody." I knew exactly what she meant and said so. Her, at least, you can talk to and get an answer back.

At first I was thinking she probably didn't even own a dress, but then I saw these fancy shoes she'd left under the bed by mistake. She looked embarrassed when I gave them to her.

I was surprised when they gave me a room of my own. Lots of times I've had to sleep on a folding cot in the kitchen or some such place, and lots of times my job wasn't just to teach, but to milk the cows and feed the pigs and chickens. Once I was supposed to do all that and cook, too. I didn't mind as much as you might think. I had worse at home when I was little. But here, all I have to do is Abel. It's like a vacation—not that I've ever had one to know what that's like.

They couldn't always have lived this way—everything gone to pieces. They have a closed-up parlor I sneaked into. There's a fancy organ there. Mice ran out of it when I went into the room. The sofa has gold-colored upholstery. There's a lamp with beaded red fringe. You can tell they never use that room. There's sandy dust all over. I'm going to clean it up and teach in there. I won't ask permission, I'll just do it and see what happens. I haven't had a whole lot of elegance in my life. *So far,* that is. It's a small room. All the rooms in this house are small except for the big eat-in kitchen where there's a big fireplace and a moth-eaten bearskin rug with the head still on it. It looks as if some dog's been chewing at it.

Of course if you want to look out at something nice, there's always those snowcapped mountains. Some people might think I'm a little bit crazy because I talk to mountains when I'm off by myself. I started when I was about three years old. I always did it after I got whipped. I never talked to the highest, just the second or third highest. When I was little I thought the highest wouldn't bother listening to a little girl with nothing but little-girl problems. I still do it that way. I wonder if I could get Abel to talk to a mountain? I wonder if there's one he likes better than all the others?

Talk or no, I'm supposed to stuff some learning down him. They said to get to know each other first, but what's to know about somebody who never says a word? He can nod and he can hum. That's what's to know. I told him, "I ask a question, and if I don't get some kind of a head shake, then one pinch to the funny bone." A pinch hurts and doesn't show. I demonstrated. That's how he ended up under the table.

I tell Abel I never knew my father either. I say, "That doesn't make me special. I was whipped regular as clock-work. Catch me not talking and they'd have put a stop to that soon enough. And *I* say, if you can hum, you can talk, and *I* say, if you think you've got everything just the way you want it here, well, not anymore you don't."

And then I go right down under the table myself and pull him out and give him another pinch to the elbow, but this time I have a good grip on him. He doesn't make a sound. I can tell I hurt him, but he doesn't look at all scared and I want him scared. I tell him I'm an old witch. I say I'm a hundred years old. I say, "Look at me. You can see the witch color in my eyes." I hold my face real close to his and he looks and then shuts his eyes after—like he doesn't want to see my witchiness. (My eyes are just like anybody else's, but he'll think they're not. You tell a little kid things like that and they just about always believe, and, even if they don't exactly believe, they half-believe.)

I say, "You watch out when it gets to be a full moon."

They already told me he might run off. I know how to handle that. I tie an old lead rope around his ankle and tie him to the organ and we get to work. "Pay attention to the old witch," I say. I keep my hand near his elbow. He knows why. At first I thought maybe he was stupid as well as mute, and that nobody in the family would admit it, but he understands fast enough.

A is for apple, juicy and red.

B is for bird, so sweet to be heard …

I change them.

A is for Abel, who's ugly as sin.

B is for bee, all ready to sting.

C is for crybaby, D is for dumb, E is for empty, F is for false, G is for *gotcha!* And I grab him. I'm the only one who laughs.

"Now draw me these letters. Or else you-know-what."

He does, and nicely, too. That's what I call one-time learning, or maybe two-time. A couple of pinches is all it takes. Most people don't know about those nerves. I guess I really *am* like a witch. But if anybody has witchy eyes, it's Abel. His eyes are sort of the same color as his hair, except darker, kind of orangy. I got a good look at them when I made him look at mine.

Next morning the big sister and brother go off to wherever it is they go—out for maybe two days (the sister says she can't say for sure how long) to bring the cows down from the mountains. She says sometimes the cows get where you wouldn't believe. After they leave, the mom cleans up the kitchen and then goes back to bed, which is her usual way. We'll have the whole place to ourselves, me and Abel. Except I can't find him. We have our biscuits with bacon grease and then he's gone. I search all over—all kinds of cubbyholes. I even search the cold cave, which looks as if it hasn't had ice in it for a long time. It's full of sawdust and oblong, rubbery eggs. Abel is small for his age (*if* they've got his age right), he'll fit into all sorts of cubbyholes. At least I get to know this place better. It really is a rundown mess. (I find out the big sister *does* sleep in the loft of the milk cow barn. She has an old hump-backed trunk up there, and a box with her clock on it, and an army cot with moth-eaten army blankets, and a sconce for her lamp. There's drawings thumbtacked to the wall. There's her drawings all over the house, and those are her paintings of mountains in the parlor.)

Well, I should have been looking up. I should have been thinking "monkey." Abel makes me think of a monkey anyway—little monkey face, and those sad eyes. Orangutan kind of hair color. Those eyes of his are going to be a lot sadder after I get my hands on him. Maybe he thinks I'm scared to get up on the roof. I don't know how he did it, but I'm going to use the ladder. At least it's not the barn roof. That's three times as high.

So we chase each other across the ridge and I win, except I tear my skirt. Abel probably tore his pants, but they already have so many tears you can't tell.

No one has ever told that child not to do *anything*. I'll bet he's climbed everything he had a mind to since—well, probably since *before* he could walk. I don't know how he survived to get to be nine.

This time I tie Abel to me and we go off for a long walk—out where his ma can't see or hear us. We sit under a willow beside the stream. There used to be a dam here, but it's been broken through and never repaired. You can see where there once was a nice pond.

I sing the alphabet song three times. Then I tell Abel to move his lips along with mine so I can see, and that I don't have to hear anything since I can read lips. (I can't really, but well enough for now.) He does. Obedient little fellow. You'd think he'd refuse. What could I do if he did except the same old pinching? I won't beat on him. I don't ever do that kind of thing. Besides, it shows. And then I don't want to be like my mother and stepfathers. Anyway, I know my pinches hurt just as much. I know because how I learned about them was that one of my stepfathers did it to me, even though nobody cared if things showed on me or not. I have the scars to prove it. I didn't learn how to pinch like that right away. I had to practice. Even on myself. When I got good at it I got to be a scary person. I always denied it when the other kids tattled on me. Lots of times a teacher looked at somebody's wrist or elbow and said, No harm done that she could see. Teachers liked me because I worked so hard, not only on my class work, but I helped with everything. I always got the top grades. I always won all the prizes. I wanted to make something of myself. Those teachers never believed anything anybody said against me. They thought the other children were jealous. They gave me good recommendations as a tutor and then, of course, my grades and prizes proved how good I am. I don't have a bad temper. I don't need one. Things usually work out my way. I'm always very calm. That scares people, too, which stands me in good stead.

It's good the brother and sister are gone because both at noon dinner and also at supper I tie Abel to his chair and the mom doesn't even notice. I knew she wouldn't. She's a terrible cook. Dinner is leftover bacon (left over from when?) and leftover biscuits. Abel eats like it's always this way. He hums as he eats and kicks the table leg. It's annoying but the mom doesn't say not to. I'll put a stop to that later. (He does this because the big brother isn't here. At breakfast, Abel ate sitting on his lap. You can see how Abel wants to be just like him—not talking and all.)

(They call that big brother Fay. No wonder the big sister is more like a man than he is.)

For supper we have beef stew. I think the big sister must have made it. At least the mom found the energy to warm it up. Or maybe it sat at the back of the stove all this time. We'll probably have it tomorrow and the next day, too. There's a lot of it. But it isn't as if I had any better fare myself most of my growing up.

That night I tie Abel to the bed, but of course he unties himself. (I used to untie myself, too.) He's gone *before* breakfast this time. I look all around again, tops of rooves and way out, but I don't find him. (I do find some old dried-up paint which I throw out, down behind the outhouse, and I find some hammers and nails and such.) Abel comes in on his own for noon dinner. I guess he got hungry without his breakfast— those biscuits and bacon grease.

I grab him and pinch him real good. Wrist, too. I know I hurt him, but what I see in his eyes isn't fear—never is. There's something calm there. Sort of as if, if he could or would talk, he'd say, "Oh." Just, "Oh," like: "So this is how it is."

I say, "Don't you want to learn anything? You want to be stupid all your life? Like you are right now? I'll bet your dead daddy wouldn't like that."

He looks away, thinking about it.

"Your dead dad would wallop you good if he knew all what you do." But Abel shakes his head, No, slowly, several times. I can almost hear him say his daddy wouldn't.

"Yes he would. You never knew him. What do you know."

But he shakes his head again.

"Your mom doesn't count. She's too tired to whup you, otherwise she'd have done it a long time ago."

He keeps on shaking his head.

"Be that as it may," I say, "now you've gone and done it. I'm going to pull out all my witching. I'm making this big magic circle. You go outside of it, you'll die in excruciating agony. *Excruciating!* So: the front fence, the rear pasture, the near ditch at the end of the vegetable garden. That leaves you more room than you need." (All I know about witching would fit in two peas.)

Then I pretend to cast a spell. I talk all sorts of nonsense. I make up a fancy sign that I scratch on some of the fence posts and the ditch gates. Then I make a couple of tiny branding irons out of fence wire, and I make a little fire, and when the brands are redhot I brand Abel D for dumb (I guess he'll learn the letter D fast enough) and then an arrow. I put these where they don't show, under his arm. They're not much bigger than a splinter—kind of a big splinter. "That arrow always points to me, even if it has to turn around to do it," I say. "Watch it good and you'll see." On myself—on the back of my hand right where he, and everybody, can see it, I burn another arrow. I tell him when he stops being dumb I'll change his D to a secret, very, very lucky sign. I tell him the arrow means I'll always be able to catch him, so I don't have to bother tying him up anymore.

After we finish with all this, I decide I'll not go on with the alphabet right now. I have a big animal book with hand-colored pictures and animal information. I sit Abel down next to me and read to him out of it, and pretty soon he's really listening. Tigers and elephants and ostriches, and, by the way he looks and listens, I don't think he's ever heard of any of them, even elephants. I think: Now I've got you, but I give him a couple of pinches to show him that, just because he's behaving himself, doesn't mean I'll stop doing it.

They have quite a few books here, but all from a long time ago. The home medical advisor says things you wouldn't believe, and half the book, maybe more, is taken up with sick horses and hoof problems. That book and the government bulletins on farming might make Abel pay attention, too, so I read to him about poison weeds that make cows have two-headed calves. There's a picture. I tell him he could read all this himself if he leaned how, "Starting with the alphabet," I say.

Just as I figured, we have that same stew again for supper.

In spite of all that pretend witching, the next morning Abel is gone again, and I find him outside my magic circle. Not only that, I find a funny little squiggly sign right under all my witch signs. Maybe I should have made a bigger brand on him that would have hurt more, like four arrows in all four directions, or five. Maybe witches have five directions. Or maybe seven.

He isn't hard to find this time. You can practically see him from the house even though he's far off. I just went to say hello to the mountains as I like to do first thing every morning, and I see him out past the horse field. At first I think he's a buzzard. He's higher up in a tree than I could ever go—up in the tiny branches at the top. When I get out there, I sit down under the tree to think what to do next. I tell him his hands will get stiff as a corpse. "That's called rigor mortis," I say, "and you'll come down in a big crash and break your neck and never walk again let alone climb anything. You'd better come down while your hands still work."

But now he's swaying back and forth like there's a hurricane up there. He's doing that on purpose. I'll be blamed if anything happens and it looks as if something will. That child is fearless. "You can't scare me," I say, "I'll just witch you down." Not that I've had much luck with witching so far, but I don't know what else to do.

So I pretend to weave another spell. He stops swaying (at least that) and looks down at me with that "Oh" kind of look, so I get louder and I start dancing around. I keep saying, "Sink," and "Low," and "Descent," between all the gobbledygook. I say, "Gravity … Gravity will get you," though I'm pretty sure Abel hasn't ever heard of that and won't until *I* tell him about it.

But all of a sudden Abel starts to make a terrible racket, shrieking and howling, and his voice is like none I've ever heard. It wobbles and wavers and clicks on and off by itself. It's scary. (But I suppose I should be happy to know he can make sounds at all.) (If anybody is a witch it has to be Abel.) But then he stops the racket and lets go of those little top-of-the-tree branches and comes crashing—or starts to—but then he grabs again and stops himself. It's like magic. (He's so light and little. I wonder if the others have noticed how thin he is?) He squats there on a bigger branch like a bird ready to take off.

I say, "You can't fly, you know," but I say it because he looks so much as if he can. If anybody ever could, though I don't believe in people flying, it would have to be Abel. "I won't ever, ever pinch you anymore." But why should he believe anything I say? "I don't want you to hurt yourself. I like you. You're the nicest person I ever did teach." And that's true, too, though maybe it's just because he keeps quiet. "I know you wonder why I've been hurting you. I just did that to make you talk." Of course I didn't. I did that to everybody I ever taught, and practically everybody I got next to. I'm thinking how I hardly ever tell the truth. "It's true," I say. "Look, this proves it."

There's a nest of beavertail cactus a ways from the tree. I go over and put both my arms right in the middle of them. I don't feel the pain. I'm too scared about Abel to feel anything, but then I realize that if I try to catch him in case he falls, my arms will prick him as if he fell right into the cactus himself. Still, I might save him. "I promise I'll never hurt you again," I say, "cross my heart." Except what will I do to make him learn—or do anything? I know he hates me. I wanted him to. I thought that would make him want to learn all the faster so I'd leave forever. "And you're not dumb. I'm sorry I said that and I'm sorry about the D. I'll change it."

But he's going to jump. I don't know how I know. His face is as impassive as it always is. He hasn't moved. He still squats on his branch, balanced, not even hanging onto anything. Then he spreads his arms like wings and drops—straight down—into mine—my prickly ones. Safe.

"See," I say, "I knew you couldn't fly."

He looks up at me with his witchy eyes—again as if to say, "Oh, so this is how it is." And then I start to cry, which I never do, and my prickles start to hurt, and he looks as if his prickles, that he got from my arms, hurt too, but he doesn't cry.

Well, their mom finally bestirs herself enough to help us get the prickers out, except there's no way we can get them all. She puts a poultice on the rest, made out of salt and turpentine and lard and tobacco and goodness knows what all else. She gives us hot wine and puts us to bed. She really seems to care about Abel. I wasn't sure she did. And she treats me kindly, too. Everybody here is kind. That is, when they remember you exist. They don't even always remember Abel.

The big sister and brother come home pretty soon. Abel is asleep from the wine and I'm kind of groggy. The big sister asks how it happened, but I pretend to be too groggy to talk about it. As I lie there, still half-drunk, I think how I like that Abel is, as they say, a clean slate, and that nobody but me will tell him anything—gravity and elephants—the whole world, mine to give. And then I get a real good idea of what to do with him. There's this little bitty circus that comes around to all the little towns. It's only one ring, but how many rings can you watch at the same time? We could go. They have plenty of money, they just don't use it for anything but cows.

Next day I tell the big sister how much Abel likes my animal book. I say Abel should go to some other places and that, as soon as our prickles are better, I can find out where the circus is. I say we should stay away maybe a week and let Abel get a good look at the world.

The big sister likes this idea a lot. She must trust me. But the mom objects. Maybe she saw more of the things I did than I realized. And she does kind of cling to Abel. I didn't see that at first. It isn't noticeable until you get to know her some, but the big sister convinces her. She says, "Talk or no, it'll be good for Abel to leave the ranch." (First chance I get I'll change that brand I put on him. Maybe just smear it some. I'll leave mine, though. I like it.)

When we're out there by ourselves, I'll work on Abel really hard. He won't get away with anything, like I won't let him hum while we're eating. And he won't get away from me; I'll bring the lead rope.

I might get him a harmonica—if he behaves himself. I'm surprised nobody thought of that before, the way he hums all the time. Except they don't think of anything. That child doesn't own one single thing. Well, there's his pumpkin patch that he waters pail by pail, dipper by dipper, and he has a couple of railroad spikes. The railroad goes right through here. They throw out the mail for five or six families as they go by, and they'll stop and pick you up, right there in the middle of nowhere, if you let them know ahead of time. That's how we'll go after we get well enough and after I find out where that circus is.

The mother brings out some old clothes from when the big brother was Abel's size. I guess without this trip nobody would have thought to get them out until Abel couldn't get his backside into his pants, which is just about right now. The so-called "new" clothes are pretty worn out, too, except for a nice mannish jacket they must have used for dress-up only. The minute Abel sees it he lights up all over. The big sister says it's just to be for good, but Abel wants to put it on right away and she lets him. Like I said, he's been treated much too kind. Why should he talk when he gets what he wants anyway, with just a gesture?

"Don't you dare climb anything with that on." I whisper it in his ear when I help him into it.

So Abel goes off, walking around as if to show the jacket off to the pigs and chickens and meadowlarks. The jacket's a lot too big. He doesn't know how funny he looks in it. The mother watches him walk away. She's frowning at him. I never know what her expressions mean (though mostly she doesn't have any expression at all, which is just like Abel). But then she gives me money to have Abel's picture taken and she says she'll give him some money and I should let him spend it on anything he wants even if it's silly. Well, am I supposed to be the teacher or not? I don't say that though.

I have only one old half-decent ... *barely* half-decent dress to wear to town. The rest of my clothes ought to be turned into rags before they fall apart completely. (A dress is what I'm going to save my money for.) This "best" dress at least is green and shows off my eyes. They're not the greatest but they're my best feature, anyway. Of course the big brother won't look up long enough to see me, but if he ever should and get to care about me at all, I'll say he has to start fixing this place up before I'll take him serious. I'll tell him right at the start he'd better not beat me or I'll be gone before he knows I'm here. And I'll say he has to begin talking, starting with a little sweet talk. He won't find me easy to get. I'll make him scurry.

Though why in the world would I care about a man like him? I generally prefer men older than I am and I usually lie about my age in the other direction. Boy/man, there's not much to him. I suppose he started out just as skinny as Abel. I don't like men like that, but when a man doesn't talk at all, and doesn't hardly look at you except a little flicker of a glance now and then, there gets to be something mysterious about him. It's kind of the same with Abel. You get to thinking they're wise. If Abel talked he'd be saying all the same dumb things nine-year-olds always do. Probably the big brother would be saying dumb things, too, and whatever he could think of to say, I've heard it all before, lots of times.

I wonder if that big brother even knows my name? The mom probably never told him, and she probably forgot it by now anyway. She doesn't care what anybody's name is—except maybe Abel's. Mary

Catherine, and I don't let people call me just plain Mary. But Fay! What kind of a name for a man is that! If he ever gets to like me I'll make him change it.

I have a hard time keeping Abel from bringing his railroad spikes along to town. I keep taking them out of his box and he keeps putting them back in until finally I tie up his box with plenty of knots and put it in my room. He's the one who has to carry it, and I don't want a worn-out boy on my hands, though I don't think it would be so easy to wear out Abel.

It's at the circus that I lose him. I just turn around and he's not there. I didn't have him tied to me. Who would need to be tied up at the circus! is what I thought. He was stuffed with red candy and red pop—red was the only kind of anything he wanted. At the hotel he even finished off his beets. First off he bought himself a man's tie, but neither of us knows how to tie it properly. Abel looked like he was going to cry when I couldn't do it. That's the first I saw him at all close to tears. He didn't even cry when I branded him. I pinched him good and that sobered him up. Maybe that's what decided him to run away again. He shouldn't be hard to find, though. I could tell the police—if it comes down to that: funny-colored hair; too-big jacket that he won't take off no matter how hot it gets; flopped over, sideways tie that he won't take off either. But I'm not going to tell anybody quite yet. I'll try to find him myself.

I think of all the things he liked best: fire eater, tallest man in the world. (The fat woman scared him. He shut his eyes. He shut his eyes for the two-headed calf, too. I couldn't make him look even with a pinch. Those things don't bother me. I can stand anything that's real and the truth.) He liked the snake charmer. *There's* something that wasn't true. I could see right away that snake wasn't even poisonous. (Out here everybody knows all about snakes. They can't fool us.) I told Abel but he didn't seem to care. "S is for sssssssnake," I said, "and looks like a snake, too." I wrote that down for him, S and SNAKE. "Pay attention. This whole thing isn't just for fun, you know. I don't care anything about fun."

I wondered if he'd gone back to the hotel? He liked looking out the window, down where people passed by all the time, day and night. (Abel has no concept of manners. I said we wouldn't eat at the hotel anymore if he didn't stop leaning so low over his food and humming and kicking the table, which drives me crazy. I pinched him good. I didn't worry he'd cry out or do anything to embarrass me. That's one good thing about him not making any sounds at all … usually.)

So after checking the side show, I start back to the hotel and I find Abel first thing, at the edge of the field where the circus is. He's getting pestered by a bunch of boys. He must hardly know what another boy his age is like. They keep pushing him and every time they do he falls over backwards with that, "Oh," look of his, and then he gets up and gets pushed over again. You'd think he'd learn not to get up.

I give my special yell. It's a really crazy yell. It's saved me lots of times. I suppose the circus people wonder what sort of animal is out here. Those boys run off right away and then I hear this funny voice saying, "Whiskey, whiskey. Comin' right up." It's a crow. That's what Abel bought with the rest of his money (he hasn't got but four pennies left—I checked his pockets): that crow and two more bottles of red pop. What will his mom think? It's not *my* fault, it's *hers* for letting him buy anything he wanted. Should I try to sell it back? Or get rid of it some way? Abel can't tell on me at least. I can do anything I want to, as when have I ever not?

It's a scraggly looking bird. I don't know why anybody would want it—except it's as run-down as everything at that ranch but the horses and the cows.

"Abel, this crow won't talk for you. It has no sense except its normal crow sense—though maybe not even that, being cooped up like it is. I'll bet it only has five or six words at the most. Of course that's a lot more than you have. Your dead daddy wouldn't like this at all. He wants *you* to do the talking. He'd whup you good if he saw you with this dumb bird."

The crow says, "Hello, hello. Whiskey. Comin' right up." It hops and flutters in a lopsided way because of its clipped wing. "Tommy wants whiskey, my good man. My good man."

"And this crow can't fly any more than you can. Are you aware of that?"

What will they think if "Whiskey. Comin' right up" are Abel's first words? Or maybe only words ever? But maybe I can use this crow some way, like: talk to a mountain, talk to a crow.

We walk down a ways and find a bench. We sit and Abel drinks his cherry pop and I drink his strawberry pop. He doesn't seem to mind.

"They won't let you take this crow into the hotel, and, anyway, it probably has lice and God knows what else."

The crow has already shat all over the top of the bench.

"Look at that," I say. "You want that all over your bed? But maybe if you talk to it—maybe then I'll find a way to get it up to our room secretly." (Just try to keep something yelling, "Whiskey, comin' right up," secret.) "I'll do the best I can. Give it a name and call it that out loud—just once is all—and I'll write it down for you." So I write ABEL and put it on him and MARY CATHERINE and put it on myself. It's not the first time I've done that for him. I've put labels on the books and the chair and table ... all over the parlor.

Abel takes the ABEL and puts it on the crow's perch.

"You mean you're naming the crow Abel?" and he nods, Yes. "You can't do that. We'll get you all mixed up."

That's the first I've seen him laugh. I didn't think he could. Or would ever want to in front of me.

"All right, then, Abel Tiny and Abel Teeny-Weeny. So if you want me to go to all the trouble and risk-of-my-neck trying to get Abel Teeny-Weeny into the hotel room with us, you have to say something. I don't care what. Say oh, or boo, or elephant for heaven's sake."

He shakes his head, No.

"Well say no, then. Just no. That's a good handy word. You can get pretty far with just that."

But it isn't as if I don't know he won't. It's not going to happen like that out of the blue. If I'm going to win every battle, I'd better make sure every battle is one I can win.

"All right, all right, we'll write things instead. We'll work till supper time and then we'll have a picnic here on the bench so we won't have to worry about getting the crow into the hotel. Ham if you like, and I won't have to be embarrassed about your head on the table and your humming. And then we'll go to the evening circus. You can stay up as long as you like." Nobody has ever told him when to go to bed anyway, but I think it's a good idea for me to treat him as if he'd been brought up like any other boy. Give him some idea of the way normal people are.

(At the hotel Abel and I are in the same room. They put in a folding army cot for him but I think he would sleep just as happily on the floor. And he hasn't got one tiny bit of modesty. He's like a wild animal. Traipses around naked as though it was the most natural thing. Nobody has thought to teach him the rudiments of anything at all. I tell him we don't do that. That he should keep his pants on except when with men and boys. "Women don't like to see that," I say. Actually I do kind of like him jumping around naked, but I'm supposed to be the teacher. And I want to shock him. People learn faster if you shock them—the learning sticks better. Learning has to hurt some. That's my theory. That's why I pinch. I'd never do it just to hurt.)

I've never had any trouble getting Abel to write out letters and words. I think he must have absorbed some things before I came. The big sister said she did read to him a little bit. She said Jonathan Swift and Robert Louis Stevenson, but she didn't have much time and mostly she was too tired. "Snowstorms," she said, "and they aren't very often. That's when we read." I suppose that was about the only time anybody paid any attention to him at all. No wonder he likes to sit and listen.

I make Abel write ELEPHANT and SNAKE and CROW and HORSE ten times each. All by himself he draws the crow and writes ABEL underneath it. Then we go back to the circus, crow and all. The crow came with a black cover so we cover him up. I hook the lead rope to Abel's belt under his jacket and tie him to this scarf kind of thing I wear around my waist. People will notice anyway. Abel is such a noticeable boy. He looks like a clown himself. His hair color doesn't even look real and, no matter how much I plaster it down, two minutes later it sticks straight up. (One of these days I'm going to cut most of it off.) So we'll get noticed anyway, and, after getting a good look at Abel, people are sure to see the lead rope.

But I must have tied a bad knot, and then I was watching the acrobats, all in white, which are my favorites, and after them the clown acrobats came, which are just as good, and maybe the same people, and suddenly there's Abel. How did this happen! Things like this don't happen to regular people. Though I guess there's nothing regular about Abel or anybody at that ranch. Abel is up by the top of the tent, hanging onto some sort of tent rope. He's got the crow on its perch in one hand. The lead rope is dangling out from under his jacket like a long, white tail. How did he climb up there with only one hand?

At the same time I see him, everybody else does. They think he's part of the clown act. They laugh and clap. Now he's up there with no hands at all, just his legs wrapped around the rope, and everybody claps all the more. He's untying the crow from the perch. There's two clown acrobats going out after him.

He lets the crow go. For a minute it looks as if even the crow thinks—or hopes—it can fly, clipped wing or not. It screams out, "Good boy," as if it was planned. It flaps like crazy, but it drops, as I knew it would—flaps just enough to break its fall some and ends up in the sawdust, hopping and flopping.

I feel my heart beating so hard I think I might die. I want to yell out for Abel to climb down and that he should use both hands for heaven's sake. I know what a good climber he is, but I'm scared even so. (I hope he doesn't have any secret railroad spikes hidden in his pockets.) I see the clowns are talking to him and I see Abel nodding Yes and No. Now the first clown has almost reached him and grabs the dangling lead rope. As if it was planned, Abel lets go right then. There he dangles, his belt up under his arms. I hope it holds.

The crowd loves it. It's the funniest act of any. I laugh, too, but mostly because Abel is safe—so far. I laugh and laugh, but I feel all wobbly. Lots of people are standing up, but I don't think I can. And then things quiet down a bit and I hear, clear as day … I hear Abel say, "Caw." And then again, and lots of times. At least it's not whiskey.

Another clown, down on the ground, has picked up the crow and is cawing out to Abel, and they have this crow conversation while the others are bringing Abel down, and then all the clowns are in it. They're using it as if it really is part of their act. Even the audience is cawing.

When he's down again, they take him back behind the bleachers, so I have to go back there, too. My legs are like … I hardly know what.

The first thing Abel sees me back there, he says "Caw," right at me. He's got this look in his eyes as if: You wanted a word? So you got one.

You can see he loves saying it. His voice sounds funny. As if he really doesn't know how to use it. Kind of an animal voice. More like a real crow than it ought to be. That makes sense, but it worries me to hear it. I'm wondering if he can manage other words. Caw doesn't take a lot of moving your mouth around. I wonder if he could say anything else that isn't an ah sort of word.

"Are you his mother?"

"Certainly not." (How could anybody think that?)

I can feel myself blushing. I hate when I do that. I don't even know why I'm doing it. Why would I blush in front of three ridiculous clowns with false noses? Of course they're acrobats. And they *are* the same ones that did the show just before, because one slips off his clown suit and under it there's the skin-tight acrobat suit. When he does that, I blush again just when I thought I was over it. I'm wondering how it would be to be married to an acrobat, and maybe even get to be one myself and wear a shiny white silky costume, then I step on Abel's dangling lead rope and almost pull him down and trip myself up, too. I'm beginning to wish I'd never heard of Abel and that tumbledown ranch and I'm ashamed of the lead rope. "He keeps climbing things," I say, and they say they noticed that. Then they say, "This is our raven, you know. Somebody stole it."

"He didn't do that. He used up all his money on it. Somebody else must have stolen it and sold it to him." (They probably don't believe me.) "But he'll give it back anyway."

Abel looks like he really *will* cry. He tries to hold it in, but this time he can't. Tears come and he's making a little animal sound. One of the clowns takes out a bandanna three times as big as the usual, and wipes the tears, but they keep coming.

"This is a special raven," the clown says. "He has a little cap and jacket. He can talk. He can turn somersaults."

So the long and the short of it is, I get rid of the crow which I never wanted to be bothered with in the first place. I grab the lead rope and we sneak out the back. I make Abel take off his jacket and tie so nobody will recognize us, but they probably will anyway. Abel doesn't mind now—he's feeling too bad about the crow.

"If you cared so much about that crow, I mean raven, why did you let it go free? Raven," I say. "Did you hear that? Did you pay attention?"

But I don't know the difference, crow or raven any more than he does. I'll have to look it up.

He just goes on making that little sound. Makes me think of a kitten.

"Well, now you've gone and done it. You're never going to see a circus again as long as you live and that's that." (At least he's making a sound. I figure any sound at all is good practice.) "And caw is not an acceptable word. Find a better one or we're going home on the next train."

But all this cawing. We can't go home with that. What if they say, "Pass the stew," and Abel says, "Caw"? What if they pick us up at the train tracks and they ask us, Did we have a good time? and Abel says, "Caw"? I have to stop him, and we have to stay here until I do.

There's still plenty of light since it's hardly eight o'clock, so I get a good hold on Abel's lead rope and start us up along the creek that runs through town. I'm thinking to go a long ways up to be out of earshot just in case Abel makes a lot of noise. He's still making that little mewling sound every time he takes a breath. He's just pretending to cry. I know all about nine-year-olds. I tell him, "Life is full of disappointments and you have to get used to it and the sooner the better. Here you have a real man's tie and a real man's jacket, not to mention getting to go to the circus. What more do you want? What do you think life is all about anyway? And *me*? What do you think *my* life is like, having to watch out for you all the time?"

Of course he just keeps on making that sound.

"Go cry into your harmonica. Have you lost it yet?" (When I bought it for him he didn't even know what it was. Who ever heard of not knowing about a harmonica? I had to show him how to suck and blow it. If he's tried it out, he hasn't done it in front of me. He did look pleased though. He had this secret little smile.)

We keep on climbing—up through the aspen and willows that line the creek. There's a well-worn path and I'm hoping we don't run into any lovers. Being on a ranch, Abel must know all that stuff, though maybe not with people. But I don't want him staring and I don't want to have to explain anything.

As we walk, I'm thinking about that crow and about how Abel doesn't have any sort of animal of his own and that he needs one. There are plenty out there at the ranch but I don't think any of them is Abel's. (A pumpkin patch just isn't the same.) Seems as if nobody even thought to get him a horse and let him go out and help push cows around. They forget how old he is like they forget everything else about him.

"You're not nine years old. You're a little dwarf and you don't even know it yourself. You're small so they think you must still be a child. On the other hand, if you really *are* a child, you can't be nine. More like seven."

Abel doesn't pay me any attention that I can tell. He's up ahead as far as the lead rope allows. If I pulled on it I could pull him down real easy.

"You ought to have a horse you know. I don't know why you don't except they forgot to give you one. And you could get your own crow. Climb up and get yourself a chick and train it from the start. Teach it your own words. You could climb up no matter how high it was."

That makes him look back at me for a second, but I can't tell what he's thinking. I do pull on the rope a little, just to see what will happen, and no great harm done but a little dirt on his so-called new pants.

I'm thinking when we're well out of earshot I'll give him what-for so he'll never dare say caw again as long as he lives, but as we walk, I begin to realize that the more I hurt him, the more he'll get even with me. He'll caw just exactly the time it'll be the worse for me, so I decide we'll just go up here for a nice walk and I'll be nice to him. Except I *have* been nice. Just about as nice as anybody could be. Has anybody else bothered to take him to the circus?

I pull on the rope again and I sit us down right then and there. (If I'm not going to give him what-for, we don't need to be far off.) I say, does he realize not one single person but me has bothered doing anything for him at all? "And am I to blame that they took back the crow? If you hadn't gone off climbing where you weren't supposed to, you'd have it still, so that's your own fault. That should teach you something. What have you learned through all this? Anything at all?"

I pinch him good even though I've decided not to anymore. Well, this will be the last time.

"Caw," I say. "Hear what that's like? Caw, caw, caw, and caw. What if that was all *I* would say? That or nothing, like you do?"

I lie back against a big rock that's still warm from the hot day.

"There's my kind of moon," I say. "That's a real witch's moon. Gibbous. I'll bet you never heard that word." (I know more words than anybody I ever knew, even my teachers.) I spell it for him, but I'm too tired to get out paper and pencil and write it down. "You'd be surprised, all the words there are in the world, and you, not saying a single one."

But I'm not in the mood for anything but listening to the creek and the circus sounds coming up from the town. You can hear the sideshow barker all the way up here. Abel sits hugging his knees, and I still have a good hold on the lead rope. I'm wondering what he's going to do next? I wonder what *I'm* going to do next? I say, "Oh Abel," a couple or three times. I don't know what I mean by that. I wrap the lead rope around my wrist and shut my eyes.

I hardly know what we ought to do for the rest of the week. I don't want to go back to the circus, considering. Well, I *do* want to, but I don't want us getting recognized all over the place. (If I had my druthers, I'd go to the circus twice a day and then help them pack up in the middle of the night. I'd join them and ditch Abel right here. I guess he'd have to say something then, off on his own. It might be the best thing I could do for him. But I promised the mom I'd take good care of him. I always do what I promise—mostly. If I don't there's got to be a real good reason.)

There's lots more things we could be doing, like the horseless bus that goes up to the next town. Abel's seen it in front of the hotel every-day—automobiles, too. You can see he likes them about as much as the circus. We could take that bus up to the town above the ridge. It's bigger and there's a book store up there and they have band concerts in the park. I used to try and get to that town every chance I had just for those. I tell Abel how we're going to do all those things and we're going to buy some books and ride the bus up a steep hill that's ten miles long. When I open my eyes he's moved two feet closer to me.

So we do all those things. Going up and coming back, Abel has himself about as far out the window as it's possible to get and still be on the bus. Up on the ridge we get as many books as we can carry. I let Abel pick out a couple on his own. I read him the titles or he picks by the pictures. He gets *Tom Swift and his Airship* and *Jokes and Riddles for*

Young People. I get him a book on volcanoes because we've been driving through lava flows and I've been telling him about them. He wanted *Peter Pan,* but I wouldn't let him get it. He already has enough trouble with flying as it is. Then I saw *Best Beloved Poems.* I wanted that for myself so I got it for Abel. It'll be good for him anyway. Uplifting—if a nine-year-old can ever be said to be uplifted.

Except for that poetry book, I read all those books a long time ago when I took up with a teacher. Or, rather, she took me away from my mother and stepfather … stepfath*ers,* I should say. She was tired, she said, of seeing me with black eyes and bruises and all shoulder blades and collar bones and half the time not in school at all. She said she always took in stray kittens so why not me? That was true, too, she did have a lot of cats. And she called me Mary Cat and, sometimes, Kitty, Kitty. I liked that, but it doesn't have enough dignity for how I'm supposed to be now. (One way or another—at the library or from the school—she got me just about every book there is.)

(I guess I'll have to get used to people thinking Abel is my child, whether I like it or not and I don't. I can't see why people think that. We don't look one tiny bit alike, thank goodness. People like him, though they laugh at him. They call him a little pixie. They're always rumpling his hair and making it stand up all the more. He's getting so he ducks his head even before anybody gets close, especially old ladies. There's a lot of "Cat got your tongue?" of course.)

Abel has never heard of a band concert before, let alone heard a band, as how could he have? After it's over he doesn't want to leave the park. He watches the musicians pack up. There's a couple who aren't a whole lot older than he is. The drummer for one. Abel can't stop staring. Even after everybody's gone, he still sits. I don't mind. He's thinking hard and I am, too. A couple of those men were nice looking and I'm wondering what it would be like to be married to a musician and maybe get to learn to play an instrument myself. (Can girls be in the band?) I'd like to play something with a deep, low sound so people would sit up and take notice. They'd say, What a big sound to come out of such a small person.

After a while I take Abel up on the bandstand and let him sit on one of the little folding chairs before they take them away. I ask him where his harmonica's got to. When he won't show it to me, I think he must have lost it. I search his pockets and it's still there, along with half a dozen bottle caps, his pennies, tinfoil, some red string, and a stone with green in it which I tell him is copper ore. (I know all that stuff.) I throw everything in the trash except the pennies and the harmonica. Then I buy him a glass of cider with ice in it. He loves ice. He never had any before now, even though they have that old cold cave.

We stay up at that town a couple of days—visit the fire house and the high school where I show Abel a globe of the world, which, I tell him, proves it's round no matter what he's been thinking all this time—and then we take the bus back to the town below and then the train home.

On the train I read to Abel out of the poetry book. He wants me to read from the joke book but I don't want to in front of the people sitting near us, so I go on with the poetry. Maybe the people nearby will hear me and see how learned I am. Erudite. That's a good word. Maybe the man sitting behind us is a school teacher. He looks as if he could be. Maybe even a college teacher. Everything about him is thin—nose, ears, fingers … He's about as pale as any man I ever saw. More like a woman who's never out of her bonnet. Maybe he has TB. He does look sick. I'd marry him anyway and nurse him to the end. I'd be faithful till his last living breath. He'd teach me things like the teacher who took me in did.

When they stop the train at the stopping place, I'm embarrassed that we're the only people getting off and in the middle of nowhere. There they all are, meeting us with their rickety old wagon and their raggedy clothes. Everybody's looking out the window at us. What will that school teacher-man be thinking about me?

Abel can't contain himself. He gives a funny sort of jump. I don't know what cutting a caper is, exactly, but it must be kind of like this, except he lands right on his bottom. He gives this jump with both feet in the air and falls right down looking shocked and surprised, but not hurt. He gets up and hugs and gets hugged. You can practically see he's aching to say something. He's breathing hard and his mouth is open. It's as if there's a bunch of words stuck right there in back of his throat. The big sister and the mother look at me like I've already done something miraculous. I'm on their good side now. Even Fay's. As usual he doesn't look at me, but I can tell.

I'M OUT TRYING to put that dam back together. I've already made a little difference in the size of the pond. I haven't told anybody I'm repairing it, though I don't suppose they'd care if I did or not. I don't worry about them catching me at it. The sister and brother are always working farther out than this, and besides, it's too nice and shady and cool and pretty for them to bother with, and who else is there?

Abel helps. He likes to. I tell him smaller stones count, too. We need them to fill in between the bigs. I'm not strong enough for the heaviest myself. Every now and then Abel climbs the highest of the cottonwoods. There must be a good view from up there. I'd climb it myself if it wasn't for the sap and the ants and the aphids, which is why I don't like cottonwoods. I wonder why Abel isn't bothered by the ant bites. It seems like he'd rather climb than care about bites.

Things are different between us now, like he knows which side his bread is buttered. And he really wants to learn to read. (Maybe that's so he won't have to sit next to me and get read to.) How we do it is, he moves his lips and I can tell pretty much when he's doing it right. I'm trying to get him to whisper it. "Breathe," I say. "Breathe it out to me." I tell him as soon as he does it that way we'll go back up to the big town and ride the bus and get more books, which is what *I* want to do. I say we'll visit the grade school on the way, but I shouldn't say that because if Abel goes to school they won't need me anymore and I like it here. I don't know whether the more I succeed, the quicker they'll fire me; or the more I succeed, the more they'll keep me on.

So he's in the treetop and I'm out in the water up to my knees—water straight down from the mountains and cold. I have to keep coming out and warming up. But even when Abel turns purple and is goosebumps all over, I have to give him a couple of good pinches to make him come out. Then I towel him off so hard he turns red instead of purple.

So there I am, out in the water with a big stone in my arms—as big as I can lift—when I find Abel's right behind me pulling on my sleeve.

Well, he's not going to get my attention that way. I dump my stone where I want it and reach down for another. Abel keeps pulling on me but I don't look back at him. He's going to have to make a noise before I'll pay him any mind. But then he goes, "Caw, caw." I'm so startled I nearly drop the stone on my toe. He hasn't made a single sound since the circus. I turn around and he points his grimy, sap-sticky finger (I'll bet he got sap all over my blouse) and I see somebody's coming. Still a ways away. A gray horse. You can just see them from behind the currant bushes. The stream makes such a rippling sound I haven't heard anything.

I say, "Good boy. Not a real word, but better than nothing."

At first I think the man riding up is the big brother, Fay. I think this partly because Abel looks so happy, but then I see this man has only one arm. As he comes closer, I see that, though he looks exactly like ... I mean *exactly* like Fay, I see he's a lot older. So then I'm thinking this must be another brother they forgot to tell me about. I'll bet he's been in the war—the war-to-end-all-wars. Everybody has. He looks to be the right age. (For a long time we didn't see any men this age around except blind men or idiots. It made me wonder if there'd ever be somebody left over for me to marry—and I still wonder.) It's been about a year since the war ended. Maybe he's been in the hospital. Why didn't they tell me about him? He's wearing a badly worn-out army shirt so I think, all the more, that he must belong with this run-down ranch.

I thought I was a little bit in love with Fay and this ranch. But when I get a good look at this one-armed man, all of a sudden I know I'm not, and I wouldn't even care if this man had a ranch or any property at all. I don't even care that he only has one arm.

(I wonder at myself sometimes, that I like a run-down place I can fix up better than a fixed-up place.)

The man says, "Hello, Abel," and "Hello, Miss," and then he puts one leg over to the other side of the saddle horn and slides off his horse, his back to the saddle, just as nice as you please. He pulls the reins over the horse's head and lays them over a tiny dead twig. I guess the horse thinks he's tied up. Then he comes and sits down on the big boulder I always sit on myself when I have to warm my feet, and he takes out a ready-made cigarette and lights it. You can see he has life-with-one-arm down to a system. He's shaking as he lights it. A lot. I have the thought I should help him or surely he'll burn himself, but I know better than to try. I don't know what shell shock is, but I figure this is part of it.

Abel comes and sits on the ground beside him and leans against him just as if he was Fay.

Now that the man is close up, I see under the shadow of his hat, that, besides no arm, he has scars across his chin and cheeks. You can see where the stitches were. It spoils his looks except I doubt there was much to spoil in the first place. He and Fay and Abel sure didn't get their fair share when looks were handed out. I wonder how the big sister got to be so big and handsome? The mother is kind of pretty, or was, but the sister looks like nobody else in the family but herself. I wonder if I dare ask her about that.

"This is a good idea," the one-armed man says. "We used to have a good time here when this was a pond." He puts his cigarette in his mouth so he can hug Abel with his one arm. (These are the huggingest men I ever saw in my whole life. Fay is more like a mother to Abel—as to hugging—than the mom.) "I'll teach you to swim," the man says, talking with his cigarette in his teeth. Abel is so pleased he has to hide his face against the one-armed man's knee.

"So you must be another brother."

"Cousin. We're across by the far mountains. Ten, maybe twelve, miles from here. I'm Hen." And to Abel, "*Uncle* Hen to you, buzzard bait," as if Abel would ever call him anything at all. "Wait a minute, not uncle. I'm cousin to Abel. I'm uncle to everybody over at our place."

Then I realize my skirt is still tucked up into my belt and my feet are bright, bright, bright red from the cold and I'm blushing, which I never do with Fay, though when has Fay ever looked straight at me?

"I'm Mary Catherine." (I'm glad I added the Catherine to my name. I did that a long time ago. I didn't like being just plain Mary. I always thought my mother probably couldn't spell any name longer or more complicated than Mary.)

I untuck my skirt and sit down on a smaller stone to towel off my feet so I can hide them in my shoes. I shake my head so my hair falls over my face to hide my blushing—*and* my nose *and* my eyebrows and goodness knows what all. I have bobbed hair—the really latest thing—and it's just right for shaking out to cover my face.

An airplane comes over. Abel jumps up and runs out from under the trees to get a good look at it. He always does that. Sometimes he gets up from dinner and runs outside right in the middle of a bite. The one-armed man just sits and studies his shirt buttons. I guess he's seen more airplanes than he wanted to. I'd like to go out with Abel to see it, but I also want to stay with this man, so I sit and look at my shoes. We keep quiet, but it's not a comfortable quietness. It goes on and on and I don't like it. I'm thinking, for sure it *is* the war. He's got his one arm around himself as if he's trying to hold himself together and maybe really needs two arms to do it. I want to ask him things—not big things, just like: how long he's been home? or how long in the hospital? But there's something a lot worse wrong with him than shaking. He doesn't want questions. He looks up just once, warning me, and I know not to ask things.

Abel stays out there watching the plane until it's more than gone, and then comes back and sits next to the man again. I say, "You'll have to talk if you want to be an airplane pilot."

I've had this conversation—monologue, I should say, six times a day if I've had it once—about everything that pops up: that he can't be a soldier, that he can't warn people a bear is coming, that he can't read to his little boy when he grows up, or, if his house is on fire and he runs to the firehouse, he can't tell the firemen where it is. "Besides," I told him, "you'll never be able to tell a lady you want to marry her, so you won't ever have any children to rescue anyway."

"Well, I don't know," the man says (he has a low, slow, careful voice that doesn't seem to go with all that shaking). "I can use the quiet. I'm uncle to a dozen nephews and nieces back home there. I can use Abel just the way he is. I have to come over here to get some peace." He puts the cigarette back in his mouth so he can hug Abel again.

But this is not good. This will make Abel feel all right about himself, which is the worst possible thing.

"Maybe if *you* said he should talk, he would." I want this man to like me, and I don't want to be starting an argument, though he doesn't seem like an arguing sort of person. Except this is not a good beginning. He'll think I'm one of those critical people.

But he says, "I suppose you're right," and then to Abel, "So talk, but not too much."

Abel has a nice giggle, though I hardly ever hear him do it.

I don't know what to say next, so I say, "What about Fay?" though

I don't care anything about Fay anymore. I really want to say, What about *you?* but he doesn't want that.

He just goes on smoking and thinking hard as if he didn't know the answer, though he must know all about Fay.

"Why is he called a girl's name, anyway?" I should be asking this of Charlotte. I wonder why I already didn't?

He just sits and looks as if he didn't hear. Or more as if he heard the question I wanted to ask him instead of what I did ask. Then he flinches—ducks his head at absolutely nothing that I can tell. He looks like Abel does when he sees an old lady about to tousle his hair. Then he says—not to anybody—"His dad ... and Abel's dad ... died saving me. A lot of good that did."

The way he says it, I know better than to say anything. Abel pulls away from him a little bit. Hugs his own knees instead of the man's ... It's not so much what the man said as the way he is.

The man finishes his cigarette and we all three sit there hardly moving. Even Abel—such a wiggly boy—hardly moving. That usually only happens when I read to him. Then the man takes his boots off and says he's going to help, and I think, how can he with just one arm? But he can. He can wrestle stones a lot bigger than I can. Some big ones we roll back in place together. We don't talk. We just grunt and gasp and blow like horses. This time the quiet is nice and cozy.

As he works, so close to me, I see that his scars go all down his neck. I wonder what his body looks like—if it's all scarred, too? All of a sudden, working on a big one together, his arm against mine ... his hand slips and is on top of mine, warm and strong, and, right then and there, I want to say, I love you. I don't want to let him get away. I'm looking right into his face, so close ... He probably thinks I'm thinking bad things about how he needs a shave and about his scars, but it's just the opposite, I like them. I want to tell him how I like everything about him. (I wouldn't even care if he beat me. I wouldn't let Fay do that, but I'd let him.) I have to make plans. I don't want him to escape. If he does I'll die.

I can see he gets along fine with just one arm, but he could do even better with somebody like me around. I want to tell him that, but of course I can't say it. Not yet anyway. (I wonder who pins up his sleeves? But probably they're permanently pinned up.) I hope he comes over and sees all the things I do for this ranch besides this dam. I've already ordered paint from Montgomery Ward's. I got white. I didn't ask. I know the house used to be a greenish gray, but white will be much better. He, Hen, will see that. Green—a bright green—can be on the shutters.

But then I say a stupid, dumb thing. I can't stand myself when I do that. If he never looks at me again, I wouldn't be surprised. I say, "It's a good thing you're right-handed," and he says, "Well, I am *now.*" I'm so embarrassed. I can't look at him when he gets back on his horse.

Just before he turns to ride off, he says, "Fayette," out of the blue. "Fay's name is Fayette." Then he goes. He doesn't say goodby, not even to Abel. I wonder what *that* means?

I start on the house painting as soon as the paint arrives so if that man, Hen, comes over he can see me doing the kind of things I do around here. I wonder if I can find a way to tell him nobody told me to do any of these things? I just do them on my own.

Abel wants to help and I think to start him on the ground beside me, but he wants to be up on the ladder—of course—which is all right with me as long as he doesn't decide he's going to try to fly off someplace.

Since I don't know what they'll think about us doing this painting, or if they don't like the color, I start out at the back. I'm hoping we can get far enough along so it would be silly not to finish before they notice what we've done. (If they ever look up long enough to notice anything.)

We paint and Abel hums, wasps hum, and I feel like humming, too. When Abel is about to paint the sills of his mom's windows, he stops humming and stares in. I say, "That's not polite," but he keeps on looking anyway. I say, "We don't do that." I'm wondering what's going on in there? What could his mom possibly be doing that would make him stare like that? Is she naked or half-naked or something of the sort? I say, "You climb down right this very minute," but he doesn't. I climb up behind him thinking to give him a good pinch to make him come. (I haven't done that in a while. I don't feel like it much anymore.) But then I think, if I do, he'll drop the paintbrush and maybe the paint can will fall, too, so I look over his shoulder to see what's so fascinating. I'm the teacher, so I ought to know what goes on.

I see the mom just lying there—completely dressed. Her eyes are open but if she was staring at us, she'd not see us. She doesn't look right. Her hair is all over the place and she's sprawled about as sprawled as a person could get, which is unlike her. She always seems very much on the dignified, proper side (not counting the spots all over the front of her dresses). Now she looks drunk, though I haven't seen a single drop of liquor around, nor smelled any. When I first hunted for Abel, I looked all over the house on purpose to find things out, but I didn't find any liquor except for half a bottle of elderberry wine they obviously keep only for medicine, and it's stayed at the same level. I checked it more than once. I tasted it though I don't drink at all. I've seen enough of the bad side of that.

So Abel and I stare in at her. Whatever it is that holds him so still and staring holds me, too. I don't know how long we stand there. Then we climb down, and no need for me to pinch him. I shut the paint can and put away the brushes. I tell Abel I'll read to him out of *Tom Swift and His Airship.* After, he can write AIRSHIP and draw airplanes for a while.

When we were in town I got myself a batch of licorice sticks. I thought to keep them secret, just for myself, but I tell Abel about them and I get him one to chew on while I read to him. At first he looks at it like he doesn't know what it is. I have to say, "You silly, it's to eat."

He chews on it just as slowly as I always do.

As I read, Abel leans over, closer and closer, until he's leaning against me just as he does with Fay and Hen. At first I lean away. I feel like pushing him off. Nobody ever did that with me before and I never wanted them to. I always think I'm hardly afraid of anything, but this … It scares me. Then I think this must be how it feels to Hen when Abel leans against him and he puts his arm around him, and then I kind of like it. Abel needs me. Well, he needs somebody anyway, and right now. I guess I'm the last resort. Even a pinching person will do.

Oriana

SHADOWS OF LEAVES. On walls and ceiling. Everyday the same. Every day different. Pines go back and forth. Poplars wobble. Shadow of a bird sometimes. Shadow of two of them sometimes. Everything two-by-two. She used to be two-by-two.

Mariposa lily, fairy duster, wake robin, bride's bonnet, winter fat ... All the names for things human beings think of. That girl picked some. Some were the same ones Abiel picked for her just after they met. Had to turn away so as not to see them. Bearskin rug, that was something to look at. One glass eye left. What happened to the other?

The rose bushes died. She let them die on purpose. Why should *they* be alive?

Bawling calves all night long and still going on. Weaning time. Big babies now, but it seems cruel even so. A mile away the mother cows cry. She didn't cry. Doesn't. Hasn't. Hasn't been a mother. Nursing Abel. Somebody brought him to her. How had he been weaned and when? It's all foggy. She's taking up space that might better be used by some useful woman.

Not taking up much space, though. Chair, then bed, then chair, then bed.

That girl hurt Abel. She does something secret. (What's her name?) She tied him up, too. Of course she herself had put harness bells on him to keep track of him. Is that so different? She hadn't kept track even so. Harness bells up on the roof. She didn't dare go after him or even call out for fear she'd scare him. Her baby ... up there and her own fault. Still in diapers. What kind of a mother would let that happen? No matter what she does, that girl is better. She pays attention. Talks to him. First she'd thought not to keep her on. Abiel wouldn't want Abel hurt. But what she, herself, does hurts him more. Abiel wouldn't have expected her to spend all day in bed. Christmas. New Year's. Every day the same. Had they had any Christmases since? If they had, they'd kept them secret. Or she didn't pay attention. Birthdays. Poor little boy. How old is he now? Imagine, not being sure! Her own son! Whatever-her-name-is can't do as badly at being a mother as she does.

Abel. So sweet. It's not her doing. Like his father even though he never saw him. Same gestures. Same look in his eyes. All the time thinking hard.

Lotti … Charlotte (Lotti wants to be called Charlotte. She must remember that). Charlotte had gone up and brought Abel down from the roof that first time. He was wearing the red shirt she had made for Fayette. Too big, all loose and floppy then, shirttail out, looking like a dress. Now it's too small. She should sew something.

What is this girl's name! She ought to speak to her. Say, "We don't do that kind of thing. Some people think it's all right, but we don't." Except she had decided to say something several times and hasn't yet. When say it? And how? Should she tell Charlotte?

But that girl isn't really cruel.

Charlotte told that girl not to do the milking. They left that so they could pretend … so *she* could pretend to herself she was being useful. Extra mouth to feed. If she could believe in Heaven and Hell, she'd join Abiel in either place. At least she'll lie beside him in Tibo and Henriette's graveyard. If they could open up the coffin and throw her in to hug his bones. She would, too. Kiss his poor crooked teeth.

But best not to say that to anybody. She has nothing to say anyway. If she could, she would will her voice to Fay and Abel, half a voice each. Better than none.

That girl is right about Abel copycatting Fay and that's her own fault. Everything is. If she'd just been a proper mother none of this would have happened.

They looked in at her. Their shadows on the wall along with the leaves. She didn't dare move. Even after they left, she didn't dare.

Cream Cup, Goldeneye … What else is there? *Mule ears, yellow throat, four-o'clock …*

He might be just around the corner. Abiel, just out of sight, that's all. Down at the hot springs. Drunk. She used to care, but she wouldn't now.

Mary Catherine

ABEL SAID MA. I didn't hear him but the mom says he did. I wonder what could have brought that on? Could it have anything to do with what we saw yesterday? For all I know Abel said Ma because of my licorice stick. Who knows what goes on in the mind of a nine-year-old?

She said he said it fast and then ran off. She says we shouldn't make a fuss when he says something else. She thinks Ma is Abel's first word ever. She kissed me when she told us about it. (She kissed me about as fast as Abel must have said Ma. I expect she wanted to run off and hide right after just like he did.)

I see, more and more, how shy she is. It's hard to get to know her since she's hardly ever around and even when she is, she doesn't seem quite really here. I doubt I'll ever know her.

Right after this, *I* hear Abel say things. He doesn't know I hear. He's alone in the parlor and I almost walk right in on him. He's humming as usual, so I don't think anything of it, but, just as I'm about to step in, I hear him make another sound and I stop while I'm still behind the half-open door.

He's lying on the floor. All I can see are his patched-up pants (*I* patched them) and his dirty bare feet, his toes tapping away to some rhythm of his own. Then I hear him say, caw, and then, Mamama-mama. Then I hear the in and out of the harmonica which I thought he'd not ever blown into and I wondered if he ever would. I don't dare move. When he's back to mostly humming, I creep away. Funny, with that humming, he always seems like a happy boy—even with my pinching—always his own music going on inside him. You'd not have thought that, considering how things are around here.

I'm making incredible progress with him but I feel both good and bad about it. I do want Abel to speak and learn to read, but now I'm wondering how to keep him from going too fast and for them to be saying I've finished my job and so, Goodby. I don't want to leave here. Ever. The house is only a little bit painted, and what if I never get to see that man, Hen, again?

Though maybe I should switch and work on Fay for a while. That was my plan before I met Hen, but I don't feel like it anymore—even though they say this whole ranch belongs to him. And I don't know how to do it anyway. I think he's avoiding me. He doesn't sit on the front steps like Charlotte and I do some evenings. My thought was (before Hen) that I'd get Fay off alone someplace and then pretend to faint or sprain my ankle. I thought, since he's that age and never so much as touched a woman (I don't think) ever before, he'd be seduced before he hardly knew it. He'd think he had to marry me. I know these folks better than they know themselves. They're not only kinder than is good for them, but much too upright to get along in this world.

But he's never off alone except in the outhouse. He and Abel sleep in one little room next to the kitchen, and he and Charlotte always work together. They like to, whether the job needs two people or not. (Charlotte told me they've worked like that ever since Fay was little, even before his father got killed.) If there's any time left over at night, Fay sits at the supper table and reads to himself. Sometimes the mom sits beside him doing absolutely nothing. She'll hold some knitting but she never knits. And she rocks even though she's not in a rocking chair. Lots of times Abel sits on Fay's lap and strokes his skimpy mustache. They laugh together, but everything is silent—they sort of pantomime sometimes, or they just laugh at nothing.

Pipe and mustache—Fay's trying to look older. That mustache is just a little bit of fuzz. I wonder why he bothers. That man, Hen, could grow a real one if he wanted to.

I'm going to ask for a day off or maybe even two. I've worked every day since I got here. They probably forgot that people usually get days off. Those two don't ever take any. I'm on their good side, though, so I think they'll give me anything I want. Also I'm hoping a few days off might slow Abel down a bit.

I'll ride over to that other ranch where Hen lives. I get goose bumps just thinking about it. I'm afraid I'll spoil everything because of being nervous. I'll talk too much and probably blush myself to pieces. I'll blush so much I don't even want to go, but, as they say, nothing ventured ...

The next time we're out on the front steps, I ask Charlotte about Hen. She likes to talk to me. I think she hasn't had anybody to really talk to until I came along. We're watching the sunset colors on the mountains across on the other side of the valley while the sun sets behind us. We watch until there's just a little bit of orange outlining the tops and then nothing left but purple. Over there is where Hen's family lives. While it's still light enough to see it, Charlotte points out the green spot where their house is. She calls him Henny. She says he's hardly ever over there.

"Henny," she says, and gives a big sigh and then she says, "Oh dear," and I say I'm sorry I asked, and she says, "That's all right," and then she says, "His poor ma."

We sit. She has her knees wide apart like a man. She's wearing pants about as worn out as Abel's are and big black boots. Her boots are new, though. The way she looks at them, you can see she likes them a lot.

"His ma says he's lost to her ... and to everybody."

Right away I think *I'll* be the one to bring him back to them.

"His whole family went to the hospital to see him and they wished they hadn't. I thought to go myself after they came home, but they told me not to. They said he acted perfectly normally—said and did all the right things, but it was as if there wasn't anybody there. At least he seems to be out of that now. Mostly. Usually. You know," she says, "We almost got married before he went off to the army. Everybody took it for granted that we would. They practically had us hitched though neither of us wanted to. They even had the date and place picked out. I never loved him *that* way. We were too much brother and sister for that other kind of love. I've pushed him around ever since we were six years old. I was terrible."

I'm thinking: And she's still doing that with Fay, but all I say is, "I can't believe it."

"Oh, not now. Not the way Henny is now. Nobody could do that to him anymore. Talk about the army making a man of you! Except—funny thing, when Henny had two hands to fight with, he never got into fights, but now that he only has one, he gets into fights all the time."

"I thought he was nice."

"Well, he is … I guess still nice." Then she pauses a long pause. The stars are coming out full force. The mountains seem to huddle in closer and look smaller as they always do when it gets dark. "But I feel I hardly know him anymore. I'm not sure what he's like."

"I really, really liked him." It's so dark now it doesn't matter whether I blush or not.

"Go to it then. It might be good for him. But just try to find him. He's probably over here as much as over home and you see how often that is. He's sometimes out at the line-riding shacks. There's one by the creek he likes best."

So that's when I ask if I can have a day off and borrow a horse. The next morning she gives me a nice shiny bay. After I mount up she says, "Go to it," over again and slaps the horse's butt so we go off at a fast, hard trot. "Bump him back," she yells, and I have to guess what she means by that. She's tough and snappy sometimes, but I like her. She doesn't mean it like some people do.

I didn't admit it to her, but I'm not the greatest rider in the world. When have I been around people who could afford to keep horses, or, if they could, when would they have let *me* ride them? I hope I don't disgrace myself some way, like ending up back home. Horses are always turning around and heading for the barn.

There's no possible way of getting lost. Charlotte showed me again which of the green spots partway up the far mountains is their house. (Not their house, just the trees around it.) I bounce along towards it. Charlotte said the horse had nice smooth gaits but I'm not a good enough rider to know the difference. They all feel bad to me.

On the way over I keep looking around for that gray horse of Hen's, but then I wonder what in the world I'll talk about if I do run into him or if he is home. Nothing I can think of seems good enough. I can't ask about anything I really want to know, and I don't know enough about cows and horses to talk about them. I guess the only thing we have in common is lifting stones. All the more reason for me to meet his family and see where he lives. Charlotte said she'd bet me two bits he wouldn't be there, which will be just as well. I'll find out lots of things about him and his family and pick up topics of conversations for later.

As I bump along, all of a sudden I wonder if he put his hand over mine on purpose. And why were we both pushing at the same stone in the first place? That was his idea. I know those kinds of men. Maybe he wanted somebody to seduce right then and there. Not marry, just ruin me like everybody else always wanted to do, including a half a dozen stepfathers. Just because he comes from a nice family doesn't mean he's not like every other man there ever was. And what have I got to offer anybody in a marrying way except that I know a lot of useless words most people never heard of? I can't even cook and never wanted to.

By the time I get there I've been thinking nothing but bad thoughts and I'm tired and dusty and sore. I freshened up when I crossed the river, but that was a while ago. I sat there a bit to rest my bottom and my legs. When I got back on the horse it hurt even more and I wondered if I should have stopped to rest at all. I was certainly not looking for that gray horse anymore. In fact I began to wonder why I was doing this. I sure won't be at my best—if there is a best, or a best of me that Hen might like.

As I ride up, and even though it's surrounded by poplars, I can see they have a big house. Three stories, and outbuildings like you wouldn't believe. I'll bet at least a dozen, big and little. And noise. Hen was right about too many nieces and nephews. I can hear them a mile away. At first I think there's some sort of game going on, with all the cheering and laughing, but then I see they're working this machine-thing that raises the hay up into the loft. If that *is* hay. If it is, it's full of alfalfa. I do know that much.

They stop when I ride up and everybody looks at me. (There's one child of every size there is.) I start to get off the horse but I'm so stiff my legs don't work and I fall flat on my you-know-what right in front of them. The little ones giggle but the big ones run over to help me up. They set me down on the front porch—which has wooden curlicues all around its edges—and hand me a glass of lemonade.

Of course, just as Charlotte warned me, Hen's not here. And a good thing, too, since I've already disgraced myself three times over. When I fell my foot got caught in the stirrup, so there I was, staring up at the big bay stomach and the horse looking down at me as if wondering what in the world I'm doing on the ground with my skirts halfway to my neck. I don't know what I'd have done if Hen had been watching.

I can tell who's which. Of the grown-ups, that is. His mother is the one who brings me a towel and a wet cloth to wipe my face with. I'm surprised at how pretty his two big sisters are even though they look a lot like him: straight black hair and longish faces, and I think, Hey, our children might not be so bad looking after all.

I tell them who I am, but they know about me already. I was hoping from Hen talking about me, but it turns out Charlotte meets them now and then. They share range land. I tell them Hen helped me with the dam. Of course the minute I say the name Hen I blush just as I was afraid I would and I'm only in front of his sisters. They look at me as though they guess right away I'm after their one-and-only precious little brother—who's not so little anymore, so what have they got to say about it? Even if he just wanted a roll in the hay? They call him Henny like Charlotte does, so I'll call him Hen. Some of those children call him Cock. That's what they called him in the war.

All those children! It's Uncle Henny this and Uncle Cock that. To hear them, it's a wonderful thing to lose an arm and to have been in one of the worst battles of all. I can see why Hen needs to get away from here.

They introduce me all around, and the sisters each have four children as if it was a contest to make sure neither got ahead of the other, children-wise.

So it looks as if Hen is rich. Except if he has to share with all these other people. I don't care about rich or not, though, just out of curiosity, I'd like to ask how big this ranch is. But that'll make the sisters even more suspicious of me than they already are. The minute I saw how much they look like Hen, I wanted to be best friends but they don't want that. At least his mother seems friendly enough. She has a thick French accent even though, she tells me, she's been over here way more than half her lifetime.

After I finish the lemonade—two big glasses (I really gulped the first one down. They'll know for sure there's nothing ladylike about me and that won't help me with the sisters.) After, they take me inside where it's cooler, in through a big hallway to a big parlor. I get glimpses into a couple of other rooms. I count up three chandeliers. There's an organ *and* a piano. I'm not sure I'd ever like to live here, and with this crowd alongside. I'd like just Hen and me in a little cottage I could fix up all by myself.

There are two big paintings of mountains. When they see me staring, they say Charlotte painted them. There's portraits she did, too. One is of an ugly dark man, eyebrows like woolly-bear caterpillars and black eyes that shine out at you. (Hen looks a little bit like that himself.) They tell me that's Abel's father. From memory. Charlotte painted it after he got killed. They say she never got to go to art school like she wanted to. (The paintings *are* kind of flat looking. Not like the ones in the art books.)

"Gored! Gored!" The children shout it as if it's the second-best thing that can happen to you after losing an arm.

"He died right here. Right in this room," they say, all talking at once. "On a couch we used to have but it got all bloody." They proudly point out where there's still a blood stain on the floor they can't get off—even from so long ago. They pull at me to come see the stain in the hall. They say they'll push aside the rug so I can see it.

The sisters say, "For heaven's sake," and Hen's mother says, "Mon Dieu," and they shoo them all back outside to their work.

Now I *do* have a question I dare ask: "How come this portrait—or one like it—isn't over there with Abel's mother?"

Hen's mother says they took it away when it was clear Abel's mother ... well, wasn't getting over it ... him.

I say, "And she still isn't, is she?"

Here's a topic of conversation they all want to talk about: What to do about Abel's mother and Abel and Fay. I tell them how Abel said Ma, and that I took him to the circus. Of course I don't tell everything about that.

Hen's mother says they don't go over there very much anymore. When Abel was a baby somebody stayed there all the time, but then it seemed Abel's mother was getting worse. The less she had to do, the less she did, and things were better when they weren't helping out so much. At least she got out of bed now and then. Charlotte keeps them informed.

Hen's mother asks me to stay for supper and overnight. (Charlotte told me she would.) The sisters look as if they don't go along with that at all. I say Yes, partly to show them I don't care how they feel about it. (I should be nice to them. Charlotte told me both their husbands died of influenza. I suppose that's one reason they're so particular about Hen, since he and his father are the only grown-up men left on the place.)

Then Hen's mother shows me things—things that Hen gave her. There's a fancy fringed scarf draped over the piano and a vase on top of it with such a raggedy bunch of flowers in it they have to be from the children. Stringy mountain dandelions and other things hardly worth leaning over to pick, already wilting. Probably wilting by the time they handed them over. There's a picture of Hen there, too, in his uniform. He has a lot of fancy stripes. I ask what they mean and his mother says he was a master sergeant … whatever that is.

"This scarf comes from Paris," his mother says. "Henny gave it to me. And this cloisonné pin." Then her eyes fill with tears and she makes exactly the same gesture Hen did but he could only half do it— arms around herself, holding herself together.

I look away.

I'm thinking: *Paris!* I know all about Parisian women. I even saw one once. People said she was, anyway. She had such pale skin she couldn't have ever been out in the sun in her life. She had an elegant, aristocratic nose. (Like Hen's, actually. And like his mother's and sister's, too.) What they say about Parisian women! And Hen was right there, in the middle of *all* of them! How can he ever be interested in somebody like me? Hand on top of mine! That was just a nothing to him. I guess I can be any old dumb way I really am. What difference does it make? I might as well just be myself. I wouldn't blush because of him if it was the last thing I do. Except here I go, doing it again anyway, and not for any reason I can tell—except Hen's mother's tears.

But all of a sudden, out of nowhere, I have this thought: Hen has gone to visit *us,* over at our ranch. Maybe even come to see me and I'm not there! Life is *always* like that. I'm in a panic. I don't care what they think about me changing my mind so fast. I can hardly stand to wait while one of the big boys saddles up for me. It's as if I itch all over.

Hen's mother begs me to stay. She says it's too far and I must be tired and the horse is tired and I haven't eaten. Even his sisters seem to want me, but I hardly hear what they're saying.

It hurts a lot when I get back on the horse but I don't care. They say to come back soon, and all the children shout, Goodby. That's enough to scare anybody off for a long time. I start right out at a trot and don't answer. I'm going to be sorry … sorry for everything including the trot, and I'm already sorry about all those Parisiennes, but this is more important than pain and Paris. It's my whole future life.

Way before I get to the resting place by the river, I'm in trouble. When I get to the trees by the bridge across the river, I check myself and I have blisters big as silver dollars by the feel of them. Broken blisters. I haven't bled through to my skirt yet, but I will soon. That'll be embarrassing.

I still have this absolutely, absolutely sure feeling that Hen is visiting back at our ranch and I also have an absolutely sure feeling that, when I get back there, he'll have gone already, though not in this direction of course, but the way I am right now, if I see that gray horse I'll hide … behind a couple of sticks of sage brush I suppose, though here by the river there's some real bushes.

I don't know what to do. I sit on the softest spot I can find and watch lizards. There goes my life. Right by me, Abel practically talking already, Hen (as Charlotte said he always is) nowhere to be seen. And I … I ought to give *myself* a good hard pinch to make myself behave. Then I think, what I'd like to do right this very minute is take off all my clothes and take an icy dip in the river.

I move us—horse and me—down away from the road to where the currant bushes grow tall and thick. I eat currants and I feel a little better. Then I take off my clothes and wade in. I'm half-wishing Hen would be behind the bushes (my figure's pretty good) but that's too much to hope for. Everything I've ever hoped was too much to hope for.

I *do* give myself a big pinch, partly so I won't hope for dumb things.

After I come out, I fold my bandanna and put it in my underwear under my riding skirt which isn't even mine. It belongs to Abel's mother. We're about the same size. Smallish. A good thing for me since Hen isn't a particularly tall man. I wonder that he can goad people into fighting with him, not being big and having only one arm. You'd think most men wouldn't stoop to that. He must bet them he can lick them even with no arm. Charlotte says he always loses … money, too, since he bets on himself.

47

Those tears of his mother's ... What if I let him have his way with me? It probably wouldn't help him. Probably nothing at all would happen to *him*, but I'd be well on my way to turning out like my mother. I'll probably turn out that way anyway. It's in the blood and nothing I can do about it. Except I've managed so far. I keep my fingers crossed about myself.

If I let Hen, and if it did help him, it would be a good deed.

His sisters don't want him to marry anybody. I could tell that, and they can see I'm about the worst there is. Where I come from shows, and probably in a lot more ways than I even know myself. And since Hen didn't care to marry Charlotte, why would he stoop to somebody like me? She can paint—bigger than any paintings I ever saw. She has wavy hair and big breasts that men always like, except she dresses so you don't notice. It would be more logical for me to make a play for Fay, and rundown places are more my type.

Except Fay compared to Hen ... is no comparison. Maybe I should work on both of them. Kill as many birds with as many stones as I can.

I T's DARK by the time I get back. Thank God for the almost-full moon. Gibbous again, but I don't feel much like a witch now. I wish I really was one. I'd witch a lot of things: first, that I should be able to stand up once I get off the horse, then, that I haven't spoiled the mom's skirt, and then, that Hen didn't come here and isn't here now and won't be here tomorrow either.

I get off and hang onto the saddle while my legs get used to holding me up. Then I see to the horse. I rub him down the way I wish somebody would rub me. (Nobody ever has, but I'll bet it feels good.) I turn him out. He's too tired for a roll in the dust, just like I'm too tired to wash up.

Charlotte is still in the kitchen reading. She often stays up late. Her lamp is often lit until all hours out in the barn, too.

It doesn't look as if anybody's been here. I don't ask but Charlotte would have told me. I guess it's easy to see how tired I am. And dirty. Charlotte brings me a pitcher of warm washing water from the back of the stove and turns down my bed. I tell her I'm sorry, but I left everything, saddle and all, on the ground by the fence. I couldn't lift a thing anymore. She just hugs me. I'm even too tired to pull away and I suppose I should be trying to get used to getting hugged. What if Hen hugged me?

The next day I'm practically an invalid. Charlotte knows without me saying. She doesn't ask a single thing about anything, like, why didn't I stay there overnight? She brings me coffee in bed and fixes me a hot bath. She tells me to soak a while. She and Fay are going out to the cows and she's left me a breakfast on the stove, and there's bread baked yesterday. It's in one of the tight-lidded cans they use to keep vermin out.

Abel sits with me as I eat. Things have changed between us even more than I thought. I'm getting worried he's going to want to sit on *my* lap one of these day. I ask him, Did he miss me yesterday? He ducks his head—almost under the table. I take that as a great big Yes. I say, "It'll be some big day when you manage to say Mary Catherine, all the way through." I tell him about my teacher calling me Cat, and Kitty, Kitty. "I wouldn't let just anybody call me those, but *you* can if you want to. If you ever get around to calling me anything."

When I finish breakfast, I hobble into the parlor so we can start on a letter to his mom about getting him an animal. Abel carries my coffee in for me. I didn't ask him to, he just does, and doesn't spill it either.

"So which do you want, Dear Ma, or Dear Mom, or Dear Mother? And that's DEAR, not DEER. This here's a deer. D is for both, but you can't draw a picture of a DEAR." (Trust Abel to figure out a way to do that.) "You don't want a DEER Mom. Or maybe you do."

I want the letter to be long and hard to write and full of big words so he'll have to work hard on it and get a lot of practice.

Abel nods Yes to—Does he want a dog? I ask him about a cat and he nods Yes again. I ask, "Horse? Bird?" Silly questions. Of course it's Yes to everything. (I want, I want, I want. He's beginning to seem like every other nine-year-old I ever knew.) "Jackknife? Motorcycle? Gramophone?" (That's what *I* want. Abel doesn't even know what it is and it's hard to explain.) "Motor car? Airplane? Applesauce?" It's not as hard to get him to giggle as it used to be.

If he talks there'll be no end to it—just like Hen said, not a single moment's peace and quiet. And he'll probably say "ain't", and "that there house", and everybody will think he learned those from me. Of course I have my pinching. I can put it to good use on bad grammar.

As it turns out, Hen was in town getting beat up the very day I was at his folks' place. Charlotte heard about it from Hen's father when they met out in the middle of nowhere like they do every so often. She called me out to the front steps that evening and told me. She said he never goes home right after. He doesn't want anybody—especially not his mother—to see him all beat up.

Then she says, "I know where he is," and I know she called me out there specially to tell me.

"Why tell me?"

"You'll be good for him."

Does she mean good for him and not me? Or does she mean because I'm *that* kind of a girl, exactly like my mother? "I don't see why, what with all those Parisian women."

"Don't be silly. If he wanted one of those he'd have brought one back. It isn't as if he isn't a hundred-percent French himself, you know."

A hundred percent! I didn't know. I don't even know what kind of a person a hundred-percent French is like. "What are you, then, and Fay and Abel?"

"They're my half brothers."

So that's why she looks so different.

"They're half-French. I don't know what I am except for Ma being Scottish. She won't talk about my father and I guess she has good reason not to. She doesn't want to be …" Charlotte looks down at her toes as if it was important that she keep an eye on them. (She's wearing those boots she seems to like so much.) We don't talk for a bit. "… be reminded," she says, "of what it was … that happened, which is why I got born."

We watch the purple shadows climb up the mountains until there's no more orange. There's a tiny line of snow just along the very tops, as if someone made a chalk outline to keep the tops apart from the sky.

I never met anybody who would admit they didn't know their own father and that maybe their father was a bad man of some sort. *I* never admit it—hardly even to myself. I've told people my father was a musician, or an actor, and hardly ever had time to come around. Nobody believed me because they knew my mother and the men who were with her, but I kept making up fathers anyway. (I never said he was dead. I needed for him to be alive.) To myself I liked to think he was a bank robber and was very rich and wanted to give me presents and come by to see me but he didn't dare because the police were watching me all the time. I even had a picture that I tore out of a library book. A man with a sort of mysterious, Mona Lisa smile. You couldn't tell if he was nice or not, but he would always have been nice to me.

"Exactly the same with me," I say. Something about Charlotte makes me want to not lie. Besides, we're a little bit the same. "Only my ma doesn't know who my father is and she doesn't care either." I'm thinking, for all I know *I* might be half-French, too. I can think that if I want to.

We sit, quiet again. We watch the barn owl take off. I'm thinking about Hen, as when am I not? "You know I don't have one single thing to offer anybody," I say. "I can't even cook." (I'm fishing for compliments. I need some right now, and she gives me some.)

"There's always enthusiasm and effort—those count for something. And you're pretty. And cooking's not so hard."

She really doesn't know me at all, and thank goodness. "Did you take a good look at my nose?"

"Oh, Mary Catherine, for heaven's sake!"

So she tells me where Hen is. It'll take more riding, but I'll be up to it by tomorrow. Anyway, I'll do it whether it hurts or not.

"Like we did last time, be sure Ma is awake and up before you leave. Set her in her chair and give her her sewing so she can pretend to be doing something. I'll bring in some wood."

(Charlotte does more of the heavy work around here than Fay. She looks strong, too, and she's brown and scarred all over—all kinds of scars.)

The next morning Fay saddles up the pretty bay for me and leaves him in the shade with the cinch loose so I can tighten up and take off right after noon dinner. Only it doesn't happen like that. That horse has to stand out there half the day, most of the time in the sun.

Abel and I work all morning on *proper* language. All about ain't and hankerings and I seen it. I have him write ten times each, I DID it, and, I SAW it, and, THOSE things, and THESE things. "It's not, 'these here things,'" I say. I tell him he should start right out talking the way his mother does and Hen's mother, too (not counting her accent). They're the best—and me, of course.

One reason I'm doing this is to slow him down some so I'll be able to stay here longer. I say, "Think before you speak. People say that all the time, but I'll bet nobody but me told it to you—ever."

I picture him all grown up and all dressed up and talking like a gentleman. Maybe he'll have a mustache. (I hope his hair won't keep on being as pink as it is now. Chances are it will darken.) Maybe he'll be a doctor or a lawyer. He'll have me to thank for everything including that he talks at all. He'll say so in front of people. He'll tell people about me even after I'm dead.

I have him write PROPER ten times. I tell him PROPER is not only how you should speak, but how you should live your life all the time.

"Manners, too," I say, "but we'll do those later. That's like not kicking the table while we're eating."

After all this hard work, I get out the Montgomery Ward catalogue. We both like looking at it. I read things to him and have him point to words with his grimy finger. (I scrub and scrub until he's all red, but he's dirty again two seconds later.) Sometimes I have him find words in it by himself. We count up prices. That way he works on numbers, too. But now I turn to the men's clothing section and show him the proper gentlemen in their dress suits and cutaway coats. After that I turn to the ladies' dresses. I've been saving my money. I know exactly which dress I want. I show Abel. He looks at me and then back to the picture and then at me again, thinks about it for a while, and then points to a different one. It's not the first time he's done that. He thinks so hard about it I keep wondering if I should really consider this other dress. I'd like to get two, but I need some of my money for fixing up this ranch.

Then we hear the sound of a horse and carriage—practically already here. We were thinking so hard about dresses we didn't notice anything until it's already at the door. We both run out. It's just an old buckboard but the lady and the man sitting there are all dressed up. At first I don't recognize her. It's been a long time and she's dressed as … like I wanted to be, sort of a flapper: A short skirt, the latest thing, but all of a sudden I'm not so sure I want one anymore. Her hair is bobbed like mine is. At least she's old and has gray that shows at the roots and plenty of wrinkles.

I say, "Maaaaaaaa." I hear it trailing off into nothing. How did she find me? And why? My dress money! I'll never catch a man without a decent dress.

"Aren't you going to ask us in for lunch?"

Of course it's exactly lunchtime.

They go right on in as if I had asked them, but I didn't. My mother sits herself down smack in the middle of the room. In fact she moves a chair so she'll be exactly in the middle. I give them the lemonade I'd made for us for lunch. They're so hot and dusty they drink it all up in two gulps. My mother introduces herself to Abel's mom and Abel's mom pays attention enough to say, "How nice of you to come," and, "How nice to meet you at last." I don't care so much about PROPER as I did a minute ago. In fact I don't care about PROPER at all.

My mother takes out a cigarette and starts smoking. I'd been thinking about taking that up, too. Women are doing it more and more now. I think it makes us look strong and modernistic, but now I don't think I'll do it. Ma's ahead of me in everything there is.

Even with that short skirt and everything skintight, my mother takes up room as if she were fat. I don't know how she can seem to take up so much space. Maybe it's the dolphins on her dress and her big yellow beads.

The man is her usual sort: too old (even for her), and big chest, big shoulders, big paunch, and big earlobes. I'll bet his thighs are as big around as my waist and I'm not a wasp waist. I've had a hard time with some of those men of Ma's. I feel sick just looking at him. I feel even worse when he ... not exactly winks at me, but sort of. No wonder I like skinny old Hen.

So there's this politeness all around and talk about the weather. Proper. Except for me. I hardly say anything. I get us our lunch that Charlotte made. I can't wait to get my mother off someplace where I can find out what she wants. But then Abel's mother goes off for her after-lunch nap. She doesn't say a word, she just gets up and goes, as if she forgot there were any guests here. And she forgot I was supposed to go off and she was supposed to stay up for a change, but now it doesn't matter.

So I decide we're alone enough for me to find out things. Abel isn't listening. He's lying on the bearskin rug, moving his lips as if talking to the bear's head. I wonder what he's telling it. Too bad I can't read lips. He's petting it, too. All of a sudden I feel so close to him. I felt this way about my teacher sometimes. I wish it was she who was visiting me instead of my mother. Someday I'll take Abel to see her.

My ma gets up and wanders around the room. "You have yourself a nice place here," she says. When she gets over by the fireplace and the bear rug, she steps on Abel's leg—I don't know if on purpose or just that she's taking up too much space. She *says* she's sorry.

"I hear you're getting paid good wages."

I'm thinking, here it comes.

I had a hope chest once. Not a chest, just a bundle. I had to give it to my mother so she wouldn't take things from my teacher. Ma didn't

think I'd have anything like that with nice things in it. I didn't like losing all that good stuff, but I did like the surprised look Ma had when
she opened the package. She thought it would be just worthless junk
because it was mine. There was a fancy hand towel I'd embroidered in
school when I was ten. I did a good job on it, too. There was a bar of
completely unused lavender soap. I was saving it for my wedding night.
I don't know what I thought my wedding night would be like back
then, but I wanted to smell nice. There was a piece of lace my teacher
gave me. I was going to make it into a wedding nightgown. I even had
a couple of dollars that I thought I'd give to my future husband. It
would be a nice present.

When I moved in with my teacher, I took the bundle with me. I
hid it pretty good, but then I had to give it to my mother to keep her
from taking things from my teacher. She said she'd tell everybody I'd
stolen the things. I started on another bundle, but this one I made especially to give to Ma just in case. I should have been doing that this
time. Except she knows I'm making money. She probably knows the
exact amount. I don't know how she finds out these things, or how she
knew I was way out here in the middle of nowhere. I felt safe out here.

She's smoking and dropping ashes all over the place even though Fay's
ash tray is right there on the table. On her second round, as she passes
the table, I see her pocket a silver spoon just as blatant as you please.
She's doing that on purpose so I'll see it and be warned.

"I've got twenty-five dollars." I don't quite, but almost.

"That's nice."

"If you leave right now and don't come back."

"Sure thing."

She's not going to go until she's good and ready and I'll have to
give my money to her anyway.

"I'll be gone from here soon, you know. Just a few weeks more."

Abel looks up startled and frightened. Right there in front of them
he says, "Caw." He comes over and leans against me like he does sometimes now.

"What a funny little boy. I heard he was odd. Simple minded,
that's what they say. Hasn't got the brains of a pea." And Abel, listening to all this.

Then I get mad. I say, "I'm about to get married." I had no idea I was going to say it until it's out. "I'll be leaving here pretty soon with my husband." Words just keep coming, all by themselves.

"Who's the lucky man?"

Of course she doesn't believe me. She won't unless I have a real person.

"Henry Ledoyt."

Oh my God, what am I saying? It'll be all over town.

Well, at least it makes Abel happy. And at least they go … with my money and my one-and-only nice scarf. Ma even takes my licorice sticks and she doesn't even like licorice.

I give up. Everything is ruined anyway. Everybody's going to hate me now. Especially Hen.

I put my forehead down on the table and rest my face in my elbow. Abel comes and pats my head like he was doing to the bear's head a minute ago. "Caw," he says, just as sweet as could be.

I stand up so fast I knock my chair over. "Abel, I have to go. Right this minute."

He looks at me as if he thinks it's for forever.

"No, I mean I have to find Hen. I'll be back. I lied. I have to tell him."

He still looks as if he doesn't understand.

"I won't leave you. Cross my heart. Did you see her take my money? I have to stay here with you and make some more." I'm thinking, of course she'll be back for that, too. *If* I stay. *If* they let me after what I said.

I sit down again and bump my forehead, hard, back on the table. I hope I get a bruise. I deserve one.

"Oh, Abel, I wanted to have a nice life in a real place like this. Just an ordinary life."

I shouldn't be saying these things to a little boy. I know better than that, but I keep on. I'd rather talk to him than anybody I know. Except maybe Charlotte. As long as he says nothing but Caw, I'll be telling him all the secrets there are about myself.

"Every single, single minute of my life I've wanted to be in a regu-lar place—like everybody else has and with things to be worked on. I don't know what to do. Everybody will hate me. Charlotte will hate me, too."

Abel shakes his head, No.

"Every single, single minute. Why do you think I worked so hard to be a teacher? It was to be here. Right here with you."

Abel leans his head down on the table next to mine. His breath is warm and makes me think of milk and hay and pitch pine. His hands are black with sap. There's even some on his cheek. He looks sticky.

"I have to go tell Henny I told a lie. I have to before anybody else tells him. You can see that."

He just keeps looking at me. I don't know if he *is* wise or just looks that way.

"I'll be back right after I tell him. You take care of your mom. Make sure she eats something. You know she likes you a lot. She loves you. She really does." He just stares. "I hope you know. She'll do what you want her to more than for anybody else. See if that isn't so."

Henny

SOMEBODY IS COMING. His horse whinnies out to them. He hides as he always does. He has hiding places all over. (There's not much vegetation except along the stream, but there is one cottonwood, his only really big tree—that's where the ants come from. There's scraggly sage. There's the wood pile. There's old tin, slanted up against the side of the old tin shack. There's lumber with rusty nails still stuck in it out back. There's a big, dirty tarp. There're rocks—all sizes, some big as a flivver.) Most times even Charlotte can't find him—or at least she lets him think she can't. He never could hide from Charlotte. When they were children he thought she was magic and a lot older even though they're the same age. She beat him up, too, over and over until he got bigger than she was, which took a long time. She keeps her mouth shut now. She knows he needs quiet and knows this is his favorite spot for it … the sound of the creek and the rustle of the aspen, rustle of little creatures. That's about as much noise as he can stand and sometimes even that's too much. Sometimes he imagines noise that isn't really there. It drives him crazy but it doesn't exist.

Papa brings food—sent by Maman. Bribes to lure him back home to the noise and confusion. Pies … cakes … Why couldn't she send him a steak sometimes? He would have gone home for a day or two now, but he has to wait until his face gets back into something Maman might recognize. There are no mirrors out here, but he can see himself in the wash basin—as if he ever washes. Sometimes … right now, he even smells bad to himself.

This time it's that girl. Charlotte must have told her he was out here. Whose side is Charlotte on anyway? After they grew up she got to be his best friend. She shouldn't have told anybody where he is.

The girl falls off her horse first thing. For a moment, mashed-up face and bad smell or not, he thinks to go help her, but she's up almost before his thought, and with a word girls don't usually say. Then she looks around as if to see if somebody heard. On her lips that damnation turns clean. On his, it's always dirtier than ever.

His gray gelding is hobbled in a grassy patch near the creek. Hops himself along from greener spot to greener spot. That girl—Mary Catherine—ties hers to a scrubby pine tree even though there's a tie line right by his front door—ties too loose and some weird kind of knot. He can even see that from where he's hiding. Didn't Charlotte tell her that's dangerous?

She's upset. Knocks hard and calls. A dozen times. "Hen, Hen, Henny," all up and down the rocks and brush. There are clean lines from tears on her cheeks.

"Please, Hen. Henny, please, please, please. Your horse is here. Please come." She waits. Calls again. "Charlotte said you might not come out, but this is important."

But this is his special, private place, and what could they possibly have to talk about? Except maybe his bruises and his black eyes. Blah, blah, blah. And not even Abel to talk at and around and over his head.

"It's important. At least to me. Please."

She circles the shack, still calling. There isn't a rattlesnake or stink bug that doesn't know his name by now. He changes hiding places, timing it with the hopping of his horse and the rustling of ground squirrels. He's lying prone. It's easier on his out-of-balance back, though no position is comfortable for long. He holds his one arm out, palm down, sights along his arm, drawing a bead on her. He's not shaking now. It always stops when he aims—even pretend aim. That's about the only time. He doesn't care much for guns, but he likes not shaking.

Pretty girl. Why would she come way out here all alone to a man she doesn't even know? Crazy man. Everybody knows that. Everybody, including himself, wonders what he's capable of. He's afraid sometimes of what's inside him. Dangerous man with medals. Decorated, the whole group—what there was left of them—decorated for simply being there. Simply that. He told Maman they were worthless, but she doesn't care. She keeps the medals anyway, arranged in a picture frame, hanging in her bedroom. There, because he refused to let her hang them in the living room where she wanted them. Course she brings them out every chance she gets.

He keeps a bead on that girl as she circles back to the door, and not one bit of trembling, but holding so still hurts his back.

Decorated for holding still and keeping out of trouble.

She sits down on his front-door stone. He dragged it over to be his doorstep. She's wearing Aunt Oriana's riding skirt and Charlotte's best straw cowboy hat. Likely she doesn't have any of her own. She takes off the hat and wipes her tears with the palm of her hand. A childlike gesture. Surely she's no threat. He ought to come out and comfort her. Maybe what she wants to tell him really *is* important.

But he can't make himself move. There were too many times when he had to make himself not move.

The sun dapples her, shining through the leaves. When she keeps quiet she seems a part of things … of nature, but then she spoils it again, though now calling more softly, as if there's no hope. "Please, Henny. Please come."

He should go on out to her if only to keep her quiet.

"I told a lie … a bad, wicked lie … About you and me."

A jay flies down right in front of her. Makes a squawking of its own. That's *his* jay (if you can ever say that about a wild creature) looking for crumbs. That jay's been on his shoulder, pecked at his ear, been on his chin and pecked at his teeth. Once hopped right into his mouth.

She stops calling, transfixed by the jay. When it's in a spot of sun, it glitters. It hops onto her shoe and turns around a couple of times. It's about to hop up to her knee. She sits utterly still. Is she, also, just as he is, no possibility of motion?

She says, "Oh, Henny," utterly discouraged now.

The bird flies up and perches right over his head as if to point him out to her. She gets up and walks all around the shack again. A little farther out this time, calling, but not so loud. She *has* given up. He hopes she has. Maybe she'll go home soon. He keeps her in the imaginary sights of his middle finger all the way around, changing his hiding place once again.

Back she comes. Tries his door. Why would it be locked?

"I'm going in." She's shouting again, so loud he thinks to cover his ears, except that takes two hands. "If you don't want me to, please say."

She waits.

He pulls an imaginary trigger. Has to get her before she goes in. *Has* to.

"I'll find paper and write you the bad thing I did."

What makes her think there's paper? But there is. His notebook. She'll find his musings. Meanderings is more the right word. Divagations. He only wrote to practice writing with his right hand. All a bunch of nonsense. And that notebook is lying open on his cot. But what had he been writing?

> *The hand that holds the hammer and the hand that holds the nail. The hand that winds the clock and the hand that holds the clock (so no clock). No wristwatch. Only one wrist. Lifting stones that day. Can lift about half the weight he could before. She must have noticed. How could she not?*
>
> *And as a lover … "His left hand is under my head, and his right hand doth embrace me." Forget the hand for under the head.*

And then there's his dirty clothes in a wad under the army cot. Books helter-skelter. She'll see the sketch he drew (back when he had a good drawing hand) of Julia, naked down beyond her belly button, on his wall in a place of honor. Like a shrine.

But perhaps she won't pry, though she doesn't seem the type not to.

> *Dead instead of me, first Uncle Bill …*

(He'd written that about a dozen times, all through the notebook, as if that was the best thing for practice writing.)

> *Then Sully, Smitty, Handy …*

She's staying in there much too long. For sure she's reading things. And written just this morning:

> *Quail woke me and something rolling acorns up and down the roof. Abel … Now there's the one-and-only quiet little kid. Now and then I try to do something for him. He's gone pretty much wild. Me, too, I guess. That girl might help him. With me it's the noise that drives me crazy, woodpeckers machine-gunning even as I write. At least it's somewhere off in the hills, so not after me. Now nobody after me but my family.*
>
> *Up in those hills once, me and Lotti—I mean Charlotte—"I'll show you mine if you show me yours." Her idea. Everything was always her idea. Good it didn't go much farther … Much. Climbed a tree*

up there and peed down, both at the same time. She tried to aim. Cursed when she couldn't. She could really curse in those days. Ever since six years old, she could curse words he never knew about. Where had she found all those words? Perhaps she made them up to impress him.

Now why jot that down? Why jot anything?

Who's wild and who's not? Who's crazy and how do you tell? Me and Abel, we have to stick together. Keep quiet together.

Dear Hen,

I don't know how to tell you except to just tell you. I'm so very, very, very sorry. My mother came. She took my money. I wanted to stop her from ever coming again so I told her I was going to be married. She didn't believe me. She never does. I thought maybe if I named a real person she'd believe, so I said it was to you. It must be all over town by now. I want to make it right ... I mean right with you and your family. I think your sisters already don't like me. What can I do to undo it? I'll do absolutely anything to fix things!

Please forgive me. Please tell me what to do.

Very, very sincerely yours,

Mary Catherine

"Henny!" She's yelling again. "Just in case you're nearby, this is what I wrote." Yells, though he's right across the way in the wood pile he made purposely to hide in and get a good view of the door at the same time. (One more crazy thing to do, out of a whole list of crazy things.) She's in his sights again, but not steady this time even though he's aiming. Bad sign.

She reads the note into the air as though to the jay. She can hardly read it she's so choked up. That's what makes him listen.

It's time. It's past time.

He comes out, his hand on his head, surrendering to superior forces.

"Oh, my God, Henny, you look awful."

"Nothing new in that."

Act normal. Say normal things. Says: "I'm sorry," and, "I don't know what to do about it either," and, "I'll have to think. I'm not getting married. That's the one sure thing I know. We have enough marrieds in the family, not to mention too many children, and who'd want to live way out here with me? No furniture, no nothing?"

She blushes. He's sorry for her. He knows she's nineteen, but right now she hardly looks fifteen. "Not even to a pretty girl like you." That makes her blush more than ever. He has the knack, but that was cruel. He should have saved it for later—if there is a later. Words and words—his as meaningless as anybody's. Could seduce her right this minute, and with just words. Could look at her with that look. She seems willing to pay most anything for her lie. Why not let her? Pick a mossy spot by the stream. The sound of water … The language of seduction—how well he knows it. Could seduce the quills off a porcupine, and it wasn't he who said it first. The whistle off a train, the scarf off Maman's piano. Maybe it comes from having two big sisters. He can charm them into almost anything, too. An ugly man needs knowhow. Some hope for Abel, then, if he learns the technique. When Abel's older, he'll give him lessons. Might even work just fine without any talk at all.

But he couldn't kiss anybody right now what with bruised lips and sore all over. Lucky girl, gets away scot-free from madman. Too bad, because she's full of sympathy. That's one way to do it, bash your face in and lose an arm.

"Oh, Henny, do you have beefsteak to put on your face?"

"If I had, I'd prefer to eat it."

Her blue-green eyes. Her hand is still over her mouth—still clutching herself after seeing his face. A nice brown hand, square, practical … a working woman's hand. Boyish, like the rest of her.

"What should I do?"

"Maybe you can get me something to eat. I'm tired of going fishing and I don't want to leave here to go get food, looking like I do."

"Oh, I will … anything you want, but what about that other? What I wrote you about?"

"Why not just say we changed our minds? We wouldn't be the first. It would be best if you say *you* changed *your* mind … after you got a real good look at me. Saw my face like it is today. And maybe you forgot I only have one arm and just remembered it in time to call things off."

There's a long pause. She doesn't know how to answer that one. She's hardly stopped blushing for even a second since he came out of hiding and now here comes another one.

She changes the subject. "Abel's alone with just his mom. I should get back."

"Abel alone is the usual thing."

"I'll get food. I'll be back tomorrow, but I might have to bring Abel."

She wants to escape from him. He can't blame her. "Fine, just so he's still not talking."

"I won't talk either. I promise I won't say a single word."

So she *did* read his meanderings. Fat chance, anyway, that she could keep her mouth shut.

What if he kisses her, holds her, gets his dirty smell and his sweat all over her, be the crazy man he is? It would be good if somebody taught her she ought to be careful of men like him out here alone.

But he can't even help her untie her horse. Bad knot that needs *at least* two hands. Let her muddle through, then. Let her go on making things harder than they have to be. He'll just take a walk off up in the hills. Or maybe follow the creek and pick himself a bunch of wild-flowers.

He should have kissed her right away instead of working at that knot and showing himself incapable of even doing that, and right in front of her. But he'd thought to let her go—let her escape him. Untie the horse and send her safely on her way.

Wildflowers and a lot of sage, too, so as to smell something other than himself. Leave right now, damn it. Damn it! Turn his back on her and leave.

Mary Catherine

I WISH, I WISH, I WISH, I WISH … I don't even know what anymore.

Henny looked so angry! I could see it in his eyes. He was going to untie my horse for me but then he stamped away and didn't even look back. I heard him say, "Damn, damn," to himself.

And all *I* did the whole time was blush.

His hut is a lot worse than I thought it would be, especially after seeing his parent's house. I don't care. I like him anyway, and I could fix it up for him. But I don't see how he lives in such a small place. Maybe ten feet by twelve?

And what about the sketch of that girl? I'll bet Hen drew it and I'll bet she sat there half-naked so he could. Maybe all naked. That's just a sort of towel in her lap. I'll bet she has golden hair. She has this wide, pure forehead, and little curls at the sides. She has sloping shoulders. Whoever drew it, drew one long smooth *perfect* line from her ear to her elbow.

I give up. I don't wish anything.

What does it matter, anyway? Pack up and leave the books for Abel. Except I promised Hen steak. I guess I'll have to make one more trip out to that tin hut. (I *would* live there if it was with him.)

As I near the barn, almost home, I see this dead baby bird. Right above it, under the eaves, there's a nest and two babies still in it. I notice the dead one because it's surrounded by tiny yellow weedish flowers that nobody would think were flowers except a child. First there's the yellow ring of weeds and after that a circle of railroad spikes. Next to the bird's head there's a pink pebble that looks like an egg. I don't know why all this makes me feel like crying. Why would I cry over a dumb dead bird when I have troubles of my own?

It's just like Abel not to even know about burying things under-ground in boxes. I'll have to teach him how we bury dead things, but I wonder if I'll have the chance. Maybe they won't let me be here after my lies, and I won't be teaching him anything else at all. Or maybe never teach anybody anything ever again because everybody will know all about my making up stories. Maybe I don't even want to teach anymore. I'll run away, far enough this time, to not ever see my mother. Far enough so I'll never have to hear about any of these people. I'll forget Hen even though he's the *only, only* one I ever … I mean *really* ever. Till now I never knew what love was. But I'll start over. I'll change myself entirely. I'll cut my hair into bangs and I hate bangs. That'll prove it. I don't care how I look anymore—even in front of Hen.

I come around the side of the barn and I see Fay there—alone for once. It's odd, but he doesn't hear me coming. He's standing beside the buckboard staring into the bed of it—which is mostly empty except for some burlap bags. He's drumming his fingers on the sides. I wonder how long he's been staring and drumming like that. I wonder if it could be me he's thinking about.

I can scare *him*. Henny scares me, but I can scare Fay, easy as pie.

He sees me as soon as I'm all the way around the barn. I get off the horse and fall down—on purpose this time. I've had a lot of practice. I can make it look real. Since he's a nice person, there's no other thing for him to do but help me up.

Of course he doesn't look at me, even as he's helping me. He's watching some spot up by the eaves. He touches me like I'm a rattlesnake, which makes me feel even more like being one. I hang onto him tight and lean my breasts against him. That'll scare him good. "I hurt my leg," I say.

He's trying to get his hands in between us to push me away, but I'm holding him so tight he can't do it. The horse doesn't like this one bit. He's not tied up yet. He dances around right next to us. It's scary, but I don't let go of Fay. Then the horse makes a high-pitched squeal I never heard a horse do before, and gallops off, saddle and all. Fay tries to grab him, but with me hanging on, he misses. Then we fall, him on top. I feel he's hard already, but that doesn't stop him from trying to get away. (I wouldn't have noticed except my stepfathers used to try and rub against me sometimes, so I know all about that.)

My nose is almost right against his nose and he still doesn't dare look at me. I hold him tight on top of me. I say, "It's all your fault Abel doesn't talk, you know." I kind of grunt it out. "You're ruining your little brother just because of some dumb old person that died years and years ago."

That makes him angry, which makes him stronger. I guess he was being polite before, or too scared to really touch me, but now he doesn't care. He's pushing at me right on my breast and he doesn't even care about that.

I say, "You're yellow."

I'm holding a bunch of his shirt in back and it rips all the way down. That's what comes of never having any new, decent clothes. I reach up and grab his hair instead. "Scaredy cat," I say.

What if Charlotte sees us? She'd know it's my fault and it'll be one more reason to send me away.

Then Fay hits me. Not just slaps. He punches me—fast, hard punches, right in my face. Knocks my head from side to side so my brains are jolted. I never thought he'd do anything like that. If any-body's going to hit me I'd rather it would be Hen. (Just like I thought before, if we ever get together, I'd let Hen beat me if he needed to.) I'm so stunned and kind of rattled that I let go and Fay runs off and here I am on the ground, dust all over Abel's mother's riding skirt and with a face that I know is about to look like Hen's—yellow and purple and scratches and scabs like his, too. Why in the world did I do that and say all that? I do so many bad things, especially lately, I can't keep track of myself. I have to change right this minute. I'll be anything Henny wants me to be. Except he hates me. He was really angry! I couldn't tell what he was going to do. He had this dangerous look, like: Get out of here as fast as you can or you'll be sorry, which I did. I didn't dare not. He didn't even help me up on the horse, just said those Damn, damns, turned his back on me, and walked away.

But it's *me* I should be trying to keep in line.

I get up and dust myself off and limp to the house. First thing I'll do is cut my bangs. That'll teach me a lesson.

Abel must have seen us. He's crying when I come in. I haven't seen him do that since the crow. I hug him. At first he just lets himself get hugged, but then he hugs me back. At least *he* still likes me. He's about the one-and-only person left anywhere who does.

Early next morning, just when I *finally* manage to get to sleep, Charlotte knocks and then comes right on in. I forget I wanted to hide my bruised face and my chopped-off bangs. She starts out saying, "Fay's gone. His bed's not ..." but then she says, "Oh my God," just as I did with Hen. "Did Henny do that? I know he's in bad shape, but I didn't think ... Not Henny!"

She comes right in and sits on the bed. I pull up the sheet so she won't see my worn out, too-small nightgown. I wouldn't be surprised if I haven't had it since I was eleven. But then I push the sheet down again, because what I've done is worse than any old nightgown ever could get to be.

"Charlotte, you'll send me away for sure."

"Why in the world?"

"It was Fay did it, but it was all my fault. If he's gone that's my fault, too. I'll leave. You don't have to tell me to."

"I'm going to need you. What did you do?"

Now I do cover my face. I pull the sheet up to my forehead. "I called him yellow. I made him help me get up and then ... well, I kind of leaned against him ... on purpose. I scared him. On purpose, and then I wouldn't let go of him."

She looks at me really hard, like, do I measure up to some yardstick of her own. "I need you," she says. "I need for you to go get Hen. Right away. If we can't rustle up Fay, I'm going to need Hen. He might as well be doing something useful."

I don't know if she means she needs me just for now—for getting Hen, or if she needs me in general in the future. And I'm thinking I can't possibly face Hen again, but I know I'll have to do it anyway. Unless I run away before-hand.

"I told him I'd get steak, and for his black eyes, too."

"Seems to me you need that more than he does. You just take him some of that corn bread and pork we had. Forget his eyes. That's his own fault. I figure he must want to look like that or he wouldn't let it happen all the time. But I don't know about you."

"He'll hide. You know how he does. And he's mad at me. Very, very mad."

She gives me that long look again, but she doesn't ask anything, thank goodness.

"You tell him Charlotte says he'd better come on out and help us find Fay, and don't shout it. He can't stand shouting."

"I know that now."

"Tell him to pull his hat way down so we don't have to look at his ugly mug."

I'm thinking, my mug, too.

"You don't sound very worried."

"Oh, for heaven's sake, Fay is seventeen. Way older than his pa and Uncle T-Bone were when they ran away west. He's probably on that gelding you rode."

"He only has that torn shirt. I tore it."

"Get along on with it."

Oriana

THEY DON'T KNOW IT, but she hears everything. Usually nothing matters, that's the reason she forgets it. Not this, though. It was about her little Fayette.

Going on up. And she's already passed where the mariposa lilies are. And the larkspur. Such a beautiful, deadly flower! Deadly!

Think about the sky instead, those little clouds that hover around the mountains. They'll gather up later on. Has Fayette got his slicker? He always forgets. But he's a grown-up now. She must remember that.

Her walking shoes feel odd after wearing nothing but slippers for so long. Her feet hurt. Abiel wanted to buy her hiking boots, but she said no. What an extravagance! Boots, and she hardly went anywhere.

Everybody except Abel gone off now—one direction or another. Fay ran away before, when they tried to get him to go to school. Nine or ten years old then. They thought he'd have to talk in school, but they couldn't make him go. Once he was found thirty miles away when somebody gave him a ride in an automobile, the first one ever around here. Abiel never got to see one. Airplanes. The whole world's changed. The war. Abiel never even got to see Abel.

Abel was in the parlor humming when she left. At least with him always humming that way, you can keep track of where he is. Maybe he was reading. Anyway, with a book. She looked in on him before she left. Pieces of green felt all over the floor because that girl is trying to fix the organ. Perhaps Abel really *is* reading by now. That girl, even with all her faults, makes progress. Or maybe *because* of her faults. Maybe she's the exact sort of person they've needed all this time. Except for last night.

That organ—fixed or not, she won't play it and that's that, so they'd better not be expecting her to. It used to be she could play any-thing, waltzes, gallops, a lot of Chopin ... Abiel would have liked her to play more. It fell away by itself. Everything changes. Sometimes one thing's important and sometimes another. But she should be teaching

Abel, he, just humming and in-and-outing on that harmonica. In-and-out, in-and-out. She feels like a harmonica herself. Breathing. All this breathing, and out of breath already.

She hasn't been up here since ... not since Abiel took her. She'd thought she'd not ever go again. Why would she?

Abel must have been conceived somewhere up here.

The old picnic tie line is down. Once a horse panicked and pulled the whole thing out, four big posts and all. Dragged them halfway up the trail. Abiel finally got him. (Why did it always have to be Abiel rescuing things? Why couldn't he sit back and let somebody else do it just once?) That was the first she'd realized just how strong a horse is. Now the wires are down, but the posts are still up.

She might have brought chicken. They all liked fried chicken. She'd thought about it. She'd thought about the milking, too. Had she done it? She usually brought fried chicken.

Lemonade. She used to bring that.

She used to sit on this very rock, Matou, Crazy, Strawberry, and all, all tied up to that tie line. The viewpoint behind her. They always climbed up to take a look at the ranch before the trail turned round the big boulders.

She climbs to the viewpoint and looks down. (Did she used to have to go on her hands and knees?) Way, way down there's a red thing climbing up. That's got to be Abel in his too-small red shirt. He's carrying the biggest canteen they have. He's got two canteens, the big and a little. She ought to go down and help him. He'd pull away and keep on carrying them by himself. You can't argue with somebody who doesn't talk at all. She never could argue with Abiel either. He would listen and then do whatever he thought he had to do. Mostly he did do what she wanted him to. Just now and then ... and going off drinking.

Little Abel and that big load of water ... She will drink some and make it lighter.

Instead she turns and hurries on up around the corner, walking faster than before. She'll be out of sight now. She mustn't be looked at, even by Abel. Sometimes he stares just like Abiel did. If she can get up to where the snow never melts she won't need water anyway. She never did like being looked at. Especially hid from Father, but hid from Mother, too. Mother, always just around the corner. Always seeing if she was doing something wrong or about to and somehow she always was. Now Abel has found her out. She mustn't be seen. Except by Abiel. Then everything will be all right.

But it's Fayette she's looking for. She must remember that. She must hurry.

Her feet are sore and her knees hurt. Lie down and take a rest. Wait for Abel. He has the water. It's shady and familiar, here under this tree. Perhaps Abel was conceived right on this very spot. There was an almost-full moon. Abiel, smoothing his mustache out of the way of their kisses. His white hair in the moonlight!

Poor Abel. From now on she'll pay more attention. She'll be a real mother to him. She'll have picnics like they used to do. With lots and lots of lemonade.

Every time Abiel came back, everything was all right. The important thing is to find him. Before it's too late. He might have pneumonia again, like when she thought she'd lost him, but she hadn't. She hadn't.

Mary Catherine

THE DESERT has that odd, sour, bitterish smell. It's raining some-place. That doesn't mean it'll rain on me. It could be pretty far away and still smell this way. (I always think that's wet sage that smells, though what do I know?)

I'm on a different horse, of course. This one's kind of balky so Charlotte actually gave me spurs. That sobered the horse up right away. I didn't use them but once. Charlotte said not to—just use them once so she'd know I had them on.

It would be fun, as I ride along, to be pretending I'm coming home to my little cottage by the stream where I live with Hen, and that I've already painted it so it doesn't look all rusty, and inside we'd have a real bed and a chair and a chest. There isn't much room so they'd all be small. Hen would have made them. (Can he, with just one arm? I would have helped him most likely.) But I'm so upset with myself I can hardly dream my own daydreams. I don't want to think about my face and my bangs, but I do. I don't want Hen to see me.

I shouldn't be thinking any of this, good or bad. I *should* be work-ing on my own character, not worrying about my looks. I should be try-ing to make myself into a more desirable person for my husband—if there ever *is* going to be a husband. Henny already knows I'm not the sort of person anybody in their right mind would marry. He probably knows—it always gets around—that I'm from the wrong side of every town there ever was. *Way* on the wrong side.

I'm not any of the things a proper woman is supposed to be. I should have virtues and refinements. I shouldn't yell like I did in front of him, there by his shack. I should be soft. Not pinch people. Is that ladylike? I *am* being a witch, and who'd want to marry a witch? No-body, that's who.

I have this book *The Art of Conversation*. I got it for Abel. I thought he might as well begin properly—not have a lot of bad habits he had to get rid of—but I'm reading it for myself, too, like: "A loud harsh voice betokens bad breeding." That's me. I told Abel to watch out for his tone of voice right from his first word. (Which, considering it's caw, there's not a lot to practice on.) In the book it said, "Nothing attracts more than a soft and sweet tone." I practice that as I ride along.

But I keep coming back to my other problems without meaning to. I'm wondering what would happen if Charlotte told me to leave the ranch and I didn't. What if I stayed here no matter what anybody said? What if I slept under a tree with a little piece of tarp over me? Could they kick me out? And what if I went right on fixing the dam and painting the house? Maybe I don't have to leave until I want to.

In any case, before I go, or even after, I'm going to see to it that Abel gets a bird and a horse and a dog and a cat. Why not all? There's lots of room.

And there are crows all over the place. Maybe they're even ravens. They're big. I should never be without a burlap bag so I can catch things. But Abel would probably be cawing all the more.

One thing, though, I'm not going to cry again. I'm simply not. Especially not in front of Hen. And I won't let him see my hair and my face this way. He thinks enough bad things about me already.

This is just flat desert with nothing much but sagebrush. If that hut wasn't so rusty I'll bet I could see it from here. Of course it's awfully close to the creek with scrubby willows and aspen around and there's lots of big rocks, some almost big enough for the whole hut to hide behind.

Henny

She's riding a different horse. It's that little mustang they'd found starving. Never did grow up to quite full size, but pretty. This one's dappled dun with black mane and tail, three black socks and one white sock. Aunt Jenny used to say, "No white feet, buy him. One white foot, try him. Two white feet, don't go nigh him …" Old wives' tales, though maybe a little truth in it as to the hardness of the hooves. Uncle Bill always said, "A good horse is never a bad color."

He wants to hide—or run off for a long walk by himself, but for sure she'll have gone out of her way to get him steak. He should stay and greet her and thank her.

He comes out to help her down. Her hat's pulled so far over her face it's a wonder she can see. Looks rakish. Why is she wearing it like that?

She waves him away. He's on the near side and she keeps looking over towards her right knee, ignores his helping hand and gets down by herself, gets the saddlebags herself though he was about to. Anything so as not to look at him. So as to hide. It doesn't work. He can see her bruises.

"I couldn't get steak. I'm sorry." She raises the saddle bags for him to take and to hide her face behind them.

When you only have one hand, everything comes down to a choice: Take the saddlebags or pull her wrist to make her lower them. She wants him to take the bags—to get rid of him. He grabs her wrist instead.

"Let me see. You're no worse off than I am."

She turns away and leans her head against the saddle. That pushes her hat back.

"I couldn't get steak."

"You said."

There's something odd about her bangs. She couldn't have used scissors. Could she? Can you cut your hair with a pocket knife?

"I brought pork slices and cornbread. Bacon, too, but it's not cooked."

"S'all right."

Her cheek against the horse, her hat falls all the way back. She might be crying.

He turns her towards him, lifts her chin. She lets him take a good look. She's as if cornered—as if there's nothing else to do but face the enemy, which is him. He can see her blush right through the bruises. He'd like to hug her as he would one of his sisters when they're unhappy, but she's so scared of him. Tears brim over even as he watches. She shakes her head, angry at herself.

"It's all right."

He does hug her, takes her by the shoulder and pulls her to him. She starts to pull away, but then she lets him hold her, puts her forehead on his shoulder. You can hardly tell she's crying except for her shaky breathing—as if she's afraid to cry any harder than that in front of him. It hurts him to stand still like this. There's always pain in his back because he's always off-kilter. They said he should exercise the other arm—what's left of it—so as to even things out. He hasn't done much of that since he left the hospital. They said it would never really stop hurting anyway, and it hasn't, as they said, no matter what he does.

He lets the pain get worse until she's had enough crying, then brings her to his doorstep stone. He thinks to sit on the ground and let her sit on the stone, but she says, "No, you sit there," so they both end up sitting on the ground with their backs against the stone. Somehow they got turned around and she leans against his handless side. She must be feeling the stump, no way 'round it. Does she think it's disgusting? this lump touching her back? Maybe she keeps blushing all the time because she's embarrassed that she finds him revolting and is afraid he'll see it in her face.

"So what happened to you?"

"Charlotte said for you to come and help us find Fay. He ran away because of me. I don't want to say why. Please don't make me say. Not right now."

What makes her think he could make her say? "To look at us, we're two of a kind."

"No. We're not. Not at all. I brought this on myself practically on purpose. I knew it was wrong."

"You think I don't know what *I* do is wrong?"

She looks right at him then. They're so close. Her blue-green eyes … Her forehead, pale, bluish, is just about the only part of her face that isn't bruised. She's not at all the kind of girl he'd ever really care about, but he thinks, as he had last time, to kiss her. It's been a long time since he sat this close to a woman that wasn't a sister or a niece or a nurse. (Everybody fell in love with the nurses. Standard procedure.) Or had his arm—stump that is—around anybody female. She's a pretty girl, though not so pretty right now. One eye's nearly swollen shut and then those bangs … every which way … bruise on her jaw … They'd both hurt too much for any kissing.

They told him he could live a full life. No reason not to. What did they mean by that? (One doctor said he'd be sixty-five percent normal, whatever that means.) What kind of a full life? How full? Full of what? Compared to what?

There was a girl once. There was dancing and lots of good music, all kinds, tangos, rags … Now maybe not ever have the kind of girl he really wanted. Maybe never dance. Who's going to want to hang onto his stump?

"I didn't think you … I thought you knew what you were doing."

"I do know. I know it's wrong and serves no purpose. I do it anyway. I hurt my mother. I hurt my whole family. I hurt myself. I know that."

"Charlotte said you want to look like this or you wouldn't keep fighting, but I don't want to. I didn't think Fay would ever do anything like this, but I scared him so—on purpose, too."

He can guess what must have scared Fay. Thinks of himself at seventeen. Ignorant farm boy. Except for French and piano, so a little more of an education than some. Well, a lot more than some, but still not knowing much about the world other than hay and horses. Fayette has all that—the French and the music. Where might he run off to? Join the army and see the world. Maybe not so bad to do that nowadays.

His back is getting sore again.

"Mary Catherine."

"What? … What? …"

There's a breeze. It's cooling off. A fine day for lovemaking, and what they say, about her mother—*know* about her mother … Maybe she's like that, too. But maybe she isn't.

"Let's eat. I'm hungry for some real food. I have a bouquet of flowers in my coffee pot. I'll take them out and make you coffee. The flowers … they're for you."

She looks about as pleased as anybody he ever saw look pleased. Blushes all over again. He picks up the saddlebags so as to turn away from his lie, or he'll be blushing, too, out of guilt.

So she's getting the food out and he's about to make coffee.

"All your books are in French."

"They are."

"Don't you ever read English?"

"I do."

"You were in Paris."

"Yes." Yes, he was in Paris.

That time, the last time she was here, he could have shot her down. He was steady and calm, looking out across his arm. Could have shot her up—up into the trees—pieces of her up with the rest of the pieces of the dead, up into what was left of the trees. Friends hanging in the trees as if taken apart and hung out to dry. Her skirt, her blouse, her shoes … Blast her up. He wouldn't look. He hadn't looked then either. Just one tiny glance and it was all—*all* burned into his brain. Seared on the back of his eyeballs. Worse things had happened. Maybe worse. How measure? But this is what keeps coming back when he least expects it. Smitty's arm. His watch. His sleeve. His wedding ring. Somebody's boot with the foot still in it. No rings on Mary Catherine's hands. No watch. He wouldn't know who's hand it was. He was knocked down by the blast. No, that was another time, before this one. This time he'd turned away. Gagged. Kept his eyes on his boots so as to not see. He'd thought about wet feet. Foot rot. Most didn't last long enough to get it. *They'd* lasted though, until … then … when they'd landed in the trees. He'd lasted. Most of him. Others were worse off. He has no right to feel sorry for himself.

He takes the flowers out of the coffee pot. There were violets all over. Not around here, just back there. Even so he has to stop, lean against the wall. Gasp, then gag. Again gag. Because of violets. Because of flowers.

"Hen. Henny. Does it hurt? I'm so thoughtless and stupid and stupid and stupid and stupid."

Say, "No." She'll not believe his no, but best, to let her think it's something simple like pain in his stump. She'd think him as crazy as he really is if she knew that that picture in his mind was as clear as she is right now. Wedding rings! Boots full of feet! You'd think he'd have gotten over it by now.

He's on his knees, says "No" again. She touches his shoulder like she's scared to—just the tips of her fingers and at arm's length.

"I'm all right." It comes out louder than he meant it. He sounds angry, even to himself. He hadn't wanted that.

She's on her knees now, too, and still afraid to come close or touch him, yet she touches. Like a wild creature, ready to run. Cornered. She won't get away. But he's the one who's cornered. "No. No!" He grabs her. Hard. Brutal. Flops her backwards on the earth floor. Falls on her, grabs at her breast, nuzzles her neck. Anything, anything to distract himself from that vision. And she will. She'll let him, but how unbutton all these little buttons? There must be a dozen. She's not helping. She's lying as if paralyzed. So, not bother with the buttons, go straight to the riding skirt. Yes, she will. She'll do it, but she doesn't help. Does she think he's a whole man? That he can butter his bread or cut his steak? Does she think he can wash under his right arm pit?

She's trembling. He is, too, but then he always is, and it's always worse after he's just seen that vision.

It isn't going to work—not with her being a scared bed post. A virgin after all—probably—in spite of who her mother is. Well, why not? Is he anything like his family? Not fair to think she has to be like hers.

He gives up. It's over anyway. He lies there on top of her, his face pressed into the earthen floor. He spits at the bits of dirt in his mouth. Over, and thank God.

She says, "You hate me, don't you. I don't blame you."

It feels good to have another human body ... a female body close to his. He'd like her to shut up, that they just lie quietly like this for a while. Not think at all. Just feel the warmth of each other.

"Rest," he says. "I don't hate you." What is she fishing for?

"Even after all the things I said and did and some things I didn't even tell you about?"

"Even after."

"But…and Fay gone." She tries to get up. "We have to go find him."

"Just rest."

"I hate myself."

"Shhhh. Rest a minute. Don't cry. Or cry if you want. It's all right."

What possessed him? She's a nice girl. Charlotte said she was a good helper. Said she couldn't get along without her. If he keeps on like this she'll run away for sure.

He raises himself on his elbow (a prop is about all that arm is good for) and kisses her forehead, the only place on her face that isn't bruised. Kisses the hacked-at bangs. Poor waif. Then he moves down so as to lay his head on her breast.

"Rest. Just rest."

At first she lies, stiff and trembling, but in a few minutes she puts her arms around him, slowly, afraid of him still, one across his shoulder and one, so tentatively, on the back of his head.

"Don't be scared. I won't. Just let me be here for a minute or so."

His right hand doth embrace … His good hand doth … As if they were lovers.

Oriana

SOMEONE IS PUTTING wet cloths on her forehead. Someone is putting water on her lips, lifting her head and helping her to drink. She keeps her eyes shut. Everything is all right now. She's found him. Whoever it was. Nobody is lost.

She wakes again and, again, there's a freshly dampened cloth on her forehead. She opens her eyes. It's not Abiel, it's her little redheaded boy, her sweet, sweet boy. Is that him muttering? Such a sweet boy. "Yes," she says. "Yes."

"Ma. Get up, Ma."

"You're my little redhead."

"Get up, Ma. You need to be over in the shade. Please, Ma."

"Yes, yes." Her littlest boy.

Mary Catherine

I DON'T KNOW WHAT Henny means by *anything!* It's all so peculiar. Like being inside somebody else's nightmare. And I don't know if he hates me or not. Sometimes men do that when they hate you. I don't understand it, but they do. I know because I once heard a man say he hated some old lady so much he wanted to knock her down and rape her. Maybe that's how Hen feels about me, but he's too nice to *really* do it—just almost.

We lie there, him with his arm around me. I watch the sunny spot from the little window move across the wall and up one of the boxes. It moves right up to the sketch of the naked girl, and I think: Well, you may be more beautiful, but *I'm* the one he's on top of right now, not you.

That's his only window. I couldn't stand that for very long—just one window, specially with such a nice view outside—but I would stand it if I had to. I wonder if you can cut holes in these tin houses. I'd do that first thing, and paint after.

The French books are piled up on the floor, one on top of the other every which way, torn strips of paper stick out of all of them. Some are close by so I can read the titles: Gide, Malarmé, De Toqueville ... I never heard of any of them, not a one. There's two in English, Thoreau and Whitman. I've heard of them. I'm good at poetry. I'm wondering how to work it into the conversation so I can show what I know.

For a minute I think Henny's gone to sleep, but then he moves to take his weight off me and right after he holds me real tight for a minute. Then he lets go and then holds me tight again. It's like a signal, but I don't know what he means.

I think about when he kissed my forehead, his lips so soft and warm. Thinking about it makes me prickle all over, except it wasn't anything like a lover's kiss, though how would I know? I've been grabbed and kissed, but, old as I am, I've never yet—*still* not yet—had anybody love me and kiss me *that* way. The people who kissed me were never the people I wished would kiss me. Not even once. I'll probably live my whole life without ever getting a real lover's kiss.

I wish he'd say something. He's not asleep. I'd like to say something but I know he wants me to keep quiet. I hardly dare move let alone ask any of the things I'd like to ask, like: What made those funny little scars all over you? And *are* they all over you?

I have that same feeling I had when Abel leaned against me after we saw his mom all sprawled out ... that Hen needs somebody and right now, but not necessarily me. Anybody would do.

I've never been this close to somebody I liked the looks of, my hand actually on the back of his head. He and Abel feel sort of the same. Bony.

If we were married, this is how it would be every night. If I was married to *anybody,* this is how it would be. I can't see any of him except his hair, so it could be anybody—anybody with hair as black and straight as an Indian's. I think about pain. I think how he shakes, though not right this minute. Is it me? Because I'm here? Or maybe you don't shake when you're resting like this. I think how I can't believe I'm lying here with somebody who's a hundred-percent French and a hundred-percent elegant.

He takes his hand off my shoulder and puts it on my breast again, and I get scared again and even sort of sick. Then he takes it off and puts it at my waist, which scares me almost as much. I didn't ever think I'd be as scared as this. Or maybe it's that I'm so scared of him in general. Maybe he's doing it on purpose to scare me.

I tell myself not to think bad thoughts. I tell myself not to look at the naked girl. I tell myself to listen: the swishing of the leaves ... I can hear the creek if I think about hearing it. I hear quail going, tobacco, tobacco, and squawks that might be the jay. I can see a bit of sky out that little window. It's clouding over and there's even more of that sour rained-on-desert smell.

I let my hand move to the back of his neck, right on his bare skin. He's damp and warm. His breathing ... the thump, thump of his heart ... Yes, I would. Even though I'm so scared, I would. For his sake, and even if he only wants to because he's mad at me.

He rolls to the side, rests his head on what's left of his arm, and looks at me long and hard and as if he's wondering what I'm thinking as much as I'm wondering about him. He's got smudges of dirt from the floor on his face. He says, "Mary Catherine," again. Again as if there's something about my name. I know there's no sense in answering.

He's about to put his hand on my cheek, but hesitates. Right then there's a huge clap of thunder. I say, "Shouldn't we be worried about Fay?"

"No," he says, and, "Shhhh."

Then he does touch, right on my bruised cheek, but so lightly it doesn't hurt. There's more thunder and then rain or maybe hail. It's hard to tell which on this tin roof. Hen looks at the ceiling and I get a good view of his straight, French nose.

"That sounds nice," he says, "but I'd better go see how the horses are doing."

He doesn't move. Then he groans a long groan-sigh. I feel it all through him. He turns so he can use his good arm to help himself get up. He's shaking again and he must be half-starved because by now even *I'm* hungry. I wonder what time it is? (He doesn't have a clock.) I wonder if I'll be stuck here all night. What will people think? But I know what. They'll think I'm just like my mother, like they always knew I'd be. "Blood will out," they'll say. (I used to hope my mother wasn't my mother for exactly this reason, but she's not the sort of person who would take in somebody else's brat. I have to be hers. She only kept me because she didn't know what else to do with me. I've also wondered if she was raising me to take over for her when she gets too old. Make money for her or find her a rich son-in-law. I always worry about that: "Blood will out.") If I stay here all night, even Hen will know I'm like my mother. I wonder how I can escape and keep on his good side at the same time?

It's raining hard—the kind of rain that soaks you in half a minute. Here in the desert that's about the only kind of rain there is. It has to be like that to reach the ground at all. Hen doesn't even put on his slicker, though it's hanging right on the back of the door. If it was anybody else (Fay for instance) I'd have yelled at him not to forget it. Just what he needs, only one arm and pneumonia.

I get the food. I lay it out on the army cot. There's no table, so it's either that or the floor. You'd think Hen would want a table and a chair so he can write in his notebook. There's room for small ones. He just doesn't bother about anything.

I try to make the food look good. I spread out the cold pork slices and arrange the cornbread beside them. I shell the hard boiled eggs, but I don't think there's even any salt and pepper here. I looked. He doesn't have but one rusty tin plate. I'll let him use that. There's two pails of clean water. I use some to start the coffee. (The fire's already laid in the stove. It's one of those squat little stoves with only one set of rings for cooking things, all there's room for in here.) He's out there longer than I thought he'd be. When he comes back in, he drips all over everything. It gets muddy right in the shack—right where we were lying. I'd say something, except it's not *my* shack. Why should I care?

"Well, *I've* still got a horse."

So that's the second horse I've lost unless Fay has the first one.

He grabs two slices of pork and puts them together as if they were a sandwich, not even looking at how nicely I've arranged things. I had thought we'd sit on the cot, one on each side of the food and have our first meal together as if it's special. He seems to think everything is ordinary and that we haven't just spent a whole afternoon on the floor in each other's arms. He eats standing up and with his fingers, but I sit down. Then I think, of course he's too wet to sit down. And then I think, he can't cut up his meat anyway.

I thought I was hungry, but it's hard to eat. Everything is dry. There's no butter or anything for the cornbread and I can't face an egg. So then I think to have some coffee, but there aren't any cups. Hen sees me looking around. "Sorry," he says. "I just drink right out of the pot, but you have to be careful not to burn yourself. Or there's a saucepan somewhere. You could use that. Or I could go get the cup from the stream."

I use the saucepan. (The coffee I made tastes terrible and of course there's no sugar or cream or milk to help it out.) Then he drinks from the spout. He doesn't say anything about how bad it tastes. He sees I'm not eating the food I took—just that one bite. If I hadn't had the coffee I would have choked.

"Are you all right?"

He's staring at me. I can't read his face. He's chewing and speculating … those black, black, French eyes. I feel sick … and trapped … and seen right into. He chews and chews, slower now. He's still holding what's left of those two slices of pork, big bites taken out of them. He reaches towards me. If he touches me, it'll have to be with pork.

All of a sudden I'm so scared I can't stand it anymore. Scared of him looking right inside me, but mostly scared of myself because I don't want to cry again and I mostly don't want to throw up right in front of him. I go out the door and start to run—up—*up* his back hill. It's steep and slippery—steeper and slipperier than I thought it would be. I'm on all fours. I don't know why I go up. It's not in the direction of anything. Maybe I'm thinking I want to make it hard for him to follow. He's close behind me anyway and gaining fast. I'm grabbing at sage to pull myself up. Then I turn my back against the bank and kick out at him.

"Wait," he says, "Wait a minute. I won't hurt you. I won't even touch you." But he *is* touching. He's trying to pull me up.

The rain has stopped and the light is weird and orange and magic. Even as I kick out I think how nice it looks, but I keep on fighting anyway. If I could just get a grip on his elbow or wrist … But I don't think my pinching would work on him and I'm not sure I want him to ever know about that.

He's trying to pull me up the bank. He's not taking me back towards the shack. "I want to show you something." So then I let him. There's not much I can do about it anyway. He has an iron grip on my wrist. We keep going. Whatever it is, is a long way up. We're away from the trees that line the creek and back in the desert. We wind around sage and chamise and Indian pipe and boulders. It's steep. I'm even more out of breath than I was when I tried to kick him away. We go up for maybe twenty minutes. Off and on the sun is out and we start to dry off. At the top he plunks me down on a big rock. It's big enough for both of us, but he sits on a different one a couple of yards away as if he really isn't going to touch me anymore. I can't run away now. I have to catch my breath first.

"There," he says. "Look at that. Isn't that nice?"

And it is. Nobody ever did this kind of thing with me before—take me somewhere just for a nice view—never once. And it's all the nicer now, in this funny orange light. The ground is orange and the yellow grass is orange. The buckwheat is oranger than ever. You can see the shiny tin roof of Henny's shack below us, all rosy. Way off across the valley and part way up the far mountains, you can see the trees that are around Hen's family's ranch, and on this side, nearer, the trees of ours. I think "ours" even though I'm about to be kicked out—unless I can do something very, very wonderful like find Fay or have Abel talking in about ten minutes.

"And there's your horse. Now how did she get way down there?"

"I don't have a horse and I never did." (Why am I letting myself sound so angry right in front of such a nice view?)

"I promise I won't touch you. Really."

I'm pretty sure he won't, except he did go kind of crazy for a minute. He hurt me, the way he slammed me down. But he was the one hurting—something awful to go down on his knees like that. All of a sudden I'm worried maybe he *will* keep his promise and never touch me again. I did like being needed and I liked ... I *do* like ... I *think* I like ... It's just that I'm so scared of it. And it's just that I've spent my whole life so far trying to avoid being pawed (and worse) by men who always think I'm like my mother.

He leans back on his good arm and we look out for a while. I think: There, if he likes quiet, he's got lots of it now—I'm not saying a word. After a while he turns around. "It's nice back this way, too."

I see the snowcapped mountains behind us, and foothills bigger than this one. One has a dozen switchbacks and a scattering of trees up just before the trail goes over the ridge. We're quiet again. It takes a while, but then I think—I *think* I see somebody up near the top under one of the trees. Maybe two people. Yes, two. Pretty soon I think one of them's wearing a dress and is lying-down and the dress is dark, and the other person, who's leaning over the lying down one is wearing red and is little.

"Henny, there's somebody up there. Henny, Abel and his mom ... They couldn't be all the way up there could they?"

He looks hard, then jumps off his rock—vaults off on his one good arm. "Come on," he says, "You go on down. I'll go get your horse and be back. Please just stay there. Pack up the food and get the canteens, they're hanging on the door under my slicker. Fill them at the creek."

He looks at me ... again, that hard, scary look—thinking about me, but I can't tell what. For a minute he doesn't move at all and I have the feeling he wants to say goodby some way or other, like maybe hug me, but he won't let himself. I look back at him, right in his eyes as if I'm not scared. I'm trying to make my eyes send out the message that it's all right—that I do wish he'd hug me or give me any sort of goodby, but I guess he can't see that.

"And eat something," he says.

He turns and I see him leap down an even steeper way than we climbed up—leaping and leaping—right over sage and rocks and everything. Big sage. I didn't know anybody could do that.

Oh, oh, I *do* love him, and he's never going to touch me ever again. He promised. Unless maybe he hurts again. But I shouldn't wish that on anybody.

My flowers! I forgot about the flowers he picked for me. They're just lying there, and all this time. They may be dead by now. I don't care if they are or not, I'll bring them with me anyway.

Oriana

Somebody has made a little shelter of pine branches over her. Somebody has put something soft under her head. Somebody is patting her elbow. Somebody is crying. It can't be her little Abel. He never cries. That's because he never has anybody to cry to. His own mother never pays attention.

She says, "Abiel, I mean Abel."

He pats her elbow a little faster and a little harder. Poor little fellow. "We'll have a good time. We'll have picnics."

Now somebody is fanning her with a hat. It feels good. And it's nice, looking up into pine branches. Mostly there's blue sky behind them. Thunder, but going away, and no rain here.

"You've been so kind. All of you, so kind." She had said that to everybody. All the time. She had remained calm. Very, very calm. And calm ever since.

Henny had come to get her. He must have been fifteen or so. He was trying to grow a mustache and not succeeding—like Fay now. He was so thin—like Fay. He was crying and didn't even care that she saw him. That's what upset her before he even said anything. He was pale ... greenish almost, and he couldn't talk at first. She got him coffee. Something terrible had happened. After he could talk, all he would say was, "It happened because of me." When she went to hug him, he pulled away. "But it happened because of *me!*" as if she shouldn't hug him.

They rode so hard she thought they might kill the horses, but she didn't care if they did or not, as long as she got there one way or another. They were too late anyway. His life's blood ... *her* life's blood all over everything. So much blood! She'd followed it down the hall. They said his last breath was only minutes before she got there, so she was that close to holding him one more time while he still lived. (If she just hadn't hugged Henny—hadn't *made* him let her hug him—she'd have been in time.)

She could see Abiel's pain—not so much in his expression as in the way his knees were drawn up and his head thrown back. Inside her there was this: No, no, no, no, like a heart beat (and ever since) as she looked at him … touched him … touched his blood. She had begun to live the day he came walking in, looking like a scarecrow (it was something in his eyes that had brought her to life, something in his smile—kindness, maybe, and humor) and she died there, right then, with him. They straightened him out so that he looked calm. She would be calm, too.

"Ma."

That can't be little Abel.

"Ma, wake up … Ma."

"You're talking."

"I know."

"I didn't think you could"

"I know."

"That's all my fault. You're a good boy. It'll be different now. We'll talk. You can tell me things. You're the only one of my children I didn't teach to play the organ. We'll do that. You're always humming. You'll like it. They sat on my lap for their lessons—at first they did. That music stood me in good stead, but we have plenty of money now. You can have anything you want. What do you want?"

"Ma, you have to get up. We have to get down back home."

"No. We have to find … I forget who."

"Fay, Ma, but he's not up here. They're all down there home by now."

"But Abiel might …"

"It's going to get dark."

"I'm too tired."

"I'll help you. You can lean on me."

"I'll lean on Abiel."

She rolls over on all fours. Her head knocks down the little pine branch shelter. She stays, kneeling like that for a minute, but then she rolls back on her side. "I can't. You go down by yourself before it gets dark. I'll be all right."

"I don't think you will be, Ma. I think you're already not all right.

Mary Catherine

I'M GOING TO WRITE all this down as soon as I get back. This might be the one-and-only really happy time of my life and I don't want to forget one single thing about it, not even little things like how Hen's shirt is wrinkled all over, washed but not ironed. (I would have ironed it for him if I'd had the chance.) Or how when the moon comes up so bright I can almost see the army color of his clothes. How the sage and bitterbrush look with their long moon-shadows, everything magic like it was before, only this time in the moonlight. Hen's horse has silver on the sides of his bit and every now and then it sparkles out when it catches the moonlight just right.

I start counting up things I want to remember and numbering them, so if I only—say—remember twenty things, but know there's thirty, I can keep trying to remember the others, like right now, how Hen looks riding ahead of me, so straight—not military, more dignified and formal, and he doesn't even know he's doing it. It's exactly what you'd think a person like him would look like riding. Maybe he even looked that way when he lay against me and I didn't know to appreciate it then.

I start way back there with my counting up, so, number one is how warm he was and how I could feel his breathing. Two is how he said "Rest," and how I *did* feel like resting when he said it. Three is his gravelly voice that I could feel as much as hear.

By the time we start up the switchbacks, I'm already up to twenty-one and I'm thinking there'll be way too many, but that's all the more reason I should keep numbering so I'll have some idea of how many to *try* to remember.

Number twenty-two is how he's silhouetted against the sky now and then so I see his longish neck. (His neck is perfect!) His hair is blowing up in a way that reminds me of Abel. I'm not so scared of him when he makes me think of Abel.

I know I ought to be worrying about them, Abel and his mom and

Fay, but I can't make myself, though I do try. I keep thinking Hen will take care of things. He can do *everything*. He saddled up his horse one-handed. Got him to take the bit. He didn't ask me to help. I don't mind horse slobber all over me, but I'm not good at getting the bit in. Hen held the head stall on top of the horse's head with his good hand and then balanced the bit on his stump, and the horse just reached out nice as could be and took it all by himself. That'll be number twenty-three. But there's one thing I won't count up. That's when he kissed me. He could have kissed a sexy kiss but this wasn't even a fatherly kiss—more a *grandfatherly* kiss—from a *very* old man. On purpose. I don't think I should hope anything at all and he already told me he wasn't going to marry anybody.

We get up to a shadowy, woodsy part and then up past that, to where there are still trees but few and far between—gnarled and leaning over away from the wind. It's a lot cooler. Since we're on the switchbacks and the trees look like the ones where I first saw Abel and his mother, I keep thinking any minute we'll find them under one of those trees.

We stop to rest the horses lots of times up here. It's steep and they're puffing. Even when we stop and wait, Hen doesn't talk. He hardly seems to know there's anybody with him. He keeps looking out and down like he thinks it's pretty. I didn't know men could be like that, thinking about the view and such. None of the men I used to know ever did.

Below us I can recognize the hill where Hen took me to show me the view. Number twenty-four will be our hill and (especially) how he leaped down it. I wonder if that hill has a name and if not, I wonder if I could name it. Like, "Leaping-down Hill," or "Leaping Man's Hill."

I want to say something about this, but I keep quiet to show him I can do it. I know I shouldn't have read in his notebook, but if I hadn't I'd be talking too much right this very minute and he wouldn't want to be with me at all.

We do talk some, a little bit, after I say I'm worried about Fay, though I'm not really. I guess I say it so Hen will think well of me because I'm worrying.

Hen says Fay will get along fine. He's a good worker and a good piano player when he's in practice. Maybe Fay can join the army. "Now that the war is over it wouldn't be so bad." Then he says, "See the world," kind of under his breath in a nasty voice, as if he wishes he hadn't seen any of it.

"Crackerjack," he says. "Fay is crackerjack on the piano." I never heard anyone use that expression before. It makes me like him all the more though I couldn't like him any better than I already do. And suddenly I know something else, too.

"*You!*" I say (I'm prickling all over). "*You* played!"

He flicks me a glance like Fay would do, except Hen's makes me think of a snake's tongue. He doesn't answer, but I know I'm right.

"You *did!* I'll bet you played even better than Fay."

W<small>E FIND THEM</small>. Abel is curled up hugging himself, naked and shivering. His clothes are wrapped around his mother. *All* these people here, and even Abel, have this kindness, even if they're only nine years old. All Abel has on is a pair of floppy hand-knit underpants. No doubt Charlotte knit them. For all her tramping around like a man, she does a lot of woman's things. Probably because somebody has to.

Looking at Abel, I can see what my teacher meant when she said I was all shoulder blades and collar bones and, I think, knobby knees and ribs, too.

Hen slides off his horse backwards the way he always does, graceful as could be, and squats down to hug Abel. I get off carefully. If I fall here I might roll all the way down the mountain. I go to Abel's mother. Before I even touch her, I know. I've never seen a dead person till now, but I know. I think Hen knew right away or he would have gone to her before he went to Abel. I guess he knows all about dead people. She looks as if made of moon-stuff, pale and glowing. Waxy. I touch her. She's moon-cool.

I know I shouldn't, but right away I think: What about me? And then I think how selfish I am. As usual. But with Abel's mother dead and if Fay stays gone, things are going to be all changed around. If I was a decent person I would be worried about Abel and not be thinking about myself. I'm just not nice, that's why nobody will ever marry me. Especially nobody who speaks French and used to play the piano. "Crackerjack" is how he must have played himself. I don't know why I waste time counting up a couple of hundred things about him.

Hen puts Abel's clothes back on him *so* gently. Abel just stands there and lets himself be dressed. (Hen is shaking like he always is. You can see it all the more because he's so gentle and slow.) They look at each other like father and son. There's hardly anything Hen does that doesn't make me love him more and more. I'll call this number thirty-three though I may have lost count.

Hen says for me to take Abel behind me and that he'll take Aunt Oriana. "There'll be buzzards at dawn. You and Abel start on down. I'll be right behind you."

He turns my horse around and puts her in a low spot so I can stand on the high side to mount, and then he swings Abel up behind me. "Hang on," he says, and Abel does—hugs me tight around my waist. It feels good. "Be careful now."

I wonder if he means me?

Charlotte is there when we get back. She doesn't ask anything, she just seems to know. She and Hen lift her mother off the horse and lay her on the porch. (She's stiff, and as if sitting up.) Charlotte says, "Oh Ma," right to her. She says it lots of times, as if scolding her for being dead. The way she looks at her, you can tell she cared about her. I never was sure about that (nor the other way around either). Then she and Hen and Abel hug each other all in one bunch—without me in it. Well, I guess that's natural. I'm just the hired help. I'm thinking how I never did belong anywhere to anybody, though maybe more here than any place else. I did sort of fit in with my teacher for a few years, but I wasn't her real family. She had a beautiful niece with ringlets down beyond her shoulders just a year older than me. And, anyway, even with her niece, she wasn't the hugging kind. All I want in the whole wide world is just to be part of a bundle—any bundle—like they are. Is that too much to ask? I guess it is.

We're worn out from being up all night. Hen carries Abel in to bed. Number thirty-four is how he looks just as tired as Abel does, all loose and rumpled—his bruises showing still, yellowish and purple. When he takes off his hat, his hair is sweated down all higgledy-piggledy.

Charlotte asks him to stay and sleep here, but he won't. He won't even have breakfast before he goes. And not even coffee. He hugs Charlotte a long, long hug, but he just flicks me one of those glances that remind me of how Fay never really looked at me. He raises his hand to me, though, so it isn't *quite* nothing, just almost nothing. How can somebody do that to somebody they lay on top of all afternoon and only yesterday? And *I'm* the one—I was the first—who saw Abel and his mother across on the hill.

After he goes I say, "You *are* in love with each other. I can see it." And Charlotte says, "We could have married any time we wanted with the blessings of everybody we know, so don't be ridiculous. I love him, you're right about that, but I love him like a brother. And I told you, I bossed him around something awful. Besides, I'm in love with somebody else."

I'm too tired to ask her who, and I'm hoping she won't say any more about anything, even that. The minute Hen left, all of a sudden I got so exhausted I could hardly stand up, let alone listen to anything. But I do think how there isn't anybody around here for her to be in love with that I can think of—nobody even halfway close to her age, and I feel sorry for her, but I feel even sorrier for myself.

I GET TO STAY ... at least for now. It's really all my fault that Abel's mother went off looking for Fay and died, because it's all my fault that Fay went off in the first place, but so far nobody has blamed me for those. Well, maybe they do but they haven't said anything. Maybe they're just too polite. All Charlotte said was she wants for me to stay with Abel while she and Hen go off to see if they can find out anything about Fay. Hen doesn't even think they should go at all, but he does it because Charlotte wants him to. Hen says it'll be good for Fay to get away from home.

He doesn't stay here more than about two minutes. Just long enough for Charlotte to tell him if he gets drunk in town and gets into another fight she'll beat him up herself, like she used to do when they were kids. She's as tall as he is. I'll bet she still can. Except I think of how he leaped down the mountain and how he leaps up on his horse. He's so strong.

They don't find a single sign of Fay. People know him in all the nearby towns, but nobody's seen him. Hen thinks he headed for the western mountains. (So Abel's mother was right. She must have had second sight.) Hen thinks maybe he's hiding out in the hills or maybe gone over to San Francisco. Hen says he could lose himself either place but he hopes it's San Francisco. "It'll do him good," he says, and, "I'll do it myself one of these days." I'll lose him for sure if he does that, but then he says he'll help out with the stock in Fay's place, and I think, good, he'll be here a lot then, but that doesn't happen. He always meets Charlotte out someplace and afterwards goes straight back to his shack from out there. I use their cookbook and practice fancy suppers every single night—special things, and I'm not so bad. I make desserts all the time, just in case, but he never comes. So then I think I won't bother doing that every day, and then I think, of course, the one-and-only time I have nothing but beans, that'll be the exact time he stays for supper, so I go on practicing special things. When a meal comes out extra fine, I feel bad. Sometimes, as I eat something good, I pretend I'm Hen, tasting how good it is and thinking how it was me that made it. At least I'm getting to be a good cook. I'll make *somebody* a good wife.

The way Charlotte looks at me—over my lemon meringue pie or my pumpkin-walnut bread, my apple betty—I know she knows why I do it. She always says, "Don't you ever give up?" and then she says, "Don't give up," and I always say, "I know he's avoiding me," and then she always says, "He avoids everybody. Haven't you learned that yet?" and I say, "But all the things I've done ... Just about everything is my fault." She gives me that look she always does and says, "Not *quite* all." (How many times do you get to have the exact same conversation?)

I haven't seen Hen even once since the funeral, which was over at his folks' house. That's where everybody is buried—all the dead babies and Abel's father. They dug up practically the same hole and put the coffins side by side. Afterwards, Hen's mother said, "It's just as well. She's where she's wanted to be all these years." She says that to everybody (she must have said it three times to me alone). It made me feel a little better about how it was all my fault. Hen's mother was just about the only person who paid any attention to me the whole time we were over there. We (Charlotte, Abel, and me—that's all that's left of us), we didn't stay the night. We had to get back to the milk cows. (Charlotte thought to leave me home to take care of things, but I wanted to come so badly she finally let me.)

Hen was all dressed up in a dark suit with a light vest. They call those vests clay-colored. I never saw anybody wearing one except the couple of times I walked through a fancy hotel just to see what it was like and watch the kind of people that got to be there. Hen looked wonderful! but he was trembling something awful. He didn't have to be trying to get a match to his cigarette for you to see it. (He did smoke through the whole thing except right when the preacher spoke over the grave.)

I numbered how he looked. I could have numbered three or four numbers. The vest itself could have been two, the color of it and the way it wrinkled crosswise over his stomach, but I was already up to forty-two so I gave it only one. But I hope I never forget how he looked even if I get up to that age, though I'm not sure I want to live to be forty-two.

Lots of times it seemed as if Hen was trying to be on the outskirts of things, but nobody would let him. Everybody hovered around him so he had to be the center wherever he went. You could see he's everybody's favorite, especially his sisters' ... precious baby brother of the family ... the one-and-only boy. (Probably he'll inherit everything and the sisters won't even care.) It's: Can I get you this? Or that? Are you thirsty? Hungry? Too hot? ... And they touch him all the time. His father, too, his hand always on Hen's shoulder.

And he fascinates the children. They hover like the grown-ups do, but they're quiet around him—as if he scares them—like he scares me. He's everybody's main concern. Even if he wanted to, I don't think he'd have had a chance to talk to me. I wondered if he made it to the outhouse by himself.

He didn't look my way at all. He could at least have *looked,* but it could be he was trying to tell me something, like: no matter what happened between us, he's not interested in a witch with a you-know-what as a mother.

It's just as well he didn't look. I had to wear my old green dress. It wouldn't hold together anymore, especially under the arms. I tried to fix it but it wouldn't fix. Charlotte lent me a shawl and I kept my elbows at my sides when I could remember to. Everybody had a nice dress but me, even the littlest girls. His sisters looked as beautiful as Hen did, but I was a sight in every way, with my hacked-off bangs and the black eye Fay gave me. If I had to face myself I'd have looked away fast.

Even Abel didn't pay attention to me. I was wishing he would. I had to stand around all by myself most of the time, holding my scarf across my front. Abel was with the biggest of the big girls. They seemed glad to have a littler person to lead around who wasn't one of their own bouncy brothers. Hen's mother was so nice to me. The one-and-only person who was. Of course she's nice to everybody. She's just plain nice. She gave me a little pin that was of a greenish beetle. "Scarab," she said. (I already knew that.) I knew it was that she felt sorry for me because of my awful dress and hacked-at bangs. I took it because it was sort of like something from Hen. I can think that if I want to.

But I just don't belong anywhere, not even with Abel. I could see that. I should remember it and not get so disappointed all the time. Every time I start thinking I belong someplace I find out I don't.

So we settle in. Nobody is happy. I thought these people weren't very happy before, but this is different—a kind of shutting down … a waiting. That suits me, too. I'm waiting (though for what!) and I don't want to go anywhere. It's good I have those (forty-nine by now) things about Hen to think back on because that's all there is I really enjoy. It makes going to bed the nicest time of any because nobody interrupts my thinking.

The funny thing is, Abel has forgotten everything I taught him so far. Flown right out of his head just like that. He sits and draws airplanes and cars on his slate and then erases them no matter how nice they are, or he blows in and out on his harmonica, not trying to play a tune. (I wonder if he knows any tunes? Nobody sings around here. I'll bet he never even heard of "Rock-a-By-Baby.") He sits in a different way, all scrunched up hugging himself just the way he was when we found him next to his dead mom. I wish he'd climb something or say caw again.

I read to him and talk to him a lot. I know I tell him things I shouldn't, about myself and my hopes. I even tell him some of those forty-nine things about Hen. "Your cousin, Hen," I say, "he has the nicest, longest neck. You have a neck like that. You look a lot like him except for your hair." I wanted to say something to please him—I know how much he likes Hen—but exactly as I say it I see it's true, and I think how Hen must have been a funny little boy, too. I'll bet his hair stuck out just like Abel's. So then I think about Hen differently, and I look at Abel differently, too. I don't think I'll *ever* pinch Abel anymore, even if I want to make him learn something fast.

Last night I cried. I cry much too much, but for once it wasn't for myself. It was for Hen. I had been thinking about dancing, and how I've only had the chance to do it a couple of times. I hardly know how. I was thinking I'd like to dance with Hen. He would be in his suit and that vest, and I would have a new dress. And then I realized it's his left hand that's gone, which I think is the hand the girl is supposed to hold, and I knew … I knew for sure he'd *never ever* let a girl hold onto his stump. What if he used to be a good dancer just like he used to play the piano? Yes, he was. I know he was. That's when I cried. I'm only just beginning to understand, but I know I *still* don't understand and that made me cry all the more.

Henny

HE'S ALMOST back to his shack. Tired and hungry, but not willing … never willing to stay and eat with Charlotte and Mary Catherine. Abel maybe. He'd eat with Abel any day, but Mary Catherine already has too many ideas. It's his own fault so now he has to discourage her. It isn't fair not to. Poor little abandonée. Charlotte says he's missing a lot of good meals made just for him, so things are bad enough already.

He's so tired, every now and then his head bobs down, but the big gray gelding knows the way and wants to get home as much as he does. No need to be awake. Is there anything to eat back at his shack? Maybe he'll not bother with eating, just flop into bed, boots and all.

Sometimes Papa will have been there, leaving food in the big tin can: just-made bread, butter, cream … Once he was so tired and hungry he drank the cream all by itself and that was supper.

Now and then there'll be a big sugary HENNY written on the bread. A niece will have made it. She'll write a note about how she made the bread just for him. His sisters send notes, too. (If you come home we'll make strawberry ice cream.) But Maman makes sure nobody comes to visit him. She knows he can't stand that. Even Papa hardly ever comes. If he hears him, he usually takes off for a walk.

He might have stayed over at Charlotte's, especially tonight. He wouldn't mind a real meal for a change, except he mustn't encourage Mary Catherine. He never should have let himself … that afternoon. And almost as bad that he took her up the hill to see the view, but she seemed so pitiful. Her face when she turned around and looked! It was a big thing to her—to be brought to see a view. A little thing like that. She was all glowy. If he stays for supper doubtless she'll glow again. He'll hurt her and she's already been hurt enough. All her life probably, considering what they say about her.

He hears groaning. He ought to get up and go help. Maybe another soldier …

He hears himself groan.

He raises his head and hears himself yell.

His arm is connected to his head in some way he never knew before. Don't move. That's always best. A friend will come. Another soldier will come and pick him up ... except it's too quiet. Wonderfully quiet. How did it get to be so quiet right in the middle of the war? He can even hear birds. Lots of them. The way they're going at it, it must be either dawn or dusk.

If it's his hand, he'll be out of it and finally. He'd just as soon lose an arm if it took that to get away from war and back home. They'd *all* give an arm or a leg. Getting home is the only thing they think about, and talk about ... and girls.

He's lying prone, his good arm twisted under him and maybe not a good arm anymore.

He ought to raise his head again to see where he is. But not yet. Is it getting dark or is it early morning?

Morning would be good. He doesn't want to lie here all night.

He's partly on a scratchy bush. Horse brush most likely. Thorny, but not a cactus, so it could be worse. Or could it?

Is he shot? He was shot once. And then there was an explosion though he can't remember that. Not even where it happened. He ended up full of splinters.

It *is* getting darker. He should get out of here.

He pulls his knees up under him, his head still on the ground—on the prickers. He tries to push himself up with his stump. He yells. He puts his forehead back into the prickly bush. He's soiled his pants. When did that happen?

Try again. Push his broken arm up along his thigh with his stump until he can hook it under his arm pit to hold it steady. Then sit back on his haunches and rest up for the next move. He can see where the break is. It hasn't gone through the skin. He can't pull it back into line by himself. He can't splint it. Can't anything.

He feels the hair rising on the back of his neck. Then sick to his stomach, and not from pain this time. What *can* he do?

It's getting darker, but he recognizes the silhouettes of the mountains and his hill. At least he's close to home. Can he open the door? It's a lever, so maybe he can. All the food is shut up tight against vermin in hard-to-open tin cans. He'll drink from the stream before he goes in ... Tries to go in.

Mary Catherine

CHARLOTTE SAID Hen didn't show up yesterday and not this morning either. She says when he says he'll be somewhere he always is. She asks me if I want to be the one to go over there with some of my good food and see what's up.

Right away I get so rattled I almost say No. I don't say anything, but even so I already feel sick to my stomach. Charlotte gives me this look when I don't answer. We're having chicken turnovers, Lyonnaise potatoes ... All straight out of Abel's mother's big, old White House Cook Book. We've just started to eat and all of a sudden I can't even look at the food, let alone eat it. I say, "What could I bring?" partly to postpone having to answer.

"I don't think he's been eating very well. Take him some coffee, too, in case he's run out. Take him anything."

"He doesn't have any pans."

"Do you want to not go?"

"Charlotte ... the thing is ... I mean I blush so much I don't know what to do." Even as I say this I can feel myself blushing. Even just in front of Charlotte. "I can't stand that. What should I do?"

"Are you going to let that stop your whole life all the time? Besides, we don't know why he didn't come. Maybe he needs help."

"He's not the sort of person I could ever help."

"What does that mean? Why not?"

"Well he's like ... well, dignified, and all his books are in French."

"Are you going to go or not?"

"I'll go."

The closer I get to that tin hut, the scareder I get and the more I feel like throwing up. I know he doesn't want to see me or he would have stayed over for a meal. Even if he needs help, he doesn't want to see me. I'm just hoping he's too polite to be nasty. Well, I *know* he is, and kind too, mostly. He's sort of an odd person. I'm not sure what he'll do. Who would lie all afternoon hugging a person as if they were a lifesaver and then give them this little nothing of a kiss, and then not come and see them for a month?

At least ... At least a lot of things. At least my bangs look a little bit better than they did. I pin them back with bobby pins. (That's a nice new thing, bobby pins.) At least I won't ... *probably* won't fall off my horse again—unless she does a big shy. At least I know how to tie up properly. Charlotte taught me and Abel how to do it, and about riding, too. She wondered why she'd never taken Abel out with the cows before. She said she just got used to never thinking about him, or always thinking he was too little for anything. Besides, he was always up in some tree or other. But she thinks he must have gotten on horses when nobody knew about it, and, she said, little kids ride so loose and easy, anyway. Abel learned everything twice as fast as I did. I knew he was smart. Every time Charlotte comes home now, he runs out to tie up for her. For a couple of minutes he looks like the boy he used to be—all energy, though he's a dreamy kind of kid sometimes, too, alternating jumpy with thoughtful. Now he's mostly just droopy.

My horse and Hen's horse whinny to each other when we're still pretty far from his hut. They like each other. Hen said his horse gets lonely. I didn't think horses would ever feel that way. Hen said lots of people have a goat when they have only one horse to keep the horse company.

Usually his horse is hobbled, but here he comes, loping right to us and nuzzles my horse. They nibble each other. He still has his saddle and bridle on, so I know there *is* something wrong. I stop feeling scared *of* Hen and start feeling scared *for* him.

His horse follows along beside us so close the stirrup bumps against my leg. I hear a funny noise and see that he has a loose shoe, just hanging by a couple of nails in front. By the looks of things, lots has gone wrong.

As I come up to his shack, I see his door isn't quite shut. Goodness knows what's gone inside. I tie up my horse, but I don't stop to get my food bundles down. I go to the door and knock. I hear an animal kind of noise, like a growl. That makes me hesitate a minute, but all the more reason I should go in and see what's going on. Anyway, it doesn't take as much courage to go in and face a bear as it does to face Hen. I don't blush for bears.

First thing I smell a bad smell. Then I see Hen on his army cot.

He's what smells. He's dusty and muddy and he has little specks of dried-up blood on one side of his face and down on his shirt. He's fallen into a pricker bush and he's messed his pants.

I kneel down next to him. I touch him—carefully. I say, "Henny."

At first he looks at me like: Who are you, anyway? And like he's still in some kind of bad dream, but then I see his face change and he knows me. It seems like maybe he tries to say my name, but nothing comes out. Then I say, "What happened?"

He tries to say something but, again, nothing comes out. Then I take a good look and see how he's holding his arm clamped under his stump and how his arm and hand are all swollen up.

I turn away so he won't see on my face where I might be showing how upset I am. I can't imagine how it must be. I keep thinking, *awful!* There's no way I can even know how awful.

I go light his stove. As always, he's already laid the fire. I get his coffee pot and start heating water. (The coffee pot has wildflowers in it again, but very dead ones. For sure these aren't for me. It makes me wonder about the other ones. I don't think they were for me either. He just said that. He picks them for himself. What a strange man!)

That uses up all the water. I go out and get some more at the creek. He has two pails. One was tipped over and I wonder if he tried to get a drink and couldn't.

When I come back and kneel down and start washing his face—in cold water—for a moment he looks at me, again, as if: Who are you? and then I see him know me again. I'm thinking I should be working on … well, his pants first, but I'm not ready to do that yet.

There are thorns in his cheek and even a couple of chunks of horse brush stuck to his shirt by their prickers. I do the best I can getting them out. When I get his face washed I see how really bad he looks: circles under his eyes—he always has them, but now they're worse than ever, and it's as if his face got thinner and his nose sharper. He badly needs a shave. I wonder if I could do that for him sometime. I don't know how, but I'd like to try. He looks so frail. I'd like to kiss him, but that wouldn't be right now for about a hundred and twenty-five reasons. Especially with what I have to do next.

"Henny," I say. "I have to get you cleaned up. I'm going to take your clothes off and wash you. Please don't mind. Have you got any clean clothes here?"

He just stares, so I look in his boxes and I do find some clean things. All wrinkly like his clothes always are.

I cover up the top part of him so he won't get cold and start with the worst. I pull his boots off and his pants and his underwear. I throw his clothes out the door. I'll wash them later.

So there he is, the whole bottom half of him, long pale legs covered all over with little straight black hairs. Straight black hairs all over him. I don't know when I've seen ... Well, I'm glad *I* get to be the one to wash him even though you wouldn't think anybody would want to do such a messy job. The funny thing is, he still looks elegant—just as much as ever—maybe even more: pale skin, long pale feet, even all those little straight hairs. What I'd like to do is take off all his clothes and see all of him at the same time, but I know I should keep him warm.

He watches me—every move I make, like a child that doesn't know you're not supposed to stare like that. Just the kind of thing that would have made me blush, but now it doesn't. Even if I did blush, I'm too busy to bother with it. I'm worried about Hen instead of thinking of myself—for a change. That ought to teach me something.

When I'm almost through with his bottom half, the coffee gets finished and I stop and bring out the cups I brought from back ... I almost thought, from back home, but I mustn't let myself think that. Nice ones. One is a mustache cup that belonged to Abel's father. I thought I'd get it out of there because it says THINK OF ME on it in gold letters, and I think they're remembering him much too much.

I lift Hen's head and help him drink. He's so thirsty! I should have thought of that first thing. I saw how he'd knocked over his pail. I'm just not thinking. After the coffee I get him water—two big cupsful in succession. He looks a little better right after. Not so much like a sad, suffering saint from an old painting and more like a French aristocrat, which I know he really is. It's his eyes that have changed mostly. There's some life in them now.

Maybe he needs food just as badly. I tell him I have fried chicken and my special bread—and potatoes, too, but they're not cooked. "I could start them in the stove."

He growls out—I don't know what—I guess it's "bread and butter." For sure that *was* him making that animal sound when I first knocked.

I cover up his bottom half and sit on the floor and feed him, bite by bite. I can't help feeling happy, here, with the good bread I baked myself, *my* butter and *my* cheese, the good smell of the fire and the crackle of it, and no bad smell anymore. And I like Hen helpless. Who would ever think: *Me!* Somebody like *me* feeding and even washing somebody like him!

Then he tries to move and winces and makes a noise that's halfway between a yell and a groan. (I wonder if that's how his voice got so hoarse. Could he have yelled out here all by himself?) I feel guilty right away about how happy I'm feeling. I put my hand on his shoulder where I hope it won't hurt him. I hold him tight until the pain seems to lesson. He croaks out, "Splint." At first I don't know what he means. Then I look around for what to use, and he says, "Kindling." This time just whispering. He looks the same greenish he did when I first washed his face. I pad the splint with pieces of blanket, and I tear strips of sheets for tying his arm to the splint. (He has sheets, but he doesn't use them. I suppose his mother made him bring them out here.)

(*I'm* not so used to sheets as I might be, but I like them.) I'm about to put the splint on when he says, "Pull it." All of a sudden his voice is strong. "Pull my arm back into shape."

"But ..." I get that scared prickly feeling again like when I first saw his broken arm. "But how will I know when to stop?"

"You won't and neither will I. Just do it."

He's in charge again. He sounds angry but this time I know why it is. It's that he's getting ready to have a lot of pain. He does scare me and pulling his arm scares me, but I'm just not going to pay any attention to myself.

He tells me where he keeps his father's homemade wine and I get him a cup full and hold it for him to drink. Then we start. At my first pull he yells such a yell! I'm completely stopped. I want to say I won't do it and that I can't, but of course I have to anyway so no sense saying it. He says "Go on" so loud you'd think I was up on the top of his hill. After that he just grunts when I pull. I know it's because he doesn't want to scare me again. I wish he'd yell. Grunting seems so held in.

I thought he was going to throw up so I put the saucepan by his head. He has me stop now and then so he can catch his breath. By the time we finish I'm sweating like a horse and I feel as if I've been in pain the whole time myself. Hen says I should sit down and have a cup of wine. I get him all splinted up first and then I do that. Of course there's no place to sit except on the floor. I've been on my knees so much, doing for Hen, it feels good to sit back. I lean against one of his boxes and shut my eyes. Henny shuts his, too. I listen to the evening bird calls, the quail's tab, tab, tab, tobacco, tobacco, and the jay's squawks. I hear something cawing and I think of Abel and how I want to get him a raven. The aspen rustle and the creek rustles. Hen looks more comfortable. But his top half has to get cleaned up before we can really rest. The wine made me sleepy so I get myself more coffee and start on his top. I wash slowly. Hen keeps his eyes shut. I'm glad he does. I take all the time I want. I look at those little scars of his that are sort of like pockmarks only not. The larger ones have the marks of stitches, and then there are those few new thorn marks.

I like his scars.

His collar bones ... Did I already give them a number?

I should stop washing him, cover him, and then clean up the shack a little. Maybe rearrange things so they'd be more convenient—and then there's the pants outside the door—but I just want to keep on washing him. I might not ever have another excuse to touch him. Besides, I can see my washing soothes him. He might wake up if I stop. The water's on the stove, so it stays nice and warm.

Later ... I don't know how much later, I get up and light the lamp. I do clean a little. I put my food in his tin food box so the mice won't get at it. I rearrange his storage boxes. (His clothes were in there all helter-skelter—just tossed in.) I've used up all the water in one of the pails so I turn it over and sit on it and look at some of the French books, but that discourages me. I was hoping for pictures, maybe of Paris, but there aren't any. I know there's an Eiffel Tower.

It's so cozy: the fire and all, and the lamplight (it's not that dark outside yet, but it's dim in here). It's like I'm the wife and my husband sleeps—though restlessly, as if he's having a lot of not-very-nice dreams or pain now and then. I know I'll have to get him to a doctor and maybe back to his home, but I don't want to. I want us to stay right here just like this and that I should be the only one looking after him.

I go out to bring in another couple loads of wood. I try to be quiet but I'm carrying too much at a time (as usual) and I drop some. Hen wakes up and right away tries to get up. I don't know if I should help him or hold him down. I say, "Don't. Don't get up."

"I have to go outside. You'll have to help me."

My God! Every other minute of my life lately I have to do some new thing I can't possibly do.

He sits on the edge of the cot and then leans way over, his head on his knees as if he's dizzy. He stays like that for maybe as long as five minutes. Then, "Make me some sort of sling" he says. I take his last clean shirt and tie the sleeves around his neck. He stands up, all wobbly. Sits down again and then stands up again. I help him and he puts his stump on my shoulder to steady himself. But then ... I can't believe he has all this energy all of a sudden. He yells and twists around, away from me, and gives a couple of hops and kicks out his one-and-only window. It's way up by the ceiling. How did he get his foot that far up? And a minute ago I thought he was going to fall over. He always does these things I never knew anybody could do. The glass breaks and he's walking on it and all he has on his feet are his socks that I put on so they wouldn't get cold. He yells again and twists around and kicks down his pile of books that I'd just made nice and neat, and then kicks over his clothes boxes, and then his pail with water left in it. The pail flies across the stove and knocks over the coffee pot and the coffee flies all over, a lot of it on me. I'm afraid he'll kick the lamp even though it's way up in its sconce—though it's not any higher than his window. I get between it and him, but I'm afraid he'll kick me, or knock me over by mistake. It's such a small hut. Or maybe not by mistake. He has a look in his eyes that scares me. I thought he was angry before, that time he walked away saying damn, but this is different.

I'm shouting, too, for him to stop and that he'll hurt himself, and then he does—he bangs himself, hard, backwards against the door. He yowls again and then he uses his stump to lift the latch and he's out. Just as I did, he starts running *up* the hill. All he has on is his shirt and his underwear and socks, and his socks are probably full of glass. I didn't put his boots on because I thought he was going to be lying down.

It's halfway to being dark. I'll lose him for sure. He's leaping up practically the way he leapt down that other time. I feel that same thrill again. Who, except Hen, could leap *up* a hill? The things he *can* do!

He isn't yelling anymore, worse luck. He's not making any noise at all, except there's the sound of swishing through the brush—a sort of rattling rattlesnake sound that always makes me stop and look, when I'm walking, to make sure there's no snake around. I'm making that sound now, too. But then the sound stops and I've lost him. I stand still. I look up at the sky where the stars are coming out. I stand there panting and then I hear him panting. I was breathing so hard at first I couldn't hear anything but me, but then I realize it's not all me. In fact it's a lot louder than me. Every breath is halfway a groan.

I practically trip over him. He's lying on his back all spread out looking up at the stars. I don't know what to do with him. I lie down— near but not too near—and look at the stars, too, and we both catch our breath. I'll bet his feet hurt, or will pretty soon. I'll have to be the one to take out the splinters of glass and whatever else got in his feet while running up this hill.

I don't want him to lie here all night. I don't want to lie here all night either, and I'll have to if he does. I can see he's already getting cold.

"Henny, we have to get back."

He stops groaning and breathes shaky breaths. "I can't," he says. The way he says it, I know he's not talking about getting on down. "I can't and I won't. I won't."

"You have to," I say, and I'm not talking about going down, either. "You will. You have to. You just have to."

He's breathing as if he might cry, and I think how it would do him good if he did, and be a good change from me being the one who cries all the time, but he doesn't, just breathes all trembly. I wonder if he ever cries even when he's off by himself. I'll bet he doesn't.

I don't know what to do about anything. All of a sudden I'm the one crying, as usual. The funny thing is, me starting to cry calms him down. Maybe he thinks I'm crying because of him and how he can't bear the way things are, but I'm really crying for myself. I'm so tired and I have to get him to go back down and I have to clean the glass out of his feet the first thing and clean up the whole hut which I already did and wipe up the coffee and the spilled water, rescue the books, get fresh water, make more coffee … I can't even *begin* to think of all the things I have to do, not to mention those shit-in pants. All I want to do is go back down and take a rest. I want somebody to make *me* coffee. I want somebody to put *me* to bed. Do for *me*.

He sits up, reaches over, and touches me with his stump, which he usually seems to be trying to avoid doing—touches like you'd do with your hand, to comfort. He's stopped thinking about himself. (That ought to be another lesson to me, in lots of ways.) He *is* cold, so I tell him I'm cold. I tell him I want to go back down but I won't leave him, so will he please come? He gets up and even helps me up. He lets me hang onto his elbow on his stump side, which I pretend I need to do. Actually, I'm holding him up as much as he's holding me. It's a steep hill and hardgoing in the dark. He didn't pay any attention to the trail on his way up. He limps. It makes me cringe just to think of glass getting ground in all the more and me being the one to have to get it out.

When we're almost down, I *do* help him pee. It's not as bad as I thought it would be. All I do is open and then close his underwear. He can manage the rest. Maybe it's not as bad as he thought, either. Maybe me having to help him with that is what made him so angry in the first place. Or maybe that made *everything* all too clear. I guess he has *lots* of good reasons to be mad. But he just can't say "I can't" and "I won't." What good will that do for anything? I have to make him stop but I don't know how. What if I could get him to make love to me? Not love me, just make love. Not marry me. I know he doesn't want that. It would just be for him, so he might forget all his can'ts and won'ts. It doesn't matter what happens to me, and maybe his sisters would like me then—not because of that (of course not!) but because I'd have cured him. I'd have brought him back home to them, and he wouldn't tremble anymore and he'd not mind noise anymore. If I love him, and I do, I have to do what's right for him.

Of course he won't feel like making love until he's some better. Though with Hen ... He's so strong! If I didn't have to get him back home, say, for a couple of weeks or so, just the two of us out here, I might really be able to make it happen. I'd be so good to him the whole time (and I already have been). I'd make him know that there is a future and lots of good things in store, bad things of course, but good things, too. He'd see that after we made love.

Back in the shack, the lamp is still lit. Nothing caught fire. (Can a tin hut burn down?)

Hen looks shocked when he sees what he did. I hear him catch his breath. He doesn't say he's sorry or even anything, and I'm glad he doesn't. It makes him seem all the more aristocratic.

I guess he can see how *I'm* feeling, just as I can see how shocked he is at himself. He says I should lie down on his cot and he'll sleep on the floor, which is nice of him to say, but I'm going to have to clean up first. There's no place to lie down anywhere. There's even glass on the cot.

I'm so discouraged. As soon as I shake out the top blanket a little bit so Hen can at least sit down, I pick up the buckets and go for water, just so I can get out of there. I can't bear looking at all that mess.

It's dark out by now. It's good I know, more or less, where the path is. Once I get my feet wet I'll know I'm there. The bank slants and it's grassy—a long stiff uncomfortable kind of lumpy grass. I sit on it anyway. I rattle around first in case of snakes or goodness knows what. I never talked to a stream, or thought to before, and lately I haven't even talked to my mountains. I thought I'd outgrown all that. It's so childish. And now that I'm really in real love you'd think I wouldn't need that anymore, but I guess I was just too busy thinking about those fifty-five things about Hen. So now I'm thinking how the stream comes from snow that's way, way, way up there, maybe from the glacier. All of a sudden I hear myself say, "I used to like horse brush." Then I say, "Hen's feet must be mincemeat and I'm the one has to clean them up." I say, "Abel's the only person who cares anything at all about me. But *you* know I shouldn't dwell on that kind of thing. *You* know how I'm trying not to think about myself all the time. I really do try. Who wants to marry a selfish person? It could be that's why I haven't already gotten married a long time ago."

The stream is chattering at me so sweet—you can almost hear the words, telling me I'm doing a good hard job and maybe I have a harder job ahead of me, but I can do it. That, in a different way, I'm just as strong as Henny is. I hadn't thought I was strong.

I could fall asleep right here, listening to the stream, but I have to get back to Hen to make sure he doesn't hurt himself again.

I get up and dip the pails in. "Now don't give me a lot of sand and weeds and baby trout," I tell the stream. Since I can't see, God knows what I've got. Probably a lot of stuff to flavor the coffee.

When I come back, Hen's trying to push his books out of the mud from the spilled water and coffee with his feet. At first I think that's because he cares a lot about them, but then I see he's pushing the books away from that notebook he was using as a journal. It's pretty wet and kicked halfway apart. He uses the swollen-up fingers of his broken-arm hand, winces, and picks it up. "Open the stove," he says. I say "No," and

I don't budge. He says, "This was just so I could practice writing with my right hand." But I won't open it. I think to snatch the book away but, the way he looks, I'm scared to. It's not just anger I see, it's that same fury—like when he kicked the window—or maybe terror. I don't dare move.

He puts the notebook down, carefully in a dry spot, as if he was going to keep it, and opens the stove himself. There are still smoldering embers in there. Glittery. His eyes are reflecting little spots of red.

The handle must still be hot, but he doesn't use the towel that's hanging right there for opening the stove. Though the notebook is partly wet, it catches right away. He doesn't shut the stove door. He squats down and stares in, angry. I'm angry, too, that he would burn all that writing up. Even if it was only for practice, it was still full of his thinking—all sorts of things I need to know about him. I wish I'd read more of it when I had the chance. I turn away and start picking the glass out of his cot. I don't want him to see anything on my face. Here I've seen his whole body naked (though only one half at a time), I've helped him pee, and still I'm scared of him even so.

He squats and watches the fire until the notebook's all burned up. When he finally turns away, he looks different—about as worn out as I feel, and ... Maybe he's given up. I don't know if that's good or bad. I don't know if that means "he can't" and "he won't" all the more, or maybe that he will. Anyway, I know I can get him to lie down now. I wrap him in his blankets. He holds his stump across his face as if to hide behind it. He's trembling more than usual, but I'm trembling, too. It's not going to be easy picking things out of his feet with both of us shivering.

It's good he has plenty of blankets so I can hang one over the broken window. I build up the fire and bring in more wood. Then I get to work on his feet.

BEFORE WE EVEN WAKE UP Charlotte and Abel are there. In fact we're so tired we don't wake up until they're right inside the shack. It's still an awful mess—things spilled all over the place. After I finished as best I could getting splinters out of Hen's feet, I collapsed. I didn't even pick up all the glass from where I lay down. I didn't have the energy to even think of *one* of the fifty-five things about Hen that I always count up every night. Besides, he was right here beside me. I could have reached up and slept with my hand right on him, but that was too hard, so I leaned my head against the leg of the cot instead. I wrapped myself in his beat-up old quilt and fell right to sleep on the floor.

It's dark inside when Charlotte comes, so we don't know it's morning. She pulls the blanket off the window and that's the first I know they're there, the light and the cold morning air blowing in.

Charlotte goes straight to Hen. She kneels down beside the cot and says, "Henny?" and then she says, "Henri?" in French, which they used to call him before he went to war. I guess she sees right away what happened—or some of what happened, anyway.

Abel comes straight to me and squats down on the still-muddy floor and takes hold of my foot.

All of a sudden Charlotte is bustling all around. I have to get up fast not to get trampled on. There's not much room for bustling, even for one person. She rattles things—making fresh coffee, cooking bacon, which I wonder if Hen will eat considering his appetite. She sends Abel out for fresh water, two pailsful. (When it suits them, they forget he's old enough to do most things, and when it suits them, they think he's twice the size he is. He's strong, but two pailsful!)

I don't know why, but none of us is talking, not even me. That "Henri" is the last thing anybody said. It seems as if we all turned into Fays and Abels. Charlotte bustles until she has Hen sitting up with pants on and a cup of coffee. (In Abel's father's mustache cup. She gives me a look. I didn't ask. I just took it.) She takes the blanket that I already partly cut up to pad the splint with and makes slippers for Hen.

She packs up his boots and what there is left of his clean clothes, which is only socks and underwear.

(Just like I knew, Hen won't eat any bacon, just toast.)

"I'm taking Henny into town. That'll be the nearest to a doctor, and there's the hospital up the grade. I think maybe he ought to be up there."

At the word hospital Hen looks up, straight at me, as if I'm the one to rescue him. He hasn't been looking at anybody since Charlotte woke us. I don't think he wants to go, but he doesn't say anything. It's like he's a child again. Charlotte said she always used to push him around but that she couldn't anymore, except it looks like she can again now.

Charlotte goes out to get Hen's horse. Even though he was loose he was standing right there with my horse as if he was tied up, too. She had taken the saddle off earlier, and now she rubs him down a little and puts it on again. She has pliers and wire cutters hooked on her saddle all the time, so she pulls off the loose shoe. She leads Hen's horse up next to a stone so Hen can get on. First he leans over the stone and loses his breakfast, then she helps him up. I feel bad, thinking about the way he used to always grab the horn and leap up in just one leap, not even using the stirrups. He looks down at me like he doesn't want to leave me—or maybe wants me to come along. Anyway, that's the way I imagine it. I hope it's true.

I look back at him real hard. Like before, I want my eyes to be saying things, like how *I* wouldn't be taking him to a hospital if he didn't want to go. *I'd* let him stay here. I'd nurse him back to health myself. Only I don't think my stares are working like I want them to. I don't think he sees what I mean.

Charlotte says for me and Abel to stay here. "Get this place cleaned up," she says. (What does she think I've been doing all this time? and over and over and over? though I admit it doesn't look it.) "And then go on back home. I don't know how long I'll be. The Jersey will need milking."

So now everything's out of my hands. I'd object … I'd argue, but I'm just the hired help. No matter how friendly Charlotte is to me and no matter that everybody gives me things, I'm paid to do what they tell me to.

I suppose now she'll be the one who gets to shave him. She'll be the one to help him pee.

I go dump hen's clothes in the stream to soak. Then I eat. I didn't before when the others did. I don't think I could have anyway, till things calmed down. I fix myself a bacon sandwich and get myself coffee (in the mustache cup) and I go out and sit on Hen's front-door rock. Abel has been picking up glass from the floor and nobody even asked him to, but now he comes out to sit beside me next to the stone. I move the mustache cup so it won't get knocked over. After all, it's got gold on it which looks like it's real.

Right away Hen's jay comes down to beg. It hops up to Abel even though I'm the one with the food. It's as if it knows Abel is the bird person. I give Abel crumbs from my sandwich. The jay hops up on his knee right away and eats out of the palm of his hand. He giggles—like it tickles. Then the jay hops on his hand. Next thing we know, it hops right on Abel's head. He giggles even more. It feels good, hearing him laugh like that, especially after last night and all that pain of Hen's.

"Abel, we'll catch him. It'll be easy. We'll take him home with us. He'll be yours. He won't ever talk, but we'll get a talking crow, too, later."

Abel says, "Caw." That's the first he's said it since his mom died, so I know this is the right thing to do.

We look for a box, but of course there isn't one that's not being used already. I knew that before we even looked. So we go to the stream and gather willow branches and I show Abel how to weave a cage. I'm glad to have something to do that isn't cleaning up the same stuff I already cleaned about sixteen times (I know that glass will *never* get out of the floor), and I'm glad not to be washing those smelly clothes. I'll do that last. If I'm lucky it'll rain and the clothes will get swept away by a sudden flood.

We make a nice little cage with a cardboard floor. (I used the covers of some of Hen's spoiled books.) We put crumbs in it and the jay walks right in. Abel giggles again. We haven't even shut the door, though, when the jay realizes it's trapped. It may be tamed, but it's never been in a cage. It has a fit exactly like the fit Hen had when he kicked the window and jumped around in the broken glass. It flies against the cage and screeches something awful, exactly like Hen's yowling. You can see it's hurting itself. I try, right away, to get him to come out. Nothing works, so I reach in and try to grab him and I get little pinch bites and scratches all over my hand. When I finally get a good hold on him and pull him out and put him on the ground, he flops around as if he can't fly anymore. I must have squeezed him too tight. Then he falls over on his side with his beak open and his little pointed tongue hanging partly out in the dust. Even dead and all mussed up, his feathers glitter in the sun.

Abel looks horrified, and I'm changing my mind about having any sort of pet bird whatsoever. I should stop *doing* things, any things at all, and now I've killed it. "Oh, Abel … We won't ever catch a bird again. Never ever."

All the time I'm thinking how the jay is like Hen. *Is* Hen, and Hen might be dying. That might be my fault, too. Maybe if I hadn't been here he'd not have kicked the window. Except without me he might have lain in his shit for days. Anyway it was Charlotte made me come. I didn't even want to. But she doesn't know what a mess I always make of everything. My mother told me that a hundred times.

I go straight to Hen's soaking pants. Now I'm glad to have this dirty job to do. It's what I deserve. Besides, they're Hen's pants. If I can't be with him to help him now, I can at least help him this way, and I can make the whole hut spick-and-span. I don't think I'm much good for anything else.

I cry as I scrub—cry and cry and cry. I killed a friendly, flying, glittery creature that was always at Hen's door. He's the one who tamed it. He'll miss it. And I made Abel feel bad all over again.

It's a while before I can say anything without sputtering, but then I tell Abel to stop picking glass out of the floor (I thought he'd go off and climb a tree, but he went right back to work), I tell him to go find a beautiful spot by the stream and dig a little hole. "We'll have a ceremony after I finish here."

Washing Hen's pants makes me think about his nice strong pale legs and those straight black hairs all over him.

I wonder how long it takes to learn French? I wonder how long it takes to get to be able to play the piano?

Later, as I'm cleaning the cabin, I think about hiding that sketch of the naked girl, but that would be one more thing taken away from Hen. I'd rather add things, except I don't know what. I'd even use my new-dress money.

After we finish cleaning up, we have the ceremony for the jay. I can't believe how it still glitters when the sun shines on it. Even though it's rumpled, it's as if its feathers are still alive. I say some of the things they said when they buried Abel's mother, or start to. "Ashes to ashes," I say, but that seems so wrong so I say, "Feather to feather, feather to sky ..." There was: Man that is born of woman lives but a little while, he flieth as a shadow ... I say, "Bird that is born of egg flieth as a jewel ... flieth as a diamond."

Abel is really listening now. "You were a kind and noble and brave bird, and Abel and I will remember you forever and ever as long as we both shall live. Amen."

We put up a little headstone and circle it with pebbles and then we sit, Abel all scrunched into himself like he always sits these days.

"Oh, Abel, what am I going to do with myself? How can I make it up to you? Please say caw just once. Say it for the bird so I won't be the only person that said anything. For the *bird!* Please!" But he won't.

I curl up like Abel—hugging my knees and my head on my knees, and then I cry again (as when do I ever not these days?). Abel comes over close and, sort of like he did before, he breathes, "Caw," right in my ear, this time so softly I almost have to guess it.

Henny

THEY STOP AND REST just before going into town. They sit by an irrigation ditch and drink the watery coffee Charlotte brought. She tries to get him to eat leftover toast. He lets her feed him a couple of bites but he's still not hungry and not willing to be fed all the time, though how eat any other way? "Maybe if we had some butter."

Charlotte eats it. Then she takes a look at his feet. "I don't know," she says. "I just don't know. I think I'd better get you right to the hospital. If you're up for it." She says, "One of these days you're going to need your feet." She sounds exactly like Uncle Bill, tone of voice and all.

Then she gets mad though she tries to hide it. Mad and sad, too, and trying to hide both. He turns away, looks down into the ditch, so she won't know he noticed her tears. There's a little bit of mud in the bottom of it that reminds him of his own floor after he kicked the pails.

"I wish you'd stop all this nonsense. I wish you'd care a little bit about yourself. I wouldn't be surprised if you hadn't broken your arm on purpose. Did you? I don't know why I'm helping you. And look at the mess you left for Mary Catherine."

"You only know about half of it."

She gives him that look he knows so well: You silly, you goose, you know-nothing, you little pip-squeak, you yellow-belly … Things she said all the time when they were kids. He got so used to them they rolled right off.

"Shit," he says. "I shit in my pants. I don't know how I broke my arm or when I messed myself. Mary Catherine cleaned me up and then spent half the night picking glass out of my feet … Poor little abandonée."

"Not so little, and she's in love with you, you know. She'll do anything you want. Henny, don't hurt her."

"If I was going to hurt her, I'd have already done it."

"What does *that* mean? What did you do? You didn't. You *didn't!*"

"You'll be glad to know I didn't."

Charlotte has tears in her eyes again. He knows because some are dropping on his feet as she puts the blanket-slippers back on him. He thinks to touch her, though there's no way to do it except with his stump. But they've never had that sort of touching relationship. They always avoided any contact—except when they fought—when she beat him up. They couldn't even stand it when they had to sit next to each other. They *always* got in a fight then. It's as if they felt too close already to bear it. The first time they'd ever hugged was when he went off to war. He'd kept himself away from any hugging after Uncle Bill got gored. He didn't deserve to get or give hugs. And he hadn't come out for Uncle Bill's funeral. Nobody could make him. Papa said Uncle Bill would have wanted him to come out. Papa said it was a trade, life for life, and Uncle Bill wanted it that way, so he was to think of himself as a gift from Uncle Bill. That's how the whole family feels still, and Papa most of all. He never wanted to be a gift. He'd rather be a nothing and be let alone. It's hard to be around his family when it's as if he's everybody's walking Christmas present. At least he's not, and never has been, that to Charlotte.

"Come on, Henny, let me help you back up on Bob. Don't look so grim. Can you make it all the way to the hospital?"

"Hospital." Hospital! … "Fix me a smoke first and give me some puffs."

Mary Catherine

ABEL AND I START BACK to the ranch. I'm feeling bad, but not quite so bad about the jay. All that cleaning and washing and fixing up made me feel at least I was good for a little something. Hen's place looks better than it ever did—at least since I saw it. I changed things. I moved the boxes around, I spread the books that had water or coffee all over them out in the sun, but, like I said, some were permanently ruined. I made bookends out of firewood I chopped to the right size and I lined the not-spoiled books up as neat as could be, sideways, not piled on top of each other like they were. (Hen was right to burn his notebook. If he hadn't, I'd have read some more in it for sure, though it's a good thing I read what I did so I not only know about keeping quiet but how he doesn't like women with high, harsh, or screechy or whiny voices. It's important that I found that out. I suppose there's a lot more I need to know that's all burned up.)

I laid the fire in the stove for next time like Hen always does. I was thinking I'd like to get him more pans and plates and how I wouldn't just take them from the ranch like I did the cups—I'd buy them. It would be a nice thing to do instead of getting myself a dress. That way I could prove to myself I'm not selfish, and get rid of my money before my mother comes back and takes it.

I could get him a clock. I could cover his boxes with pretty cloth and they'd look like real furniture. I could sit on his front step–stone and see if another jay comes by and I could tame it.

Going home, Abel rides behind me and hugs me around my waist like he did before. I pretend it's Hen doing that and make myself get scared all over again even though it's just thinking.

As we come in around the barn, right away we see a strange horse in the yard, and there's this little sort of basket and something in it that

squeaks like anything as soon as we get near it. Abel jumps down before I hardly begin to think how to get off and he has the lid open and
the piglet in his arms right away. First thing I think is, I hope that
wasn't supposed to be dinner.

Then Hen's sister, the one named Madelaine, comes to the door.
She's so … dressed! Black and white and tweed, Her neck is longish,
like Hen's, and she's showing it off. Her fine black hair is piled up, but
bobbed hair like mine is more the latest thing these days. The cat's
meow.

She calls out to Abel right away, "It's for you." She's even brought
him one of those canes you use for pushing pigs around. "You can take
it to the fair and then you can eat it or sell it."

Why didn't *I* think of a piglet? But I wouldn't ever have, and I don't
have any piglets to give away anyway. (They have absolutely *everything*
over there.) All Abel ever got from me is a dead blue jay. Maybe if I get
Abel a puppy it'll grow up and eat the piglet. But then I tell myself to
behave myself even in my thoughts.

"It's a prize Hampshire," she says. "You'll probably win a blue rib-
bon."

To me she says, "Charlotte won't be back for a couple of days,
maybe more. They went up to the hospital. Charlotte said his feet were
getting blood poisoning." The way she says it, for sure she blames me,
but that's the one thing I don't think is my fault. I don't say that,
though. She probably blames me for Hen breaking his arm, too.

I'm wondering how Madelaine got the news so fast, except that always happens around here.

One nice thing, though, she's done the milking and fixed us a
supper.

"I'll stay and help for a day or two."

I wish she wouldn't, and why does she have to be so dressed up?
That's the kind of clothes Hen must be used to seeing on women, not
my kind of clothes. Well, at least the piglet will help take Abel's mind
off the jay and maybe off his dead mother some, too. You can see how
happy he is with it. He's lying on the porch with his head down next to
it, moving his lips like he does with the head of the bear rug. Then he
brings it into the house and Madelaine says, "You can't bring that pig in
here," but I say, "Yes, he can," and she says, "Of course not," but I say,

"Enough bad has happened to Abel already without he can't bring the piglet in."

But this is Hen's sister, that I want to like me and that I want to try to like even though I don't. Of course, when you think about all the noisy children over at her place, and all the pigs, if you said Yes to piglets there'd be a dozen of them in the house. "Oh, all right," I say, but then I think of Abel and I take it back. "No, I'm sorry, but Abel has to have it with him. I'll clean up after it." (I'm already in practice for that sort of thing.) "I'm really sorry, but Abel *needs* to have it inside."

She gives up. She must be twice as old as I am, but she gives up anyway. Maybe something in the way I said it, or maybe it *is* sort of my home here, or maybe she sees I'm right, Abel does need it. I should say something nice. I'll thank her for the milking and for making us supper. I'll compliment her food, though there's no possible way it can be as good as what I've been cooking lately, and I don't even like to cook.

Henny

THAT HOSPITAL—and now this little hospital ...

Things seem almost as bad as they did last time. At least there's a window that looks right out into the top of a tree. And quiet. That's the important thing. There never was any quiet back there, in the hospital or out.

There are birds in the tree. When the late afternoon sun is just right, shadows of birds pass right over him. One must be a mockingbird the way it goes on and on. If he could write, right now he'd write down its song to see if it really does never repeat itself. You have to listen hard to try to find out. It takes his mind off things.

A nurse shaved him and then brought a mirror. He saw—his own wild eyes. He even scared himself, all neat and clean and freshly shaved and crazy. "Wait," he said, and made her bring the mirror back. Study the monster. It's a wonder they took him in, showing himself to sick people, scaring the children. He must hold himself together, but he's all coiled up inside.

And Mary Catherine's in love with him even so. He could see that for himself. Even Charlotte knows about it. Why does everybody want to marry off the monster? and to just about anybody? As if whoever would go so far as to marry him could tame the beast. ("Bring him back among the living," they keep saying.) But if he'd wanted to marry he could have done it back in France, except her parents wouldn't put up with him, let alone with him taking her back to America. She didn't want to leave France herself. Maybe he should have stayed there, except at that time all he wanted was to get back home and back to his family. And here he is living as a hermit, so, so much for the idea of home.

Mary Catherine ... He'd never known a person who appreciated things as much as she does, where all you have to do is take her to a view and pick some wildflowers. It makes you want to do more things for her. It would be fun to take her to a really big town and a fancy restaurant, or, actually, to a little town and any restaurant—any view. Except that would make her like him all the more. Doesn't she see how he scowls? Can't she see he might do harm? He almost did. He did! To himself and almost to her, too.

And here she is, stuck in his head in some way, especially after the last two days. Without her, God knows what would have become of him. He wants to make her happy … because she owns nothing, because she's frightened, because she doesn't even know what happiness is. What would she do if he got her a dress? It would have to be anonymous. He could give her lots of things that way. She'd never know they had come from the madman.

The thoughts of giving please him … lying here half-asleep, looking out at the top of the tree. It's dark outside now, but the lamp in the sconce across from him shines light out on the leaves. He drifts in and out of sleep. Perhaps he's feverish.

Somebody comes between him and the light. A fuzzy person, like a mountain man. Has it really been that long? Can you get that fuzzy in just a month or so? Fayette sits on the chair Charlotte left not so long ago. He's actually going to say something … Except he doesn't. Should he, himself, speak first or give Fay plenty of space and time?

He'll speak first. "Ol' Buddy." And then, "Where've you been?"

They wait. Fay breathes out hard a couple of times.

"You'd better escape while you can. Charlotte's coming back any minute."

She's gone to get things to make a book holder so he can read and turn the pages by himself, and to get magazines and books. He doesn't feel like reading. He'd rather watch the treetop.

Fay finally actually gets some words out. "Jewel Lake. Ruby Lake." His voice grew up while he was keeping silent. Logical, but a surprise. It's like Uncle Bill's, deep and gravelly. "I came back to get fishing line and hooks." He's talking almost like a normal person—just a little jerky.

"Don't do that. Don't come back. Go to San Francisco. You need to get out and see the world. It's not likely you'll lose an arm or two doing that now."

"Maybe, but I'll need fishing line anyway. Is Mary Catherine still around?"

"Yes, and you stay away—for now, anyway. I won't tell on you."

"They said you weren't doing so good."

"I'm good."

He can see on Fay's face that he doesn't believe it. Maybe he's worse off than he thinks.

"I'm *fine.*"

If Fay keeps looking at him like that, he *will* start feeling bad, and how come nobody talks about how he looked in the mirror—as if he's about to bite somebody?

"You go find a girl of your own." He can't believe he's saying that—as if Mary Catherine is his girl. He doesn't want a girl, least of all her.

"I hit her."

"You had a reason."

"She told you?"

"No, not exactly. I figured some things out. She's sorry. You know about your ma?"

"I heard."

"She guessed where you were. She was headed straight out to Jewel."

"That was where we used to have our picnics ... back when we had picnics."

He's always felt, just like with Charlotte (she was as if his closest "sister," both being exactly the same age) ... He'd never wanted to be the youngest in his family. First he conjured up an imaginary little brother and then he took Fayette as his little brother. Somebody he could teach things to, tell things to, fatherless little boy and all because of him. And here he is, still doing that. He'd like to fill him up with "good" advice: Go someplace and live a little. Don't just be a hermit—at least not yet. He, himself, is the hermit, but at least he'd lived some first. More than he wanted to. But who is he, to tell other people what to do?

"Do what you have to do ... or not do, Ol' Buddy." And that's the best advice he ever gave anybody.

Maybe he *is* sicker than he thought. He keeps fading away into sleep even with Fay right here.

"Take care," Fay says. "You take care now." He reaches over and squeezes his shoulder just the way Papa does all the time. "I'd better go so I don't meet Charlotte. You take care now."

If he had something to reach out with besides his ugly stump, he would wave some way.

Charlotte is back and making a fuss with the nurses. She usually doesn't get angry like that anymore. She looks almost like he did in the mirror.

They're wrapping him up in quilts. They're bringing in a little stove. He feels like crying. He hasn't done that since Uncle Bill's funeral when he wouldn't come out because he couldn't stop blubbering. He'd stuffed his pillow slip in his mouth, blown his nose all over it, washed it out himself so nobody would know. That was the last time. There wasn't much sense in crying over a gone arm.

They're making a tent over his feet and putting compresses on them. He *is* crying, but nobody seems to notice. They're all too busy with his feet, and just as well. It's not exactly crying, just tears running down into his ears. They hardly seem part of himself. They just happen.

Then Charlotte notices. She wipes at them. It's a while before they stop, but she doesn't get tired. Good ol' buddy, Charlotte.

Mary Catherine

CHARLOTTE IS STAYING AWAY a long time because of Hen's blood poisoning. I should have worked a lot harder getting the glass out of his feet that night. I shouldn't have let myself be so tired. He might die all because I didn't stay up and keep at it. Of course it wasn't me, kicked out the window, though Madelaine would prefer to think I did it.

It's funny how I'm never thinking about other men like I used to all the time before Hen. I had pictures I'd saved of boys I liked the looks of. I'd been collecting them over the years. I think I've been in love since I first remember anything at all. I didn't take (tear out and steal) just any pictures. I've only gathered eight in all this time, so I didn't steal many, or ruin many books. I'd line them up every now and then and arrange them in the order of who I liked the looks of best at that particular moment. Every single one of those boys was a *lot* better looking than Hen (and none of them had scars all over them or lost a piece of themselves). But, even so, I don't care about any of those pictures anymore. I even forgot about them, but as soon as I remembered, I burned them up.

Madelaine says their mother is up at the hospital practically permanently, and sometimes their father, though he's over here quite a bit helping out. Some of the bigger Ledoyt boys come here, too. They've moved most of our stock in with theirs. (I say "our" though nothing is mine.) I'm doing all the cooking. I like it when Hen's father and the big boys come over for a meal. For a change I have some special people to cook for, and I sure do impress them ... all of them. I might even win Madelaine over. I'll bet she didn't think I could do this fancy stuff. She doesn't say anything, but Hen's dad does. He puts his hand on my shoulder exactly like he did to Hen all the time when we had the funeral, and tells me how good everything is. He eats two or three desserts. He once finished off a whole half a pie that I was thinking to have for another meal. He shouldn't because he's on the heavy side, not like Hen.

I still keep on pretending to myself that I'm cooking for Hen. I even pretend, when Hen's father puts his hand on my shoulder, that it's Hen doing it and that all his dad's praise about the food is what Hen would be saying.

Madelaine is thinking to go up to see her brother. I want to go so badly I don't know what to do with myself. It takes my appetite away no matter how good the food is. It's just like life's always been, with wanting and wanting and feeling sick from so much wanting. Feeling sick from wanting is my whole life and always has been.

What if I ask for a day off to go see Hen? Madelaine will just say she hasn't been up there yet either and it's *her* brother and *nobody* of mine. What if I just go? It's far, but if I leave right after the supper dishes, hike half the night to the crossroads, and catch the morning bus to town … (the bus comes all the way to the village now). All I want is just one little tiny glimpse of him. Nobody has to know. I know I'm supposed to stay here and look after Abel, but I'm not sure I can make myself *not* go.

Except I'd better let Madelaine go first. Then she can't say, "But even *I* haven't had a chance to see him yet."

So she does go, partly because I kept urging her to. I didn't tell her I'd be going right afterwards. I did say I'd like a day off pretty soon, after she comes back. She probably guesses why anyway.

Madelaine is a hundred times more educated than I am. You can easily tell. No wonder Hen isn't interested in me, and even if he was, he shouldn't be.

When Madelaine comes back, right away I ask her how things are up there. She says he's getting some bit better, but she starts to cry anyway. All of a sudden I feel close to her. I know how she feels. I get her warm water to wash up with and I make fresh coffee like Charlotte always does for me. While she was gone I made sand tarts and a lemon pie. I tell her I did it for her. That pleases her, but mainly I was hoping Hen's dad would come.

After she gets all settled down, I ask her right out. I say, "I want to see him."

She looks at me exactly like I knew she would, and we're back where we started, with her not wanting me to get too close to her baby brother. I see in her eyes that I'm just the low-down hired help and I should stay in my place—that I don't have any reason to think of myself as part of the family, which is true. But don't I deserve a day off? All the more since I'm *not* family. *I* shouldn't have to work around the clock just because *they* have need to. I'm not even supposed to have to bake pies.

So I say, "I'm supposed to have a day off and I'll come right back. I promise I won't do one thing else."

If she has any fairness in her at all, she can't say No, no matter how much she wants to. I can see her struggling with what's right. She knows, though, that I could just go off like I thought to do in the first place.

"All right," she says, "but there's nothing to see. All he does is sleep, and don't you be bothering him any."

Madelaine and Abel take me to the crossroads. Abel is to ride my horse back and then they'll come for me that night. I'll have only a couple of hours there before I'll have to catch the bus home.

At the hospital I stand in the doorway to Hen's room. Madelaine was right, all there is to see is a lump in the bed. He's lying on his side facing the window, so there's just a lump with rumpled black hair on top. I'm scared all over again though I can't even see an eyebrow. There's a sort of tent over his feet made out of the blankets and there's a stove with a teapot on it and steam going into the tent part.

I stand by the door for a bit, but I feel so weak-kneed I have to sit down. As I move towards the chair, I come between Hen and the window, and my shadow must have wakened him. He opens his eyes and looks straight at me. He's glad to see me. Really, really glad. It's right on his face, plain as day.

He's usually not very countrified in his talk, but now he says, "Howdy." I don't say anything. He says, "Mary Catherine," like he does sometimes for no reason.

Then I remember my sand tarts and my gingersnaps that I brought for him. I put them on the bedside table. That gives me something to do. I wish I'd brought flowers. I forgot people do that. He has a lot already, but I'd have liked him to have mine. One bunch is scraggly wildflowers—from his younger nephews and nieces for sure. Just looking at it makes me think of noise and confusion.

"Sit down ... Please."

"I have to catch the bus back in a little bit."

"The nurse'll bring you tea or coffee ... or cider if you want."

He's trying to scrunch himself up so as to sit higher, but he can't. "That extra pillow there." And then it's like he's going to say, Please, but he says "Mary Catherine" again instead.

I put my arms around him ... *arms around him!* and put the pillow behind him. He's warm and damp. When I go back to the chair I can feel him on me where the breeze from the window dries his sweat.

There's nothing to talk about. I knew there wouldn't be, and I'm so scared that even if I could think of something, I wouldn't say it. He must know how I feel because he reaches out to me with his broken arm. Like he wants me to hold his hand ... just his fingers that is, the cast comes way down.

"Don't worry," he says. "I can move it around a little without any problems."

I pull the chair closer and touch his fingers. They're sweaty like the rest of him, and I think maybe it's because he's still sick, but then it is hot in here, even with the window open, what with the little stove going, and he's got blankets on, too.

Holding his hand certainly doesn't help me with my being scared. I want to enjoy it right now and remember it later, but it makes me too nervous. I have to look out the window at the tree to feel even a little bit calmer. His fingers are ... like they say about electricity ... like some magic flows out from them through mine and into my whole body.

He signals twice with his fingers, exactly like when he gave me those two hard hugs in a row and I don't know what he means now anymore than I did before. Then he says, as if he's reading my mind— or more likely my face—"It's all right. Don't worry."

I take a big breath and I feel some better. Then he shuts his eyes and I feel even more better with him not looking at me. I can begin to appreciate that I'm holding his hand and sitting beside him and I can look at his long eyelashes on his pale, pale cheeks. (Girls are supposed to be the ones with long lashes, but from what I've seen it's always men who really have them.) With his eyes shut like this I don't feel I have to think of things to say. I don't have to try to be clever and educated, which I used to think I was before I met these people.

But all of a sudden … and they startle and shock me … Charlotte and Hen's mother … Hen doesn't snatch away his hand, but I snatch mine away. I stand up. I twist around. I say, "I have to catch the bus," which is ridiculous since everybody knows it doesn't leave for another hour. Charlotte grabs my elbow, but I twist around again so she can't hang on. I run out. I run until I can't see the hospital anymore. After that I walk. I wonder what Hen's mother thinks about me *now?* Holding hands with her son like that? I wonder what she thinks it means? I should have stayed and told her it doesn't mean a thing. But she's never critical. It feels good to be around her. I never knew anybody like that. I wonder if I could ever be that way? Except I have all these feelings that get the better of me.

I walk until bus time. I'm so mad at myself! I not only didn't bring flowers, I didn't think to ask Hen how he was, so I don't even know! And all I said the whole time … *all* I said was, "I have to catch the bus." The absolute only thing. Saying it twice doesn't make it any better.

I don't know if I'm glad I went to see Hen or not, except I do have more stuff to think about when I go to bed—if I can get my own mistakes out of my head and keep on thinking things about him. Mostly I just tell myself how dumb I was and how I could have said this or that or the other. Anything would have been better than what I did say.

I wonder how long I was there? All that way for just twenty minutes or so? And then spending most of my time walking around in the desert?

I wonder what Hen told his mother about holding hands with me. I don't think he talks with his family much. It seemed, when I saw him there at the funeral, that he wanted to get away from everybody. I'll bet he didn't tell them anything.

Everything is back to … I suppose you'd call it normal. I wish it wasn't. It'll probably be this way for a long time, though I guess this is how life is supposed to be. When Hen comes home they're going to take him straight to his family's ranch, and I'm not going over there for anything. I'll have to wait till he goes out to his shack.

It hasn't been all bad with Madelaine here. I did win her over a little bit with my cooking and with all I do. I finished painting the whole house *and* the outhouse. I fixed the organ so it finally works. There's still a little wheezy leak somewhere, but I'll find it one of these days. Madelaine was impressed. She played it, and then *I* was impressed. I can't play a note of anything. They *all* play around here. Abel's mother taught everybody.

All that work kept me from feeling too bad that I have to spend my whole life waiting. And I can do a lot more daydreaming with Madelaine around than with Charlotte here, because Madelaine doesn't want to talk much, and I don't want to talk with her either. I should. I could be finding out all sorts of things I need to know about Hen. *If* she'd tell me anything.

Abel started being a little more like Abel and began to pay attention to his lessons, and I have to admit ... had to admit to Madelaine that the piglet was a good idea. Of course there'll be a problem when it gets to be a sow, but that'll be a while yet. Abel and I wrote Madelaine a thank-you note about the piglet.

(It was just weaned, but Abel wanted to bottle-feed it, so we tried and it went back to that right away, no problem. Now it'll probably never want to be weaned. I can just imagine this two-hundred-and-fifty-pound sow still being bottle-fed, and probably walking all over Abel, who won't have grown an inch.)

I'm reading him *Cinderella* and *Sleeping Beauty* and *The Three Little Pigs* ... All those things. (And we've read *Tom Swift and his Airship* twice now.) I talked about witches when I first came, but I know Abel never even knew what a witch was. I guess he knows now. He's back to sitting close and leaning up against me all nice and warm and listening to beat the band. I thought it would be good for him to catch up on these stories that other kids know all about, and I wanted him to forget, a little bit, about his mom being dead and Fay being gone. When we read even Madelaine listens, educated as she is. We sing some of those baby songs Abel missed out on. Madelaine plays them for us and Abel hums along.

I haven't pinched him once in all this time. I haven't even felt like it. My goal is to be like Hen's mother—be the kind of person that's really, truly kind. That scarab pin she gave me. That was a completely-for-no-reason nice thing.

Being like Hen's mother is another way *not* to be like my mother.

I know … I just know Hen will want to get back to his shack as soon as he can so as to have some peace and quiet. Wouldn't it be nice if I could have it all fixed up for him, like with a bookcase and curtains and a rug? But thinking about a rug makes me think how we were, hugging, there on the floor. With a rug we wouldn't have had so much dirt all over us. But if I got a rug, that might mean something to Hen. Like a suggestion, so that's the one thing I can't get even though it's important. I don't want him thinking things.

Abel and I go out there by ourselves. I don't tell Madelaine where we're going and I don't have to worry that Abel will talk about it. I bring a picnic—all stuff that Abel likes best: cold pancake sandwiches and lemonade. For Hen—for later—I bring salt and pepper and honey and sugar so there'll be some there. I bring three tins of peaches so Hen will have something nice to come back to. I didn't just take them from our place. I paid for them myself down in the village.

We take two horses because there's lots to carry and Abel wants to bring his piglet. I tell him it's all right as long as he thinks of a name for it on the way and calls it that out loud. I say if he says its name a lot, it'll get to know it and come when he calls her. "Pigs are smart," I say, though I really don't know anything about them. I've just heard that.

Abel says "Caw?" like it's a question and I say, "Is that supposed to be its name?" He nods and I say, "You know perfectly well caw won't do. Anything but caw." I say.

So we go riding along with Abel thinking hard, and me keeping quiet to let him, and finally he says, "Cock?"

"Good boy, but no, Cock is what they used to call your cousin Hen. We can't have two cocks."

Then Abel starts to giggle. It's been a while since he's done that so I know it's a good sign. "Cat," he says.

I look at him. I don't know what he's talking about—not for sure.

"Cat, cat, cat." He's laughing so hard he almost falls off his horse and he's looking like the joke's on me. I laugh, too. I guess more *at* than *with*.

"Well, at least it's something you can already write. Why not call the pig Pig?"

That sets him off all over again. Maybe he really is feebleminded like they say in town. But then I think it's just being nine years old, which is not all *that* far from being an idiot.

We ride along and pretty soon I get into my talking mood. I know I'm just using Abel for my own purposes—like he's part of my daydreaming. I start saying all sorts of things I shouldn't, as usual. I might even be one of the reasons he isn't learning to talk. When somebody else is making all the noise and doesn't leave another person any space of their own, they haven't got much choice. I even tell Abel that I know I shouldn't talk so much and that I know I should be talking about things *he* might care about, not always be saying what *I* want to say. So then, just for him, I tell him what we'll do when we go to the village to get some more things for Hen. How we'll have ice cream. How if we had any ice at our place we could make some ourselves. *If* we had an ice cream freezer. Then I tell him how you need salt to make it colder, except I don't know why that works and we should look it up if we get to a library some day. But then I go on about how I'll be spending all my money, except at least there won't be any leftover for my mother to take.

I talk so much I'm glad Hen isn't here. He wouldn't like me one bit, but he doesn't anyway. So, of course, I say that to Abel, too. I say, "If Hen cared for me at all he'd have come to eat some of my good cooking, wouldn't he?" (I should stop talking for two minutes just for practice.) "He knows about my food. Charlotte told him, but he wouldn't even come for even just one good meal." Then there's that hand-holding at the hospital. What does *that* mean? So I tell Abel about that. Actually, it's that I can't *not* talk about it. Who else is there to tell? I can't tell Madelaine. Abel is the only person I could ever say these things to.

"Abel, when you get to talking, you can go on and on as much as you like and I'll listen. I owe you. And you could learn to say 'Shut up' to me." (I say that, but I don't shut up anyway.) "Say it. Say 'Shut up,' like you ought."

We do all sorts of things out there at Hen's. We picnic by the creek, we see another jay, but it's not as tame. We leave crumbs all over so maybe it'll get started and it does get started. Abel is sad when he first sees it, but then he likes it. He gets it to come up to his toes. We clean up more glass out of Hen's floor. (I think again to take down that sketch of the naked girl, put her in the stove and use her to make the coffee. I look at her a long time. I have to admit there is something special about her— a kind of delicacy I don't have. It goes with how Hen is. You can practically see how educated she is. She has an educated forehead. And she looks to have naturally curly hair. Even in the black and white lines of the drawing, you can tell that her hair is a nice light color, blond or reddish, and very fine. There's nothing coarse about her. I don't look like much compared to her. Even if I got more educated, would I look more educated? I don't think so.)

I need to do something nice after looking at this girl, so I take Abel up the hill to see the view. I carry Cat-the-Pig partway, though mostly she follows us, nice as a dog. I don't want to leave her by herself. Something might come around and eat her, and I don't want any more bad things happening to Abel. (We saw a coyote family on our way over. I hate the way they eat things, sometimes just the stomach, like that's the best part. Coyote candy.)

We sit on the very same big stone that Hen sat me down on. Up there the breeze is blowing, nice and soft. Just right, and all of a sudden I'm thinking: I love you, I love you, I love you, and I don't know why I'm doing that except because of the view and the breeze and the sky and because it was Hen who showed me this place. I love you, I love you, as if that girl on the wall doesn't mean anything, though how could she not? But, at least for right now, I'm just in love with everything.

"Oh, Abel, do you think I'll ever get to be in love with anybody who loves me back? I mean I like you very, very much. I love you even, but I'm thinking about that other kind of love. Sometimes I'm glad you don't talk. I do want you to talk ... I really do, but sometimes it's nice that you don't."

He leans up against me like he does and looks at me as if he knows exactly what I mean. I keep forgetting he's only nine.

A couple of days after Abel and I come back from Hen's hut, Hen goes home from the hospital, back to his family's ranch to recover, Madelaine leaves, and Charlotte comes back here.

Right away Abel gets even more like he used to be. He's not sitting all curled up all the time. We start writing a lot about pigs, some of it the real stuff from government bulletins. Charlotte doesn't mind Cat-the-Pig in the house (I knew she wouldn't), though she says it makes her think more than ever about how a dog or a cat would be nice. She says it's good we kept it inside because otherwise something would have eaten it for sure, considering we don't have a good pen.

The very first night Charlotte is back, she and I sit, like we do, on the porch and I ask her about Hen. First I just ask how he is and she says, "Not very happy—as if he ever is these days." But then I ask her, What about Hen holding my hand? What did she think it meant? And what did Hen's mother say about it? Which is what I really want to know the most.

"How would I know? You're the one whose hand he held. And Aunt Henriette didn't say a word. She wouldn't, though I must admit we did give each other a look, whatever *that* meant. And we wouldn't have said anything right there in front of Hen."

"Is she against me? I know his sisters are. Are *you* against me?"

"I've already told you a long time ago, and I feel exactly like Hen's mother does. We'd be glad for anybody that could get Hen out of where he is. Even *you* for heaven's sake."

Which I know is supposed to be a joke, but I take it as the truth (which it partly is) and say, "I know I'm not like all of you. I didn't grow up nice with nice people." (It took just about all this time for me to really understand this and I know it more and more, the longer I'm here.) "And then my mother … I'll ruin his life. If, that is … if anything happens. I just know I will."

I'm thinking she'll say, Don't be silly, like she usually does when I say things like that, but she says, "Who knows?" instead. "One never knows. His life doesn't amount to much anyway, the way it is now. What's to ruin?"

A few days later, we hear that Hen has gone back to his hut even though nobody thought he was at all well enough. They couldn't stop him. But they're just happy he didn't sneak off to town and get in a fight again, which they couldn't have stopped either.

Everybody else is worried, but I'm not—not really. I'm happy because he's alone out there and I'm going right out. And, since they say he still isn't well, maybe I can do things for him to make him like me and need me. And I want to bring him some of my fancy cooking, which he hasn't even eaten one single time, but now he'll have to.

I'm not hurrying. I'm so happy, my saddlebags full up with good things. I'm savoring the trip, heading out towards a person who held my hand, and it's *almost* with Charlotte's and even Hen's mother's blessing, as far as I can tell. But the closer I get, the scareder I get. I want it to be nice and for us to sit down and eat my special food, maybe by the stream where Abel and I picnicked. (I brought only things Hen wouldn't have to cut.)

I'm pretty close when I hear music. At first I think I must be making it up, especially since it's my favorite kind of music. It's off and on, as if blowing with the wind, and then, as I near, it's mostly on. Piano music, but I know that can't be, and it certainly can't be that Hen is playing. And how would a piano get way out here? It's jazz. Or maybe ragtime. I'm not sure I know the difference.

I go slower. I turn west, off the trail so I'll come to the shack by way of the stream and from behind the trees that line it. I want to sneak up on him. It's a gramophone! I just know it is. Exactly what I've always wanted.

I dismount and tie the horse to an aspen. I walk down along the creek. Its sound will hide the noises of my coming. I guess the music will, too. I want to see what's up before I let on I'm here. That way I can turn around and leave if I need to and nobody'd be the wiser.

I see him. The gramophone is set on his front-door stone and he's dancing. As if with a girl. Slowly. A sort of shuffling, but in a really stylish way—kind of jazzy. Just the way I *knew* he'd dance, being who he is. Crackerjack, like he said about Fay, that's how he dances. He's hardly taking up any space, just the little sandy spot in front of his hut.

He's curved forward a little and his arm not quite around himself,

as if he had a girl in it. I want to run right in and be the one he's dancing with. Except you could just as well think he was curved over like
that in pain.

The music stops and he winds up the gramophone and puts the
needle back on the exact same record. There's a bottle of wine by the
door that I hadn't noticed until he takes a swig before he dances again.
The music is on the happy side—it *is* ragtime—slowish ragtime, and
Hen *is* hurting. Now he's hugging himself tighter, holding himself together, exactly the way Abel was when he was always curled up after his
mom died. Hen's head is up, looking at the sky, but I'll bet his eyes are
shut. I'm not close enough to tell for sure, but he looks like a blind
man. The happy music fooled me at first. This is agony, I see that now,
and he's doing it on purpose, like when he picks fights. He wants to
hurt. He wants to wallow in his sorrows. I don't think he should be
doing this, but I don't dare go in and stop it. Besides, I'm looking right
straight into somebody else's daydream. I shouldn't even keep on looking. It hurts to watch. I go down on my knees because of how he looks
and how the music is and I know … it wasn't *pain* kind of pain when he
went down on his knees that time and then knocked me down with
him. It was *this* kind of pain.

I curl up, my cheek in the sand. Will this have to be one of my
memories? Will I have to know about it until the day I die? The
stream, such a nice rippling sound, and the music that I love the most,
and Hen in agony, trying to hold himself together?

The record ends and swishes around, sounding like the stream.
This time he doesn't go put the record on right away. I get up to see.
He's just standing there, leaning over, but then he does wind it up and
put the needle back on.

This is *not good!* It's enough!

I hardly realize what I'm doing. I hadn't thought to do it. In fact I'd
thought *not* to do it. That I shouldn't. That I should leave and never let
him know I'd seen into his bad dream, but I run out to him, running
and yelling like the witch I really am. "Stop it, stop it, stop it, stop it!" I
throw myself at him. I grab him, my arms around him, hard. "Stop. I
love you."

Then, and it's like an unconscious spasm … Or maybe they teach
you that in the army. He throws me from him. It's not like when Fay

139

hit me. This is how a really grown-up man hits out. Like for keeps. He throws me … yards away. I land on my back, my breath knocked out of me from both front and back. I can't breathe. As I try to catch my breath I think, Thank God having my breath knocked out hasn't happened but twice before.

So I'm rolled into a ball, gasping, and he's saying, "I'm sorry, I'm sorry." Shouting it like I was shouting "Stop, stop." He kneels beside me. I'm all curled up in my own kind of agony. It takes a while. He gets me fresh cold water from the creek, but I can't drink until I can breathe. When he finally dares touch me, he puts his hand on my ankle. Even when I can talk, I don't. We look at each other and then his eyes are flickering all around. Have I embarrassed him terribly, coming in on him like I did? He hasn't said a thing except "I'm sorry" all this time, yelling it right into my face as if I'm not going to believe him. But *I* should be saying it to *him*. I'm the one who sneaked up on him on purpose and kept watching even when I knew I shouldn't.

Here he is looking as if he doesn't have any idea what to do or say, which is not like him at all. Most times he seems to know exactly what to do and does it with a kind of know-how. Purposeful, is how he is. (Charlotte said he never was like that before the army. She said he was a master sergeant for a while at the end, so he knows how to push people around.)

He's shaking pretty badly. I'm thinking how he's still sick. He looks sick, too. He's very pale, but then he's been out of the sun for a long time.

The gramophone has unwound completely by now. The only sound is the creek. Our yelling must have scared off all the little things that rustle. We're quiet for a while. Until I feel I should say something or nothing will happen forever.

"They said you really ought to still be at home."

"I *am* home."

"I brought you a nice meal."

"I don't need it."

"I know you don't. And apple walnut cake."

"I don't need it."

He sounds angry. I suppose we both sound that way—all my "Stop its" at the top of my voice and all his "I'm sorrys" at the top of his. And I'm wondering if he's had too much to drink.

But how come *he* always gets to be the one who has some sort of fit? I've felt sorry and sorry and *sorry* for him for so long and here he is—even right this minute—feeling maybe sorrier for himself, or at least just as sorry, than anybody else feels, and that's all right, I know it is, except enough's enough.

He's spoiling my whole nice day and he's spoiled dozens of wonderful meals I made just for him. We could be listening to wonderful music, which I never get to do. We could be dancing, except I know he won't. He couldn't stand that, not if I have to hang onto his stump. I just want to grab him and shake him and yell some more. And what if it would be good for him if I got angry? His family never does. They're too careful around him. They're more afraid of him than I am.

"You could be dead," I say. "Everybody else is dead. You could be blind, you could be gassed so you'd never speak again, you could have lost *both* arms. Mostly you could just be dead like everybody else. You might as well be, the way you go on. Did you ever wonder how long you're going to keep this up? Did you ever think: another day? another week? another month? a year? It's *been* a year." It feels good to yell all this true stuff at him. "Did you say to yourself, I'll start living next year? You ought to pick a date and decide that's the end of it. I haven't had the greatest life in the world myself, you know." But that's not fair to say to someone who lost an arm, and probably all his friends are dead, and they say it was the noise that never stopped, night and day, that would drive you crazy. Thousands—millions of bombs. "I know your life is worse. I know that, but you have a family that loves you. You have a real, honest-to-God mother. I'd trade places with you any day for your mother alone." (I would, too, and I could cry about my life right now, except then I'd be doing exactly what Hen keeps doing.)

I'm not angry anymore, but maybe he is. He has a funny look I haven't seen before. What did I do to bring that on, I wonder? He looks both frightened and calculating at the same time. He's squinting, thinking. He has plans. He gets up and pulls me up, too. I can smell the wine on his breath he's that close, but he doesn't seem at all drunk. Just the opposite.

"So you want to? So we will."

(*That* sounds like a master sergeant.)

He's going to use me to escape thinking about things—to escape hearing anything I say or anything I said. It's just like before … that afternoon on the floor. I'm to be the distraction—again. That's all. There's nothing of love in what he wants to do, just determination. It's all thought out. I should *never* have said "I love you."

He leads me to the hut, shuts the door, and bolts it. Too sure. Too quiet. I can see the muscles of his jaw working.

I'm worried about the horse. I'm worried about my food out there. Something will eat it for sure. But I guess I'm really mostly worried about myself ... and about him, too. But this *is* what I wanted. Only not like this.

He does everything slowly and staring at me, unbuttoning my blouse (this time it only has six buttons), my skirt, undressing me down to my stained and torn underwear that I was hoping he'd never see. But I'm too scared to worry about it now, and he doesn't look as if he sees anything anyway.

He keeps looking at me with this staring, mean look. Maybe he's doing it all out of rage. Or maybe this is the shell shocked way of love. Maybe this is his only way possible.

When I'm down to nothing on at all, he takes all the blankets off his cot, spreads them out on the floor, and then undresses himself. I want to shout "Stop it, stop it" again, but what if this is what will help him? What if it's his only way possible? And Charlotte said, "Go to." She *might* have meant this. And what if this will make him love me?

We're completely naked. I'm too scared to blush—for myself or for him. (I'm not too scared not to think how beautiful he is.) He pulls me down on the blankets. He's not cruel, but it's all so thought out! So decided and so precise! Even his hand on my breast, as if: I will now put my hand right here. And then on my stomach and then down there. He doesn't even kiss me, not once, and then we're together. It hurts and it's hard to do, but he does it. Then we're as close as anybody could possibly get. There just isn't any closer. I feel every bit of him. It hurts so much I wish it would be over. And all the time there's that sketch of the naked girl looking down on us. There's nothing else to look at. I shut my eyes.

Then he does kiss me, all wet and gooey and needy, not loving, but I do begin to feel ... because of his neediness. I love. This is me, loving and being loved. And this is Hen. Not the way I wanted it, but it *is* Hen ... not some stepfather or other, like I was always afraid would happen for my first time.

And this is Hen finishing. I think of bucking horses, and the groaning sounds a horse makes sometimes. And this is Hen, holding me almost as if he cared. Kissing my cheek. As if he cared. His arm across me as if he cared. This is Hen, warm, relaxed against me, just like Abel when I read to him. And this is Hen, asleep. My Hen. *Sort* of mine—a little bit. Who am I, the hired help, to ask for more than this? And if it does get him out of how he is, then my life will have been at least a little bit worthwhile. Of course it might not help him at all, but for now, with my arms around him, I can think anything I want.

I must have dozed a little bit, too. I wake up (of course looking straight up at that sketch of the naked girl. She's prettier than me all over her). I move away from Hen a little but he doesn't notice. He's absolutely sound asleep, so floppy he looks as if he's never slept but a couple of minutes in his whole life and is busy catching up from day one. I'm beginning to think maybe it really *was* good for him … doing that. Maybe he's cured now, and all due to me. Though maybe it's the opposite and he's sleeping like this because he's still so sick. I don't suppose, really, it was the best thing for him to do while still recovering.

I push myself out from under his arm and there's his stump, right in front of me. It's not pretty. I know him well enough to know that's what he thinks, too. I make myself look at it: the folded skin with the sewing marks. I want to find a way to show him I don't mind. I need for him to know.

I examine it a long time and then I ease myself away and get up and right away I see the blood stains all over his blankets … from me. I knew I was all sticky, but I didn't think it was blood. I guess most of my time out here is going to always be washing things out, though I can't do that till he wakes up, which looks as if it won't be any time soon.

I start to dress, but there's so much blood! I had no idea it would be like this. And it keeps coming. Could it be the time of the month starting so early? I have to find a rag. I rig up something using one of Hen's towels. Another, a big one, I use to cover Hen up a little even though I'd rather have him naked so I can look at him. So thin and muscley and hairy (a good kind of hairy, not at all like any of my fuzzy stepfathers). But if he's still sick, he shouldn't get chilled, and the blankets are all under him and bloody besides.

(Everybody has very nice towels here. When I was with my mother, we just used our worn-out clothes. She's better off now, though.)

Then I go out and bring my horse down and tie her up to Hen's line, unsaddle her, and give her a good rubdown and some of Hen's grain. (I wish I had hobbles like Hen does. I'd put them on and let her hop herself around.) I bring my food inside. The ants found it, but Hen doesn't have to know. He wouldn't care anyway.

I'm bleeding all over Abel's mother's skirt, though I guess it's my skirt now. Not the most up-to-the-minute style, needless to say. Even so, and even though it's mine now, I don't want to spoil it. Hen has a pair of clean black pants. I'll wash them out afterwards ... along with everything else. Maybe this really is the time of the month even though it's not supposed to be. Or else I just never knew how bad it would be. I thought a drop or two. (I've had to guess at just about everything. My ma never told me a thing even though she made a lot of sexual comments. Mostly I never knew what she was talking about.)

I bring in the gramophone and the records and the wine and arrange everything nice and neat. (Hen is still looking as if he never did sleep but once till now. I wonder just how drunk he was? *If* drunk? He didn't seem drunk. I wouldn't want it all to have been just because of being drunk. I want him to remember it.) I move things around so the records will be easy to get at. I put the gramophone on top of one of his boxes where it'll be easy to get at, too. I put my stew (nice and soft and cut-up meat) on his stove to warm. I try to keep quiet through all this but I do bump around a little, but Hen still looks like he'll never wake up.

I have coffee and eat some of my walnut bars. He's sleeping practically a whole night's sleep in one afternoon. That's all due to me. He must have needed it.

Finally he wakes up. The first thing he says is, "That smells good," about my stew. Then he sits up and puts his hand right on the bloody spot, which must be dry by now, and must feel stiff. He looks at it and then looks up at me.

"Mary Catherine."

"Don't worry. I'll take care of it, I promise. I'll wash it right away."

"Mary Catherine. Mary Catherine."

He keeps doing that—saying people's names all the time for hardly any reason. (I'm glad I made mine longer.)

He reaches for me and I sit down beside him—not on the blood— and he hugs me, this time as if he cares about me, but I know it's really because he's sorry for me because of the blood. Even so, it's nice to be kissed in a sweet way and then to have your hand kissed, whatever that means. I could think it's because of him being French, but I know kissing the *palm* of your hand isn't the French thing.

I lean my face into his neck and I think: *I'm a fallen woman!* I'm a fallen woman just like my mother and it's not like I thought, because I don't even care.

Henny

H<small>E WAS DETACHED</small> ... as if watching himself. Floating two yards above himself and a little behind, looking over his own right shoulder. A puppet master with himself as puppet. He had been too disconnected to be angry at what she'd said. Nothing seemed to have much to do with him. The whole world around him might as well not exist. He's in some hazy other world where everything merges into everything else. Nothing matters. He's been this way before a few times, especially over there and then again in the hospital, floating up where nothing can touch him. Nothing hurts. Even sounds go away.

But if he really is the puppet master of himself, why hadn't he stopped himself? It was as if the puppet master was as helpless as the puppet, a frozen creature incapable of any emotion. He had choreographed himself, gesture by gesture, into a lovemaking he'd not felt—until the end. By then, a need, and then a sort of love, and then a sudden gratefulness, and then pity for the little waif. *His* little waif. For some reason or other, his, and almost from the start. He'd wondered why they'd hired a girl with such a mother and such a reputation in the first place, but she wasn't like that at all. Charlotte must have seen it and felt sorry for her, so Charlotte's little waif, too. And now this blood. He hadn't realized there'd be so much. In some countries they'd hang these blankets out for show, proud of it. Even if he did that and had a place to do it, nobody would believe it. There were always stories going around. He had proved them untrue, but he couldn't prove it to anybody but himself. Had he done it to prove it? That would have been a nasty thing. He owes her and now more than ever. Nasty! Worse than nasty. Mean and hurtful. He owed her before for looking after him, washing him and his shitty clothes. Washed his blankets then, too, and now again. He should do them. Why should that always be her job? He owes her more than he can ever give, and he wants to give, but not so it would seem like payment as though she was a whore. That's what she'll think. She's on the edge of that thought all the time. She'd see gifts as an insult.

How she looked naked … Compact. Her breasts not as rounded—not as sexy as Julia's. Soft when he rested his cheek on them. Her working woman's body, like her strong, square hands. Not like Julia. Julia would never have made a farm wife. She wouldn't put up with that, but back then he wasn't going to be a farmer, though he'd never told his parents. They'd have been upset. He was supposed to be the heir. *The* heir, and here he was the only one who didn't give a damn about the ranch. It was lucky he'd never told them. And now … That's all he knows how to do. Mary Catherine, she's the farmer's wife type. Just what he never wanted. To her it would be a big step up. And babies. Julia wanted only one, at the most, which was about all he'd be able to put up with, too. Mary Catherine would take whatever came along and think it the best that ever happened.

Julia had admired him for all his non-farmer aspects—for his music and because he knew French literature as well as she did though she was the Parisian. He hadn't realized until the army how well-read he was compared not only to other farm boys but to two thirds of most everybody. He hadn't understood how much Aunt Oriana had given them of music and his mother had given them of French. Given and given, but he was a taker, even of other people's lives, even Uncle Bill's, and now here he is, the taker, seducing young virgins.

Mary Catherine is right, of course, all those things she'd said, scolding him. She didn't tell him anything he doesn't already know. Of course he should pick a date and end all this. She'd said, why not right now? Why *not* now? Just as she'd said, he's not as badly off as most. He's already thought about that a lot. But it started before, all the way back with Uncle Bill. He has no right to always be the one left alive … still alive and seducing people.

And he wants her again even as he scolds himself for it. Wants and doesn't want. "A rooster, a horse, and a woman should be chosen for their type," the saying goes, and she's not at all his type. But he hardly knows what the puppet master's going to do next, nor which is the slave and which the master. Wouldn't it be something, though, to take her places? Like to the opera! Her eyes would shine out. She'd shine out all over, maybe even more than after that view he took her to. But how can he make her see it's not payment for being his whore? That'll be her first thought. But what if that *is* why he'd be doing it—that she's his whore? What is he doing, anyway, and wants to again? So just stop.

Stop everything. Come down—out from behind his own left shoulder—and stop, like she said, and why not right now?

"Mary Catherine."

And she will, *again,* even now. He can see it on her face.

"Mary Catherine."

He owes her at least a real kiss. The puppet master will choreograph a real kiss for her.

Mary Catherine

SOMETHING IS very, very, very wrong with Hen. He *is* crazy. I don't even have to know what crazy is, which I don't, to know for sure. I can feel it. I can see it. Sometimes there's … It's like nothing at all in his eyes. He's just a blank. How could I have been telling him how he should act and that he should stop this right away when he's so crazy? He scares me all the time, but this emptiness inside him scares me even more. I wouldn't call what he did making love, but at least it wasn't making hate. It wasn't anything … though, at the last, there was a minute or two when it did seem like love—a *little* like it. And after sleeping, he went at it all over again. But I didn't believe one bit in that kiss he gave me even though it almost was a real one, and then he kissed me up and down, and it was good he had his eyes shut because I didn't want another view of how he wasn't even there. If his eyes had been open, he'd have looked as if I was a mathematical problem of some sort that had to be solved.

I began to feel things, though, and for a while I didn't care if he was in there with himself or not.

We lie still again, after this second time, his hand on my breast. Now and then he moves his fingers a little bit as if he likes how I feel. I don't think he can be looking so empty now, lying so still, breathing so softly on my neck. I hope not, anyway.

I know he doesn't want to hear what I'm about to say, but I'm going to say it anyway. I need to say it for myself, and I wonder, after all this, what he'll say about it *now?* I said it already, when he was dancing except, back then, I don't think he even noticed. I say, "I love you."

He takes his hand away from my breast and turns on his back. "Don't say that!" He really *is* angry now. "Don't ever say that again. Not ever."

"Why not?"

"There's no future in it. I told you that already."

"I don't care. I never had a future anyway."

"Just don't say it."

He gets up fast, just like that, and dresses, so I do, too, even though it's *my* turn to feel like sleeping the rest of the day away. I put his old black pants back on. He doesn't look at me, which is just as well. Then I start to pick up the bloody blankets but he takes them from me. "I'll do these," he says. When he looks at me now, there *is* something in his eyes but I don't know what. He's squinting, like he does when he's thinking hard, puzzling over me.

Then, "Go home," he says. "Go on. Please."

How can he say that after all we did together? I don't want to leave him now. Why does he want me to go?

"Go on. Get out of here."

How can he want that?

"I need to be by myself. That's all. That's *all!*"

There's a path that goes along by the stream. That's where he walks off. First he says, "I'm not angry. I need to think," in an angry voice. In half a minute he's behind the willows.

I wash my pots and pans and my other clothes. I do the blankets, though he said he would. I do everything slowly. You can't do things any slower than this. I'm hoping … wishing, he'll come back. I tie my things to my saddle. I put the horse in a little low spot with me in a higher part and mount up. I start out, away from the hut, as slowly as I can go even though it's about to get dark and I'll be sorry. Then I hear him coming back. I hear him yell, "Wait!" and I feel such relief! All of a sudden I can breathe again, and I don't care how dark it is by the time I get home.

He comes up to me and grabs my knee. "Go home and pack your good things—for maybe a couple or three days. I'll come by for you. We're going some place nice."

For half a minute I feel wonderful, and then I feel all mixed up, partly because he looks so sad—not at all as if he might have any fun going some place nice with me. But at least he doesn't look crazy.

Of course right away my biggest worry is that I haven't any clothes, and that Hen'll be wearing his dark suit and his beautiful clay-colored vest, and I'll disgrace him. Pack your good things, he said. I can't stand it. I can't answer him anything at all, because there's no way I can go anywhere. I don't have one single good thing. Charlotte is much too big for me to borrow anything from her. (We already tried. Her things are pretty plain, anyway, and she only likes men's colors.) And Abel's mother's old clothes are all from before the war when skirts practically dragged on the ground and there's all this old fashioned lace at the collars.

I don't answer a single thing. I turn away and ride off fast. If it wasn't for Abel I'd never come back to anywhere around here. Is this supposed to be love? There's nothing but aggravation in it ... for both of us, it looks like. Besides, Hen didn't say *when* he'd come for me. Knowing him, it won't be right away. All I ever do is wait. What's the use of waiting when you don't have one single decent dress to your name?

I don't want to go anywhere with him, and clothes are not the only reason, though it's a big one. Charlotte would laugh at me. She'd say, am I going to run away because I blush and don't have anything to wear? And I'd have to answer, "Partly I am." I will not—absolutely *not* go anywhere nice in my old green dress—not with Hen in his clay-colored vest anyway. If Hen can say, "I can't and I won't" then I can say that, too.

What if Hen had asked me to go off to some place nice with him right then—right that very minute, me wearing his old black pants and bleeding all over everything? I'd have gone and not a second thought, even though I know he doesn't love me, else why wouldn't he let me say it? He said, "Never, ever, ever say that again." Those were his *exact* words.

Nothing in the whole world could have made me want to leave but a thing like this. I painted the whole house and shutters, too. I nailed the outhouse back together. I planted columbines all around the front door. I was right there when people died. In fact I saw them first. If not for me, then *lots* of things. The whole place feels like it's a little bit mine, and these people ... Abel, more than a little bit mine. If Abel could say boo, he might even say so himself. Nobody ever treated me so kind as them. Even Hen, peculiar but mostly kind ... Crazy and kind, but I don't know if I want to be around him when he turns blank again.

It isn't until I get halfway down the trail that I start to shake. Just about as badly as Hen at his worst. Hen said he needed to think, but I can't think at all. I hardly know where I am. I would have ridden right past our ranch if the horse didn't know where to go. She trots up to the pasture gate and waits for me to get down and unsaddle and turn her out. At first I just sit there, goodness knows how long. She's patient. When I do get down, the saddle seems twice as heavy as usual and it's not even that late.

There's this nice, lamplight glow coming from the house. It looks *so* cozy. It looks exactly like coming home should be. And then, before I even open the door, I smell biscuits. Inside it looks perfect, too. Charlotte is at the table, drawing. (I've never seen her doing that and I haven't ever seen any new drawings around either.) She's sketching Abel. He's asleep on the bear rug with the piglet in his arms. The way he looks is enough to make a person cry. I don't, but there must be something on my face—some look or other which I don't have any idea what. I'm wondering, can it show? What Hen and I did? Or maybe it's that I'm wearing Hen's old pants with a rope for a belt, or maybe it's all this shaking, but Charlotte gets up, right away, and comes to hug me.

"Mary Catherine!"

Now *everybody's* going around saying my name for no reason whatsoever.

I pull away. "I'm leaving. Don't ask what happened."

"What did he do? Did he hurt you? I've been worried he might. Did he? ... He didn't!"

"No, Charlotte. No. It wasn't his fault. It was as much mine as his. Really." I sit down because I can't stand up a minute longer. "Do I have to talk about it?"

"He did, didn't he."

"It's not his fault!" I shout it.

"Of *course* it is."

"It's not. If you'd seen him, you'd know."

"I've seen him. I know."

We're both talking so loud I think we'll wake Abel up. We already woke up the pig. Except Abel can sleep through most anything.

"Don't try to defend him. He's a grown-up. He knows better."

"Yes, but he's not ... He's not right. And I could have left. I could have fought him off. I just didn't want to."

"You don't look like you had a good time."

She's right about *that,* and Hen didn't look that way either. "I wanted him to be happy … *happier.* I know he doesn't love me. I'm not asking him for that, and I guess I know he won't be happy either."

"Well, I'm going over there first thing in the morning."

"Charlotte! Please, please don't. If you tell him he ought to marry me, I won't. Ever. That'll be the end of it. I know he doesn't want to. He already told me he wouldn't."

"At least he's not lying to you."

"I knew what I was getting into."

"Oh, Mary Catherine, you don't know anything. What'll I do with you!"

"He's crazy, Charlotte. He really is. I saw it. Right in the middle of … what we did. You *know* he is. Everybody knows. If you go out there it'll only make things worse. I'll leave here for sure. I won't be able to face him after you talk to him. He'll think I told you to go talk to him. I'll have to leave. Besides, he's coming here anyway. I don't know when. I was hoping to be gone by then."

"Please stay. Abel needs you. We both need you, you know that. I could go out just to see how he is. That's all. I wouldn't say a single word about you."

"If you do, it'll make things a lot more complicated than they are."

"They're complicated already. Or maybe they're utterly simple. I'm so mad at him! What right? And you. So young and …"

She doesn't finish, so I'm thinking, And what? foolish? ignorant? not his class of person at all? It has to be something like that or she would have finished her sentence. Except I know she likes me. So then I do start to cry. Charlotte makes me some cambric tea, which reminds of that teacher and when I wasn't feeling well at her house.

"Please don't go running off yet. Abel misses you whenever you're gone. You've been good for him. Go have a good sleep. Please."

She carries Abel into his bed and then the pig. She fills the wash basin in my room with warm water and then comes and gets me and my tea. Sits me on the bed.

"You've helped us. *All* of us. With Fay gone, and Ma … at least she used to milk and cook a little. This whole place will fall apart without you … even more than before. I can't run it by myself. I love this place and I love being in charge of it. I'm good at it. I know you'll laugh at me saying that. I know I'm only good at the stock part. We make a good team, you and I. Let me just go take a look at Hen. I promise I won't say a word."

I don't believe her—what will she talk about except me?—but she's going to go no matter what, and I'm too tired to think about it anymore.

"Well, take him those strawberries."

"You're the crazy one. He deserves a lump of coal."

Henny

HE SPENT A BAD NIGHT. Got drunk on wine, which never makes him feel good, but that doesn't stop him from doing it. He was already a little drunk even before he decided to get drunk. Used up the last of Papa's wine, and just as well it's gone.

This calls for making plans. But there's a wall he can't think himself beyond. A bad habit from the war when there wasn't any future to think about anyway. He would think: home—all he had to do was get home and everything would be all right. Home was the only thing he looked forward to. Now he *is* home and still lives as if waiting for some wonderful thing like coming home—some home that never existed and never would. A child's sort of memory as if from before Uncle Bill died when everything was Paradise, and Uncle Bill was the man he wanted to grow up to be exactly like.

He's been thinking of taking off—like Fay did—and never coming back. Not to start life over, more to *not* start over, and in a place where nobody would expect things of him, nobody would think about him at all, or be disappointed in him. If his family knew about yesterday they'd be even more disappointed than they already are, and they'd be thinking about him all the more.

He should be getting out of bed. He's doing an Aunt Oriana, and it's not the first time.

If he had his notebook he'd write in it. Even if he had one little piece of paper he'd write, write that he's not ever going to take that picture of Julia down. He doesn't want to and it'll show Mary Catherine how things stand. She needs to know. But why is he thinking she'll ever be out here again?

It's just that she walked in on him at a bad time. Having her come yelling down at him … It's a wonder he didn't break her neck.

She let him, though she was frightened. He must have looked like he did in the mirror in the hospital when he even scared himself. She said, I love you. But there's no love in *him*. Maybe never will be. He doesn't even *want* to love—ever again. He doesn't care what happens, but Mary Catherine does, and he owes her. So then just do something for her. See the town, see a moving picture. She'll love that. (Love! For her it's easy.) Go home and get his good clothes and the carriage and some of Madelaine's clothes—his smallest sister. Nice dresses.

But Mary Catherine won't stand for that. Neither one of them will stand for it. He can see them—both of them—refusing to have anything to do with it.

Did she like it? Did she feel something? If she did, it wasn't because of anything he did in any sort of loving way. This time it'll be the opposite. The trip will be for her. He'll keep himself in line and not bother her with anything to do with sex. Everything will be to make it up to her for all she's had to put up with from him.

There's squawking outside. That's a different jay—not as tame as the one that disappeared. Nature. Things go off and die. Things get killed. It's just like war. No, not at all like war. Hidden, nice and quiet deaths. One squawk or none, and that's the end of it.

Someone's banging at the door. "Henny, are you all right?" He'd thought at first it might be Mary Catherine, come back to ... to what? He'd thought, maybe to make love again, but it's Charlotte. Probably come to ball him out, but there's nothing new she could say. She's right. Everybody's right. He knows it all already: Just because you have shell shock doesn't mean you can do the first thing that comes to mind. You think if you tremble enough, all will be forgiven. Well, not by me it won't. Not by anybody. This is the last straw and you know it ... And he does, too. And you took advantage of somebody who loves you. How could you? You're crazy.

"Of course I'm all right. Why wouldn't I be?"

"Let me in."

"I'm dressing."

"It's just me."

He throws on his pants and shirt, though with only one arm, you can't exactly "throw things on." It takes him just as long as usual.

"I'm coming."

"I've already ridden all the way over here and you're still in bed?"

She's got bundles, but as soon as she puts them down, she gives him such a look! She knows all about it. He never could keep anything from Charlotte. She always knew.

"Mary Catherine told you."

"She didn't have to. She came in, all … She hardly knew which way was up. I mean really. I had to help her sit down."

"I should have known you'd figure it out."

"We've known each other too long."

"I guess so."

"I promised Mary Catherine I wouldn't say a single word about it, so I won't, but *Henny! Henny!*"

She's opening up the packages: putting out strawberries, and cream, and then his black pants, already all cleaned up and even ironed.

Strawberries and cream … lovers' food?

"I couldn't keep Mary Catherine from sending these to you, though I tried. I told her, better she should eat them herself—give herself a nice treat, she needs one—but she wanted you to have them. I guess that's love. She's not very happy but she still loves you. You don't look very happy either. You look as if you had a bad night. Guilty conscience, I presume."

He shrugs. What's to answer?

"I'm trying to keep Mary Catherine from running away."

That shocks him. It's because of him. He hurt her that much. Yet all the different things she's done for him … He *needs* to do something for her. It's the only thing he wants. He never looks forward to much of anything, but this he does, as if the look on her face could fill the emptiness inside him. As if, if he can't feel feelings of his own, he could use hers.

Charlotte sits on the floor and leans back against the cot. She's wearing the exact same kind of black pants as he is and a loose farmer shirt. Why can't she show a little bit of her figure for once. Every time he sees her he thinks that. Here she is, knees apart, big black boots … In her own way she must be as crazy as he is. But, not true. She's living a real life.

He sits down beside her in the same position.

"Eat your strawberries."

But he can't now, not in front of her, especially since she won't take any.

"I won't marry her. She knows that. Lotti, I can't be married. I can't go out and be with people."

"Well what *are* you going to do? I mean about the future?"

"I don't have one and I don't want one."

There's places in his mind he can't make himself go. It's that same wall—there all during the war. If there was to be a future, thinking about it would just take up thought that was needed someplace else.

"Use your big fat head for once. Are you thinking with your elbow? Well, I know what you're thinking with."

But he wasn't. Or maybe. But he was hardly there at all. In fact he doesn't remember it in any real way.

"Eat your strawberries, for heaven's sake. I'll make the coffee. You look like you need it."

But what if she does run away?

"Charlotte, I want to take her to town, to the opera, and have us stay in the Boston—separate rooms I mean. I want to take her to some of those restaurants, especially the French one, and the one in the hotel where they have a trio playing.

"You think she'll get happy just like that?"

"No, but she'll like it. But, yes, I think she *will* be happy—at least about all that. I want you to make her stay until I come for her."

"I don't know if I should help you or not. I don't know why I'm even talking about all this. I promised I wouldn't."

"Who's side are you on?"

"That's just it. She needs somebody on her side for a change. Oh, Henny, I don't even know why I still like you at all. I don't know why I'm even talking to you as if you were a reasonable person. But … It would be a nice thing for her, no doubt about it. She hasn't been any-where. Maybe I'll do it—try to keep her here I mean. I can't make her do anything any more than I can make *you* behave yourself. But I want her to stay for my sake. We'll lose the ranch if there's nobody to help look after it. I'll need you, too, if I'm to keep things together. Or maybe I'll have to hire some of your nephews. I just don't want to let go of this place. I love doing this. I mean I'd like to be an artist even more but I love doing this, too."

She turns sideways and rests her head into his cot, but then turns back again. "You ought to wash your blankets. They stink."

He thinks about Mary Catherine and all that washing and yet some of the blankets must still stink. Or it's him. When did he last wash himself?

"It's me most likely."

"I wish I could have studied art. Even *I* can see the difference between my painting and trained artists."

"What happened to L.D.?"

"Oh, he pops in now and then, once a year. On his way to painting in the mountains. He gets more famous every time I see him. I don't suppose he'll bother with me much longer."

Charlotte stares at her boots and then gets up and stands in the doorway and takes a big breath. "You know your whole shack stinks. I don't know how Mary Catherine can stand you—in *lots* of ways."

"Didn't Oriana's mother leave you art school money?"

"I'm keeping it for Abel or Fay. Maybe they'll want to go to college one of these days."

"You know Fay couldn't. He hasn't been to school a single day in his life. You could still go to art school, you know. Why not? I think you should."

"We'd *really* lose the ranch then. It's nice and fresh and breezy out here."

They step out into the sunshine. Charlotte gives her horse a couple of rubs on the poll and then a stroke on the rump as they pass by.

"I don't think it matters how rich and famous L.D. gets. You're … I know you don't want to hear it, but you really are a beautiful woman. I knew that back when we were ten years old. Before even."

"I have to go up to see your view before I leave."

For sure she doesn't want to talk or think about how she looks.

Just then, as they start up the slope, a little sand storm blows by. The wind swirls his laundry on the horse tie line around and around and around until it's completely wrapped round the line. At least his clothes aren't blown away. (It wouldn't be the first time he's lost things.)

Sand in his eyes and ears and mouth. Charlotte rushes back and holds the door for him to come, but he turns into the wind.

"Henny, come back. Are you crazy?"

"Every now and then. Usually. Why even ask?"

But his words blow away. He's pelted with leaves and sticks as well as the sand. He can't see. If you have to go on, you just go on. Rain or sand, or wet feet with foot rot, you don't think about it, you just do it. You go on. That's the way life always is.

"You nit-wit." She's there, behind him, turning him around. Pushing him inside, slamming the door. "What was *that* all about? You *are* crazy. What are we going to do with you? Both of you. Poor Mary Catherine, and here you are, too smelly and crazy for anybody to live with for a half a minute."

They wipe their faces with his more-or-less clean towel, dripping wet so as to get the sand out of their eyes. Charlotte makes a face. Maybe the towel smells, too.

"I must say you do need a wife around here."

The dust devil has passed by, but they don't go out again. They sit on the floor as they did. The strawberries and cream are still on the cot. Charlotte eats two though she said she wouldn't touch them.

"I won't marry."

"What if your parents knew about this? What would they do?"

"You going to tell them?"

"Of course not."

"I'll make it up to her. I want to. I don't suppose she ever saw moving pictures. I want her to have a good time. Maybe see Charlie Chaplin."

"Well, that would do you both some good."

"Make her stay. Tell her to at least wait until I talk to her—at least that. Just a couple of days. I need to go home first."

"She's upset about nothing to wear. And Henny that's not just nothing for a girl. Would you go to those places in your Levi's?"

"I want to get her a dress, but I don't know how. You know what she'll think if I buy her anything like that."

"She already thinks it. Maybe you should let her alone for a while."

"But if she's going to take off ... I need to see her. I need to talk to her before she does."

"What for, for heaven's sake!"

"No. I promise. Not for anything like that."

"Henny, Mary Catherine isn't in a state to fight you off or stop you or to want to. She has enough troubles without ... without getting even more attached to you."

"I know. That's what I want to talk to her about."

"I don't trust you. Not for a half a minute. Eat your strawberries before I eat them for you. I can't stand to see them sit here anymore."

"I can't. I'll save them for later."

"The deer mice and the ants will get them. I'll go, so you can enjoy them by yourself if that's what you're waiting for. If you ever enjoy anything."

Mary Catherine

I'M SO MIXED UP I can't think at all. I thought I knew exactly what I wanted and it was Hen. And I did like … well, the second time—even though it hurt. I don't know if Hen liked it or not—except he did it twice. I guess that's a sign of something. But I don't know what I want anymore. I really ought to leave before Charlotte comes back and starts persuading me into things before I've had a chance to find out what I think myself.

I never thought love would be so sad and serious. If I'd known it was going to be like this I might not have been looking forward to it so much. I thought it would be playful. Sometimes, anyway. I thought we'd laugh a lot and have fun together. We'd tickle each other, we'd chase each other around, I'd run and he'd try to catch me, and there'd be lots more nice views to take each other up to. I thought life would just be pure joy from the minute we both loved, onwards for forever. I mean I know Hen won't dance with me ever. That's too much to even think about and I'm *not* thinking about it. Why think about something that would be so painful to him? And I know he won't be happy *all* the time, but I thought maybe just now and then.

I thought I'd be dancing around, inside myself at least, and I'd belong somewhere because of loving and being loved, but I don't belong anywhere anymore than I did before. Even less, because I have to leave. That's what gets in the way of my thinking anything at all. And that sadness of Hen's—and I made him sadder than ever. I should leave so he won't feel so bad. I'd be doing him a favor. Charlotte already said a long time ago that nobody and nothing could make him happy. She warned me, but I didn't believe her till now.

So today just goes along all by itself. I'm floating in it as if there isn't such a thing as time, and as if there isn't anything I need to think about at all. Everything is slow. There's no hurry. It's as if time itself is saying,

"All in good time." I notice everything. The clouds have that funny circular look they say is typical over mountains, but I've seen clouds like this all my life so they're just regular to me. Quail coo to their little cotton-ball babies and the babies trot after them as fast as their little toothpick legs will go. It's as if the smallest things—or big things, too—as if everything is *very* important, and I only began to notice that. I wonder if this is just for today or if this is how I'll see things from now on. I wonder if it's because of what Hen and I did. If that changed my whole view. I wonder if even more things have changed and I haven't noticed yet. I wonder if this is how things *really* are. But they *are!* All you have to do is notice. It's as if it's always silvery moonlight, or always that orange look, like after it rains. It would be nice if I keep on seeing this way. Except I can't think. Maybe this is instead of thinking. I don't know, maybe I'd rather be thinking.

And what about love in all this? Has that got anything to do with anything?

It's nice to be alone with Abel now, and nice that he's quiet. I appreciate that more and more. I need him. I need to read to him and teach him and for us to go out and work on the dam some more. He needs me, too. He leans against me and I put my arm around him. Now that I'm leaving I can do that. It doesn't matter much what I do.

We have Cat-the-Pig with us all the time. At the pond, we all take baths. The pig seems more and more like a dog. It sticks with us like Abel is its mother. It even squeaks and waves its hoof to beg.

I move lots more stones. I need the hard work and the cold feet. I need scraped-up hands and arms. By now you can actually see that the pond is a little bit bigger. If I stay here, we'll have a big pond in no time. But I should prepare Abel for the worst.

I tell him I'm leaving soon, but I'll come back and visit him lots of times, I promise. I'll make good money so I can take him places like we did before, ride the bus and go to a band concert. I wouldn't have money for a hotel, but maybe we could camp out some place. And I say, "You have the pig for company now."

I'm giving him a good rubdown to dry him off and warm him up. He's looking at me, big eyed—those orangy, witchy eyes. Before I can stop him, he's hugging me hard—half-naked skinny little kid. Strong skinny arms. Maybe I *do* belong some place after all—at least some place with Abel in it.

I say, "I love you," and I'm happy to get to say it to somebody who doesn't say, "Don't ever say that to me again."

But after supper I start thinking—well, more daydreaming as usual. (Charlotte isn't back yet and Abel is using her big drawing pad and drawing the pig. She doesn't mind even though that paper is expensive. Wouldn't you know, that paper is from France. The way people throw away their money around here!)

I start thinking what it would be like if I went with Hen. I didn't want to be thinking about that. I'll spoil all my own ideas. Hen didn't say what we'd do or where we'd go except that it would be some place nice and I should get my good clothes ready, so I make up all sorts of things: Me, sitting across from him in restaurants, and looking at his chest with the clay-colored vest over it. I'm watching his long-fingers, which look so graceful and strong at the same time. The perfect piano-playing hand. (Would I have to cut his meat?) I think of us having a picnic out someplace pretty, sitting side by side looking at a nice view. We hold hands. I make it better and better. Hen is smiling. He's laughing!

I'm making myself ache to go. What if it really would be like that and I ran away and didn't get to have any of it? What if we saw a moving picture and I would have missed it! I'm the only person I know who's never seen one.

I'll go! I'll just go. I can always run away after.

Three days later Hen comes for me. He's very quiet. Mostly he doesn't look at me, and when he does he stares like he did before, wondering about me. I'll just let him wonder.

He trots up in a fancy carriage and a matched team of brushed and shiny bays (horse colored, we always called that color). I know—I just *know* everybody in his family knows all about us, though I hope not *all*. I'll bet the children polished things up and braided the tails and manes. Even the hooves are polished.

There's a buffalo robe lined in red wool for a lap robe, though it's so warm we won't need it or … what is he thinking to use it for? There's silver on the horses' headstalls. If I didn't know he was rich before, just looking at this carriage and these horses would prove it. And everything all shiny and clean—just for me—for his you-know-what. At least I'll have my own old dress. Nobody could be a fallen woman and have a dress like mine. My mother has lots of nice things nowadays—now she has a better class of man. (When I was little I didn't even have socks. She always had cigarettes, but I never had socks. I'll bet I could have had two pairs, even, for just one pack.) And then I don't think a fallen woman would have scratches and bruises all over her hands and arms and a fresh crop of broken fingernails.

Hen looks so morose. Well, *I'm* going to have a good time no matter what.

And why should I stop loving him just because he doesn't want to hear about it? I can love inside myself. He doesn't have to know. I'll stop when I feel like it.

As we trot along I watch his profile: his slanty forehead, sophisticated nose … He has buckteeth but I don't mind. (He's really not at all a handsome man, but I like his looks better than anybody I've ever known and I like how he looks older than he is. I suppose that's because of all his hardships.) He's wearing a fancy, black, aristocratic hat that goes with his nose. I look at his little scars. Since he doesn't look at me at all, I get to watch him all I want.

It's a breezy morning. Wind always makes horses frisky. One of them shies at every other bush out of sheer exuberance. I feel pretty frisky myself even though I've hardly slept for the last two nights. I *am* going to have a good time. I just insist on it no matter what.

We have this conversation in bits and pieces, and a lot of long silences between. We go for three or four miles before he says anything at all. Then, first, he says, "I," and then he says, "You," and a while after that he says, "You know you shouldn't …" Then another mile goes by and he says, "You shouldn't let me hurt you."

In the distance I can see the hill we climbed, up behind his shack, and all of a sudden I feel such love for him. That was the sweetest thing, and the flowers … Maybe they really *were* for me. I want us to hug, or even just hold hands. But the team is spirited so Hen has to keep track of them all the time. He'll not *ever* be able to hold my hand as we drive, when he only has one for holding the reins.

"I owe you more than I can ever repay. You know that. You probably saved my life. You must know."

Well, if he owes me such a nice time, why doesn't he try to look happy? He could at least make the effort. It won't be for more than a couple of days. Does he think I like to see his face all stony? But of course that's the way he usually is.

"I won't touch you again, I promise. Fight me off if you have to. Hit me hard. I'll come out of it."

Well, I don't know, he might throw me a couple of yards by mistake like last time ... But what if I want him to make love to me? And maybe this time I don't want it for him, but for myself.

"I hurt everybody I get close to. I always have, since a long time ago. Since I was a boy."

I had thought to mostly keep quiet, but then I do say something. "Things can change," I say, but he just grunts. It's a nasty, ironic grunt.

We turn off the road down to the big river and sit by the weeds. Hen gets out a picnic. His mother made it for us, little finger-sized potatoes and a kind of cold pie Hen says is French. It has hard-boiled eggs and vegetables in it. I'm sure there's nothing like it in Abel's mother's cookbook. I thought *I* was the good cook around here, but I don't begrudge his mother being better. She's too nice for begrudgings.

"My mother did something else," he says. "It isn't that she knows what happened, she doesn't, but she wanted to give you this because she's grateful about you cleaning me up and helping me and staying with me. She wants to do things for you."

There's a box wrapped up in pretty paper. I guess if it's from his mother and she doesn't know, it can't be because I'm a fallen woman.

I'm hoping so hard I don't want to open it. I might like my hopes better. It's one of those times when you want to be alone in case it's something wonderful or something that disappoints you. You want to have time to prepare your face for other people either way. But it *is* ... Better than my hopes. There's a silky, cream-colored blouse with a lacy collar. It looks as if she really thought about what would look good on me, because it will. It's new, too. Nobody else ever wore it before. It even has the label, which says it's silk, still on it.

I say, "Oh, my God." That's all I can say. He's reading things in my face. He almost looks happy. He practically smiles.

"I brought you some other clothes, too."

I know where he scrounged them up. They belong to his sisters and I won't wear them. Besides, I have this blouse. I say, "No." I'm not going to argue about a thing like this. It's just, No. I may be a fallen woman, but I haven't yet fallen so far that I would wear things belonging to his sisters.

"I'll take this blouse from your mother, but nothing else."

"But Mary Catherine, think what you've done. How you stayed up all night picking glass out of my feet. Please don't worry that I give things to you."

"No. It's just plain No, and that's that."

"Maybe you'll change your mind later when we get there. And you'll need white gloves in some places. I have those, too."

White gloves! What have I gotten myself into!

W E HAVE TO STOP at a little inn halfway down. They know him there, which makes me wonder—about a lot of things—like how many women has he taken to town like this and stopped here with? But I know I'm not the first woman he ever had. After all, he was in Paris.

I'm so tired I just flop into bed. He said there'd be separate rooms and there are. At first I wasn't sure what to feel about that. It's clear he doesn't want us to get to be too close. Right now I'm glad of that, though. I'm even too tired to have any supper. Hen wants me to but I just can't. I'm too worn out, and it's as if the wonderful thing of sitting across from him eating, like I've always imagined, would be wasted on me in my state. I want to save it for later when I can appreciate it. Hen has warm milk and cinnamon toast sent up to my room. He never asked what I wanted, but I *did* want exactly that.

For the first time in several nights I just sleep and sleep, even though it's a strange place and a strange bed and you wouldn't think I'd be able to for lots of reasons, including that Hen is in the next room. You'd think I'd be a nervous wreck just from that.

A lady wakes me early in the morning. She just walks right in with coffee and eggs and bacon (on a tray right to my bed), so I won't be having breakfast with Hen either, but this is nice anyway. Better, be- cause I bring the tray to the window where I can eat and look out at Hen. He's already up and dressed and harnessing up all by himself, even though now he's in his fancy clothes. (Yesterday he just wore his usual wrinkled clothes, which are mostly left-over uniforms.) He's not wearing that clay-colored vest I was hoping he would, but another one just as nice. By the looks from here, it's black velvet and he has a gold chain for his watch going across it. For such a messy man, back there at his shack, he sure can get dressed up. I wonder what I should put on? I guess I'll wear my old green and see what happens. That lady with the breakfast tray is better dressed than I'll be.

Well, nothing happens, just that I feel bad about myself, and glad Hen wraps a blanket around me to keep me from the morning air. But maybe it's to hide me. I wish now I *had* said I'd take one of his sister's dresses. After all, if I don't mind being a fallen woman, why do I mind taking presents for being it? And he's right, he owes me. God knows how long he'd have lain there only half-conscious. I'm not surprised he wants to pay me back, but he doesn't have to. I just plain love him.

Finally … *finally* all the stuff I daydream about starts happening, and better even than I thought it would be; me, across from him in the hotel dining room (and they have an elevator!). I'm looking at his velvet vest and gold watch chain. I'm wearing his sister's slinky, fringy dress. I've never had anything like it. Of course there's my shoes … I keep my feet under the table as best I can. And my hands, all banged up one way or another, skinned knuckles and all, and then there's that burned-in arrow where I branded myself. It's kind of smeary. Maybe he can't tell what it's supposed to be.

"I'm sorry about my hands."

"They're fine."

(That's just polite talk.) "They're worse than the waiter's."

That makes him smile—for once.

I can't help smiling too, because of the pillars and the trio playing and the white, starched tablecloth and all the glasses and silverware and the silver salt and pepper shakers … And Hen looks more beautiful than ever, and I think how *I've* been as close to this person … just as close as anybody could possibly get.

I keep quiet. I watch to see which fork to use. I don't make a single move without seeing the way he does things first. I don't want to disgrace him. By the time this trip is over I think I'll know everything there is to know about fancy places. I thought I knew what proper was, but now I know I never did.

I just can't keep from smiling all the time, and the more I smile, the more he can't help smiling too. He looks as happy as I've ever seen him. I know his smile is as much *at* me as *with* me, but I don't mind. Me, having a good time, is what's making him happy.

The only problem is, I can't eat. Hardly a mouthful. I'm so nervous—sitting here, across from him, in this place—I can hardly bear it.

I nibble a couple of radishes. I sip a little wine and then a little water. (I'm scared of wine. I've seen what it does to people all too often. I never drink so I don't know what it'll do to me.)

So I have to tell him I can't eat. I just can't. He reaches across the table and takes my hand. It's like at the hospital, the same two squeezes, and he doesn't say a word.

Next day we see a Charlie Chaplin moving pictures. We eat at a French restaurant and Hen speaks French to the waiters, and I think how this actual, French-speaking person, right here, made love to me not so long ago, though of course it wasn't really love.

The day after that we get me a new dress, and new shoes. They're for the opera. Hen wanted to get them and I guess it really was good to do it, because it made him smile a lot, which, of course, was because *I* was smiling so much. Every time I think about it I just start smiling all over again. He picked everything out. I let him. I wanted it to be a dress that pleased him more than it pleased me because he's the one I want to look good for. But it pleases me as much as it possibly could. It's the most elegant thing I ever saw. Three different tans, and some gray, and fringe of course, and a little bit of Indian red here and there in triangle shapes. And he got me a headband so it doesn't matter what my bangs are like. I never thought to have a beaded headband. I feel like an entirely different person. Not like a fallen woman. I'm a flapper. I know that's all pretend, but nice to think anyway. People probably think we're married.

He doesn't touch me at all, all this time, not even to hold my hand like he did at the first dinner. In the moving pictures I saw a lot of men with their arms around their girls' shoulders, or just across the back of the girls' seats. Hen didn't even do that. I leaned towards him so at least my shoulder was against his.

And then we go to the opera! Aida, with *very* famous singers, though I never heard of a one. (Galli-Curci and Tito Schipa, and me in my new dress. Galli-Curci … *All* of them have great names.) It's about real lovers, not like Hen and me.

There's this huge purple curtain, and when it goes up, there's Egypt. Really Egypt! All tan like our desert right here (kind of like the colors of my new dress), and big tan pillars decorated in red and blue, and I knew it was *exactly* Egypt. A little bit later there's a scene that has the actual Nile and what looks like real waves going by, up and down, and even clouds going by, too.

As usual, Hen is watching me a lot, with a little almost-secret smile but *I* can see it. He's probably watching my eyes pop out. I'm the entertainment for him. But he's the entertainment for me, too. I like to see him smiling.

He whispers to me what they're singing about—just enough to keep me on track. Every time he leans so close, breathing on me, I prickle all over. I want to touch the velvet vest over his stomach and chest.

The last scene is the most remarkable thing I ever saw. The stage is divided crosswise so you see the temple upstairs and the tomb underneath. At first all the lights are bright in the upstairs part, and then, when the hero is put in the tomb, that part lights up and the upstairs gets dim. Hen tells me how Aida goes into the tomb to die with her lover. How it's true, too, the Egyptians really buried people alive just like that. I would go into a tomb with Hen without a second thought. I'd especially do it right now with the music and all, but I know he doesn't want me to say anything of that sort. It's so hard not to say things, but I manage it. I haven't said much this whole trip. I'm getting into good habits.

So they wall the hero up inside the tomb and at first he doesn't know Aida is in there, and then he discovers her and they hug and kiss and sing—everything at the same time. They're real honest-to-goodness lovers. He kisses her hands all over, top *and* bottom. The music is so sad I don't know what to do. It all seems to be about Hen and me in some way, but, like Hen said, nothing will come of me loving him. We'll never have the chance to get entombed together. And if we ever were, Hen would just say, "Oh, it's you again," and turn away. "And don't, for heaven's sake, say that word love."

I can hardly watch anymore though I do, and when it ends I have to sit there while everybody else leaves. Hen gives me his big handkerchief, and I try to keep my tears off my new dress. Finally Hen sort of picks me up and makes me leave. He walks me back to the hotel for coffee and, when that doesn't help me stop crying, he takes me out for a drive in the midnight air. We go up to a nice view which makes me cry all the more though I don't know why, and then he finally—*finally* he puts his arm around me, and *finally* with real feelings, and it's as if we've—both of us—been aching to do this all this whole time, even Hen. He actually means it. He kisses my tears. He gets his own cheeks all wet from me so, when I kiss him back, I taste my own saltiness. I know what's going to happen, and that we won't be in two rooms—at least not for this night.

We make love—real love this time, both of us in his room. I had been worried about my poor old nightgown, but I didn't have to worry. We don't wear anything. It's better than I ever imagined real love would be—and I did a lot of imagining, though I never did imagine such a beautiful, hairy body. I still cry now and then, partly for the lovers in Aida and partly for … I don't know what. Maybe out of relief to be in his arms in a real loving way at last and relief at how sweet Hen can be.

Then he's blowing on my stomach on purpose to make me laugh, and after that he's tickling my feet with his toes. All of a sudden he seems like an entirely different person. I laugh partly because of how he looks, making faces at me. It's a Hen I never knew could be. He kisses the tips of every single finger. He nuzzles me all over, pretending to be a puppy. He growls and barks and sort of bites. I feel … well, not beautiful, I know exactly how I look (which isn't like the girl in the sketch. *That's* real beauty), but like beauty doesn't matter any more. I don't exactly believe in his love. And I think he's done all this before. If I was the first person he ever loved, he'd not know to think up all these things. I think he learned it from some girl. Probably that girl in the sketch, but I don't care. It's nice, and I like seeing him like this. I don't think he'd do all this unless he *sort of* cared. Maybe he got resigned to me. We'll probably hold hands at every single chance we get from now on.

Hen not only has his arm around me, but his bare feet cupped around mine, too.

"Can I name our hill?"

"What 'our hill?' Do we have a hill?"

"You know, the hill you took me up to … to the view. Behind your hut. Or does it have a name already?"

"They call it Lost Dog Hill, but it's yours to name. We'll change it."

"It isn't that I've thought of a name yet. I keep remembering how nice it was up there, and how you leaped down. I keep thinking: Leaping-Down Hill, or Viewpoint Hill."

"Better than Lost Dog."

And then Hen is sleeping so soundly I wonder if it'll be like the time he slept the whole afternoon away, but *I* watch dawn come. I don't want to fall asleep and miss any of this. I do sleep a little by mistake off and on, but I don't want to waste a single minute not noticing his arm around me and how I'm tucked in so close against him. And it's all due to Aida. I never thought I'd get to see an opera, let alone like it.

There's something else I want to do so badly but I don't dare ask for lots of reasons. Especially after that time by his hut when Hen was feeling bad about himself. Besides, I'm already so happy it would be immoral to think of having even one more happy thing. But what I want is to go someplace with the kind of music Hen was playing on the gramophone out there—some place where they dance to it. I know he wouldn't dance with me, I'd never ask him to do that. Except I'm worried about what might happen to him in a place playing the same music. He might have another fit of some kind.

I loved going to Aida, but I want to do something modernistic, too.

But it turns out I don't have to say anything about it. It happens by itself. Hen gets to talking to one of the waiters and gets handed this little modernistic card about a colored man and his jazz band performing on a back street down the block from our hotel. The minute Hen has it he starts shaking twice as much as usual. I had been thinking maybe I was making him a bit better, what with all this lovemaking and laughing, but I guess not.

Something did happen just before this, as if Hen *had* changed some way. At supper he ordered steak. All this time it's clear he's been careful to order things he can eat easily and not ask for any help, but he got steak and then asked if I would cut it for him. This was the first he's asked for help or confessed to not being able to do something.

So we go to this ragtime band thing. It's in a small, basement place. There's not even a sign that says it's there. Hen says there are lots of places exactly like this in Paris. That surprises me. I thought things were big and glittery there, but I should have known because this is exactly right for a jazz-type place. But in Paris they don't have to hide that they serve alcohol.

Even when we first walk in, I see in Henny's eyes that he's upset ... the upright piano ... the dark, smoky walls ... (the air is already smoky enough to be kind of foggy) ... For a minute Henny looks at me the exact same way he looked when Charlotte was about to haul him off to the hospital, startled and yearning, I don't know for what. I get worried. If he needs to leave, I'll let him take me out of here no matter how much I want to stay. I reach to hold his hand but, though the look on his face says, I need you—or somebody—he turns away fast.

He's a little better when the music begins and he's had something to drink, and he starts explaining things to me. He likes to do that. The black thing is called a clarinet and the big horn-thing is a tuba, but not the kind they have in marching bands. (They have all sorts of things to drink here. I guess it's what you call a speakeasy.) When they sing "Willie the Weeper," Hen explains how it's all about drugs. He says, "Smell. You can smell griefers right now."

"Did you ever smoke that?"

"Little bit. Hear the way the left hand on the piano is playing? That's called a walking bass. Know who Mr. Johnson is? It's the cops."

He's all flushed and glittery eyed, and he can't sit still. Sometimes he's sort of singing. His voice is terrible, mostly just gravelly sounds. ("Ain't that a shame, to leave Bill Bailey out in the rain," and, "Mr. Johnson, turn me loose ...") Except for all that, it's the same as when we were at Aida, him leaning towards me the same way, but after last night, I feel easier with him than I was, and I *do* touch his velvet vest this time, right over his stomach, and he puts his sweaty, shaking hand over mine—so shaky it's scary. I put my other hand over his to hold him still. It doesn't help much.

But something wonderful happens … something *else* wonderful besides this place. (Actually, by this time I'm used to lots of wonderful things.) Hen gets a little drunker and excited about the music and when the musicians take a break, and everybody's wandering around not paying attention, he goes up on stage and starts playing the piano with his one hand. Right away everybody sees how good he is and they come back and sit down to listen. He's just as good or better than the real piano player. I thought he'd be good, but I had no idea what that really meant. I'm thinking, *this* is crackerjack! Somebody yells out, "The cat's pajamas!" And somebody goes, "Meow." And he can't even be in practice. Then the regular piano player comes back just because of Hen and starts playing the left-hand part for him. Now my eyes must be popping out even more than ever. Hen can do so many absolutely amazing things! And always better than I ever thought.

The regular musicians all come back just so they can play with him. They don't let him stop. Nobody in the whole place wants him to stop, and they keep bringing him this mixture of beer and whiskey that he's already been drinking. They move me over to a table near the stage and bring me a drink, too, my first one ever, but after just one, I decide all I want is sarsaparilla, so I drink a lot of that.

Even though I'm right beside the stage, Hen has completely forgotten about me. I'll bet he wouldn't know who I was or even care, if I went over to him now.

This goes on and on. A couple of times he and the man doing the left hand do classical pieces. That colored man and Hen just know all there is to know about every kind of music. It gets later and later and it didn't even start till late in the first place. I don't think they'll ever stop. Except I can see Hen is getting drunker and drunker. First he was all excited about himself and having a good time like I've never seen him have before, even when trying to make me laugh last night. He was laughing out loud and grinning every time he looked over at the man doing the left hand. They were playing at outdoing each other, and talking to each other this real black kind of talk. But Hen is getting drunker and pretty soon he's looking angry. Can't they see what's happening? All of a sudden he gives this terrible yell and slams his hand and his stump down on the piano keys, banging out a lot of noise. Then he tries to tip the piano over! And he almost does it, but the man next to him grabs him—everybody on the stage comes to hold him and some not on stage, but he swings around as if he's being attacked from all sides and starts fighting with everybody and punches the closest person, which of course is the smily man who was playing left hand for him. Everybody grabs him and he fights and yells—crazy yells until—just like that—he passes out even though nobody hit him. I saw the whole thing. I was right there trying to help hold him, and I know nobody hit him. (They're the ones to have bruises, the way Hen hit out at them.)

They carry him backstage and I go back, too. When I see myself in the dressing room mirror, I hardly know myself. I completely forgot I was wearing that headband. There I am, the flapper, lipstick and all. But what a silly thing to be admiring yourself when your lover is passed out on a scratchy horsehair couch, with somebody's jacket thrown over him.

Everybody is so nice to me. Most of the musicians are colored, but they call me Honey, and treat me like a bosom friend. A couple of men take us back to the hotel and carry Hen up the back stairs and put him to bed. I don't tell them I have a different room. I pretend I'm the wife. I ask if I can tip them. (I don't know anything about tipping, but Hen's been tipping people right and left. I would have had to take something from Hen's pocketbook. I don't have a single cent.) They think that's the funniest thing they ever heard and won't let me. They say it was pleasure enough to play with him. They don't even seem surprised about him having his fit and hitting everybody. They think it's perfectly natural. They say they'd have fits, too, if they could play like that and only had one hand to do it with. They say they should be paying him for letting them play along. They say he made the night special. They say, "You keep him playing, you hear? Don't let him stop." (I don't tell them he's already stopped.) They call me "Lucky lady," because of Hen. I already know that. I even like it that I have Hen right here helpless. I have *the* piano player, the one-and-only. I can kiss the hand that plays. This hand … this actual hand that plays, has touched me all over my body. I can curl myself up beside the very man, and stroke him, kiss his scratchy unshaven cheeks, his collar bones, and I don't have to feel shy like I usually do.

I undress him—down to those little black straight hairs all over him. I take a few minutes to look at him and then I cover him up. I lie down beside him and put his wonderful piano hand on my stomach. I say "I love you, I love you" a dozen times. He can't hear me—I can say anything I want. I go to sleep wondering how in the world I ever got to be right exactly here! I feel so good I can't hardly bear it.

When I wake up, he's not here. I never know what he'll do next so I get worried. I wouldn't put it past him to leave me to find my own way home. Maybe I won't go home at all. Maybe I'll stay here. I'll go back to those nice black people and look for a job with them. Anything. Making beds or washing clothes if they want. They were about as nice to me as anybody could be. They called me Honey all the time. The only trouble is, I really am in love with Hen.

I'm not just worried about myself. For sure Hen has a giant hangover and maybe he feels bad about everything that happened last night, even though—or *especially* because he was having such a good time. If he remembers how wonderful it was, he'll feel terrible that it can't be that way all the time.

I find him harnessing up—looking just as grim as I expected. He's back to wearing his old unironed army clothes. The only fancy thing is that elegant black hat—low over his eyes.

He looks sick. I guess he *is* sick. That doesn't stop him banging around the horses. Or maybe he bangs because he's sick. They don't like it. He's usually gentle and slow with them—with everybody. (I'm thinking how he was with Abel when he dressed him, there up in the mountains.) And he's so shaky. Worse again. And kind of jerky.

He doesn't look at me and I know better than to say a single word. He just puts our stuff in the carriage (he's too polite not to help me up, though I don't need it) and we trot off, no breakfast, no coffee, no anything. It's as if he wants to feel just as bad as he possibly can. If I dared I'd try to talk him into a cup of tea, as much for his sake as for my own.

It isn't till late in the day that he seems to feel some better. That doesn't make him sociable, though. I think he wishes I wasn't with him. But I'm not going to let him spoil my memories. I have so many good things to think about, and I have a wonderful new dress, and new shoes, I saw moving pictures, I saw an opera, and I was there for the best of all, Hen's playing. I can hardly believe I did all the things I did. I wonder what Charlotte will say when I tell her? Of course not about everything. (Best of all was being made love to in a really and truly loving way.)

I don't mind his not talking. It gives me lots of time of think and remember. I'm not going to try to count up good things anymore. There's just too many of them.

Finally we stop to eat. It's almost supper time, and we haven't had a thing so far. I eat a lot: soup and ham and white potatoes and sweet potatoes and corn and cornbread and biscuits and pie. Hen just has soup. (He's shaking so much most of it spills back into the bowl. I wish I dared reach out to him—for even just a half a minute. But I know he doesn't want me to.) After he has most of the soup, and coffee, he looks some better. He even can smile at me for eating so much. And he turns solicitous again, sad and morose and sick and solicitous and kind. I know he's sorry for me, but that's another form of kindness. I don't mind people being sorry for me. My teacher was sorry for me. Charlotte was sorry for me when she hired me. I never understood why people always say they don't want pity. Pity's just fine. I want it. What's the difference between pity and just plain kindness?

I wonder what Hen's thinking—about last night? I wonder if he remembers it? It would be horrible if he thought of it as torture—like when he was listening to music there by his hut, trying to hurt himself with what he loved best. But last night he really was having fun, so fun *is* possible. I want to scold him again, but I don't know what to say that I haven't already said. I've known people who go on and on and say the exact same things all their lives. I could get to be that way myself with telling Hen how he should behave. I ought to stop right now.

I thought maybe my dream would come true and Hen and I would live out there in his hut together and I'd be planting things and fishing and taming blue jays and we'd build another room onto it, but he drives me straight back to Charlotte and Abel and the ranch and not a single word about anything. I'm not going to care. I had a good time anyway. I even almost got enough "I love yous" said to him when he was passed out.

He hands me down from the carriage as if I'm just some hitchhiker he picked up along the way. (Doesn't making all that love mean any-thing? But I know what men are and why should Hen be any different? Except whenever he's not in some odd state he is kind. Gentle. Char-lotte said she pushed him around all the time before the war and I can see how that could have been true. He would have let her, purely out of kindness.)

Abel is so glad to see me I do feel I've come back to my own home. Charlotte is glad to see me, too. Even Cat-the-Pig is glad. Charlotte reaches up and grabs Hen's knee, but he just drives off fast, right out from under her hand, not a word, and not a glance back at us. At me.

Charlotte stares after him. "Well then damn it to you, too," she says, and turns to me. "So what's going on with old grumpy?"

"He's had a hangover for two days. He hardly said a word all the way home."

"Trust Henny to find the speakeasy first thing."

"*Last* thing. But, you have to see my dress. Abel, I have a dress even better than all the ones in the catalogue put together." But I'm fooling myself. I'm pretending everything is rosy. All I've done for the last two days is watch Hen frowning to himself, and hoped things.

So this is it, then. This is how it ends, not even a kiss goodby or a hand squeeze, let alone a backward glance. I guess I shouldn't be surprised. I guess I'm *not* surprised. If I was like those nice black folks, I'd be think-ing: Why, of course, if we had his problems we'd be just like he is.

It's all over town—probably all over *all* the towns—that Hen took a woman on a trip with him and that they stayed at a hotel together and that the woman is me. I suppose they even know we stayed in the same room. (Even if we hadn't, they'd have said that.) Charlotte told me everybody knows and she asks me, "What did Hen say? What's going to happen now?" But I tell her Hen has always said he wouldn't marry me. "So that's that."

Not being with Hen and not knowing what's going on makes me upset enough without having to answer questions I don't have any an-swers for anyway.

"And don't talk about it because I don't want to think about it."

She actually doesn't talk about it. She goes around muttering to herself but she doesn't say anything. She's mad at Hen, not because he took me to town and slept with me—I think she knew he would no matter that he said it wasn't what this trip was about—but because he isn't planning on marrying me, which she thought all this was going to lead up to. Or it sure seems she thought that. She must know there aren't any answers that I could have. I don't think Hen has any either. I used to think he knew everything, but now I know him well enough to know he might have even fewer answers than I do. Or he doesn't *want* to have answers. Or he doesn't want there to *be* any answers—to anything.

We get back to our usual routine (I get so tired of always—*always* being here waiting for Hen some way or other). Charlotte with the stock and me, milking the cow and cooking and working on teaching Abel every single thing I ever learned. If it wasn't for Abel I don't know what I'd do. He sticks around with me a lot now and helps me cook and milk. Once in a while Charlotte takes him out to work with the cows. Sometimes she has me help out with them, too. I like doing that. There's so much to learn. We shut the pig up in the house when we're all gone out. (The pig has her own place to make her messes in. I never knew a pig would be so good at that. She always cries when we leave and squeaks like crazy when we come back.) Sometimes Abel and I go out to work on the dam, but I usually just sit on the stone and daydream. Abel climbs his big tree and I imagine he's looking out and seeing Hen riding up to us like before and any minute now Hen and I will move stones together.

My mother comes out again (with a different fat man), but I'm not worried this time. There isn't any money around. I saw to that. I already ordered my dress and I ordered a little metal elephant for Abel. I know he's going to like it. I have too much on my mind and I feel so changed I can't be bothered worrying about my mother. I know all about what being a woman is now, and mine is a real, true love forever and ever. And I'm not afraid of the man she's with. He wouldn't dare touch me. Everybody knows I belong to Henny Ledoyt—belong *some* sort of way or other. (One nice thing out of all of this—though why should anybody be afraid of a man with one arm who loses every fight he's ever in?)

My mother looks at me funny—studies me, and asks how I've been feeling lately. "You know," she says, "those T-Bone Ledoyts have plenty of money."

I don't stoop to answering.

"You've got yourself in good with them. If you had your head screwed on straight … You look a little pale. Are you all right?"

I have a *lot* of reasons to look pale but I'm not going to tell her one single one of them.

"Are you sure you feel all right?"

"Why wouldn't I?"

"If you play your cards right …"

"I don't play cards."

I hope she can see she doesn't scare me at all anymore. *I've* been loved.

So they wander around a bit. They stare into the parlor where, right at the moment, the pig is resting. (We don't keep the parlor shut up anymore. Charlotte and I feel the same about most things like that.) My mother doesn't say anything, but she looks disgusted.

"I *am* your mother, you know."

"*May be* …"

Will I have to give her something to make her leave? But if I do that every single time she comes, I'll never be rid of her. Except I probably won't ever be rid of her anyway.

"That's a nice scarab pin you're wearing. They say it's for good luck. I could use a little luck."

She's asked for the wrong thing this time. "I'll never part with this—ever. Look, I'm even wearing it on my apron."

The man comes at me as if to take it. I grab a chair and get ready to defend myself. I'm so mad I'm ready to fight to the death. But suddenly, as if from the ceiling, Abel drops down or leaps out, I don't know how, and he's wrapped around the man's head screaming like … Talk about witches, this is worse! He even scares me, but I have my wits about me enough to push the chair hard into the man's stomach and knock him over, easy as anything.

He's big, but he gives up in a hurry. It must not feel so good having

Abel stuck on your head like that. My ma doesn't do anything but stare. I think her heels are too high and her skirt is too tight for her to move much.

So right away they leave in a hurry and Abel and I laugh and hug and cry and laugh. "You saved me. You're my hero. You're exactly like Tom Swift."

"Mary Kitty. Mary, Kitty Kitty Kitty Katty."

We're both too excited *not* to talk.

"I knew it! I knew you could talk."

"Don't tell."

"Why not?"

"Don't."

I guess I *sort* of understand. And I feel flattered, too. I mean Abel and I … we're a bundle.

"All right, but talk to Charlotte pretty soon. Don't wait forever. Promise."

He nods.

"Is that all you've got to say for today?"

He nods again. And we hug and laugh again, and dance around holding hands, and then I go to make the best dessert I can think of, and Abel's favorite, which is grape pie, which is very hard to make. I wanted to do the hardest thing. And while it's cooking we drink tons of lemonade and I start reading *Tom Swift and his Airship* to Abel over again for the exact fourth time, or is it the fifth?

But there's something I have to tell Charlotte, which I didn't tell my mother but I think my mother guessed or hoped was true. That's why she came. I don't want to have to know this all by myself. I want to tell Charlotte what I can't tell her. I just can't but I have to. There's nobody else to tell. She's already mad at Hen and she'll get angrier than ever. I should just run away and take care of this by myself. I still could. I could run away even after I tell her. One reason I don't want to is Abel, especially now that he talked. The other reason of course is Henny. He might come by any day. Maybe take me away to his hut or maybe to some secret place of his own that I don't know anything about. What if he changed his mind about marrying and I was gone? Or what if he needed me?

So we're sitting on the porch steps like we do, looking across to the mountains where the green spot that's Hen's family's ranch is, and I tell her. She says "Damn," and hits the steps railing so hard she hurts herself and grabs her hand and swears something awful. She gets up and stamps around in her big black boots and kicks things. She seems even more like a man than ever. She says if Hen had any tiny shred of morality he'd marry me, but that if he had a shred of morality he wouldn't have done this in the first place if he wasn't going to marry. She keeps saying, "He's crazier than I thought," and, "Stark raving mad," and, "I *used* to like him." She wants to go out to his shack right now, tonight, but I keep telling her please not to, and that this time I mean it, and I'll never ask her for another thing in all my life, so please. I keep saying he *always* said he wouldn't marry me. I tell her I knew what I was doing, but she keeps saying that I didn't, and that I'm too young to know anything and this proves it. Hen said she used to call him You Ninny and You Nitwit all the time, and now that's what she's calling me.

"But, Charlotte, since he won't marry, there's absolutely no other way for him to have a woman. It *has* to be with somebody like me." (This is the first I've thought such a thought, but I know it's true. It's absolutely reasonable. Charlotte should see that.) "He has to have a ... a *whore* like me or nobody at all."

I talk as if Hen and I are going to stay together some way or other, but of course I don't know if this is the very end of it or not. Maybe that was it, and I'm all paid back for the good things I did. And I guess, value for value, I am. It's true, too, I had enough happiness in six days to last a good long time.

"But it's *me*, Charlotte. It's not *you*, it's just me. Just me! It doesn't matter."

"You have to tell him."

Part of me doesn't want Charlotte rushing all around *doing* things, and part of me wants her to.

"I won't, and you mustn't either. Actually, I'm scared to, you know how he is. He might disappear forever just like Fay."

"Fifty dollars Fay comes back one of these days. And, Mary Catherine, it's only fair for Henny's mother to know, too. She's the grandma."

"Grandma! Oh, for heaven's sakes!" Does everybody have to be a part of it? "Well, maybe just his mother then. Just her. But he won't marry. You mustn't ask him to. He *can't.* I wouldn't let him anyway. I won't marry him. I just won't!"

"You're such a nincompoop."

Charlotte says he won't ever think … it will never—not once in a million years—occur to him that such a thing as this could ever happen. "I know him well enough to know how his mind works, which is not very well. This just isn't one of his possibilities."

"Please don't go tell. I'll never ask for a thing ever again."

Of course she goes right over to Hen's shack the very next morning. When I get up she's already gone, but she comes back practically before Abel and I have finished milking. She looks odd. I get worried before she says a word.

"He's gone! I don't think he's been there for days. I wondered why he hasn't been around helping out with the cows."

Where is he! I don't even know where he is! At least I *thought* I knew where he was. At least that, and it was a comfort, though I didn't know it until now. I was thinking of him out there with his view-hill behind his shack and the sound of the creek and his books and his gramophone. I'll die. No I won't. I won't let myself. I feel all tingly.

Next thing I know I'm lying on the rough dirty barn floor with a wad of hay behind my head and Charlotte is wiping my face with a wet cloth and Abel is patting my hand and saying "Coo."

For a minute I forget what this is all about. I say, "Oh Abel, tell me something real." Though I know he won't in front of Charlotte.

Charlotte looks so worried, and then I remember. She keeps saying "Oh my God," and when she sees I've come to, she keeps saying "Are you all right!" It's not a question—more like a command. Like I just *have* to be all right. All of a sudden I can see something. Charlotte wants this baby as much as I do. Maybe more. Not that I don't want it—it's something permanent of Hen's—but because I still can't figure out what this is all about and I'm scared—too scared to think about it. (I do think about it, but not in any real way. I've been in a daze ever since we came back from town. I go up and down from hilariously happy to incredibly depressed.) I wonder why Charlotte wants this baby so much? What does the baby mean to her? And she wants Hen to marry me. And if this is all true, that she cares so much, I guess I really do have a family here. I can see it in the way these two look at me … At least for sure the baby has.

Nobody knows where Hen is, not even his own family. Of course they don't usually know anyway. Right away they invite me out to stay a while but I don't want to go. I'm scared of what they may be thinking of me, seeing I'm their son's whore and all. I wonder what they want me there for? They never did like me, but Charlotte thinks I ought to go. She says the baby belongs to them, too. (I'm not sure I like that idea, but I guess it's true.) She'll come with me, and see how things are and we'll come right home if I want to.

"But Charlotte, there's another problem, which is I'm feeling kind of tired and sick. I'd rather be sick here than there. If I throw up there, I don't even know where to do it."

"Believe me, they have a place."

"But in front of all those people!"

"We can just make a onenighter of it, but I think you ought to go. And, Mary Catherine, they don't think you're just Henny's whore, I know they don't, not any more than I do."

We all go, even Abel and Cat-the-Pig. Charlotte insists we go in the buckboard for my sake, but it isn't much smoother than riding a horse even though she put in all our cushions and bed pillows. Abel and I cuddle up in the back. He cuddles up to me all the time now and I don't mind. The baby'll be like that, too, I'll bet. It'll be somebody that belongs to me forever.

But I feel horrible anyway. In every way. I just don't care about anything. I miss Hen so much more than when I *thought* I knew where he was. He could even be in San Francisco where he said he might go someday and get himself lost. What if I went there, too, and tried to find him? Except I know it's a big, big town. But I'm not sure I really *can* live without him. And it's even worse out there, with pictures of him all around and two sisters that look sort of like him only pretty. And what if Hen is hurting even more than I am? What if he needs me and pulls away from me exactly because he does?

Cuddling up to Abel always makes me feel better. There won't be anybody over there like Abel who knows me and likes me in spite of everything I've done—pinching and branding him even. Now that I've been here and known these people all this time, I can't even conceive of doing such a thing as that branding. Pinching ... that was for his own good, but even so, I don't ever feel like it anymore.

"Abel, talk to me. Just anything."

I was hoping he'd say something in front of Charlotte to surprise her, but he has that secret, pixielike smile. He likes to be fooling everybody. He says, "Cat, Cat, Cat, Cat, Cat," real fast, and giggles, and the pig grunts as if it knows its name, which it probably does.

"You're a little dickens," which is exactly what he wants to be—you can see it on his face.

Everything is changed over at Hen's ranch. It's clear *everybody* knows about me even though Charlotte says she only told his mother. I should have figured. I mean his mother would tell his father and his father would tell the sisters and his sisters would tell the hired man and the kitchen maid. But everybody's on my side now. I can't believe it. I never thought they'd all get so angry at Hen—not their precious baby boy. It makes me want to stand up for him. I mean, I knew what I was doing, don't they see that? I tell Madelaine that the very second time I saw him Hen told me he wouldn't marry anybody, and she says, "That doesn't matter. It was a bad, immoral, wicked thing to do *especially* after saying he wouldn't marry. I can't believe he's my brother." She sounds exactly like Charlotte.

Why don't they blame me? Isn't that the usual way?—that I'm the one who seduced him? And maybe I did. I certainly wanted to—in a sort of way.

In twenty minutes over there I get so pampered I feel sicker than ever because everybody reminds me of it by asking how I feel all the time.

And the confusion of all those children … It's clear they all know about me too and want to get a good look at me, though I can't imagine what they think they're going to see. And no matter how the sisters scold them, you just can't keep eight children quiet. Even the scolding makes a lot of noise. Even when they're scolding in whispers.

His mother keeps telling me not to worry about a thing, that they'll take care of me, but I know what she really means is they'll take care of the baby.

But that's not fair. She's a good person and she really is concerned about me. She touches my shoulder just as Hen did when he leaned close at the opera to explain things to me. (I could cry right then and there, but I manage not to. I mean I have to grow up now whether I want to or not.) Give her a couple of minutes and she holds my hand more than Hen did in six days. She can't let go of me. That night I sit next to her at their huge dining room table in their huge dining room with the chandelier. Right across from me there's a picture of Hen in his master sergeant uniform—with two arms. His hands are folded, resting on his lap. (Strong long piano-playing fingers. It makes me cry to see them. Everything makes me cry.) The photo has been colored so it looks completely real.

Thank goodness I don't have to wonder what to talk about. Everybody is talking at once except Abel and me and Hen's mother. I can keep as quiet as I please and just look at that picture of Hen. It's a good thing I have a napkin and can pretend to wipe my mouth a lot.

I'd give anything for that picture. I have to have it. I need it. I don't have a picture of Hen. If it just wasn't in such a prominent place … I deserve it don't I? I have to figure out how to get it without anybody knowing. Except I'm trying to be grown-up now. Except I *need* it. More than they do. They have others.

But Hen's mother guesses. She hands it over after breakfast the next day, silver frame and all. I should have known she would. I'm just not like these people, the way I always think of stealing first and never think of asking.

She sits me down right then and shows me pictures of Henny as a starved-looking little boy—looking just like Abel. "He was always so thin, though he ate like a horse. Of course he worked hard, too. Papa had him out with the cows by the time he was six."

Looking at the pictures makes her sad. (It makes me sad, too.) She shakes her head, No, every time she turns a page. It's as if everything she sees is No, no, no. "How he used to be," she says, and, "Poor Henny." She says, "Oh dear," even when she's looking at a picture of Hen making funny faces for the camera. She wipes her eyes. Especially at the pictures when he's cutting up. I've been selfish, thinking I'm the only one that aches. I guess she's ached for a lot longer than I have.

"We used to be so close. I used to worry he was a 'momma's boy.' I guess that was useless worry, just like most worry is. And then, when we went to the hospital that time when he'd just come back to this country, he was like a different person. Like a—I don't know—a machine, not a man. The look in his eyes … like nothing was there."

"I've see him like that. Like he's not in his skin. It scares me."

"It scares me, too."

I guess I *do* have somebody to hug around here, but I still miss Abel (they've already started back home) and I'll miss sitting on the steps talking to Charlotte. There's things I can say to her that I could never tell Hen's mother … And I shouldn't worry Hen's mother with *my* worries.

"Don't you worry about a thing," she says. "Like I said, worry is just a waste of good thinking that you can use on something else."

So time goes by. I don't keep track. Every day seems too long.

Even with his mother and everybody so nice to me, the more I'm here, the more I don't want to be. Besides, the more I'm here, the more the baby doesn't seem to belong to me at all—nor to Hen either, for that matter. It's just theirs. I don't know why they care. There are already so many children over here. (Like Hen said, they don't need any more—what *did* he say, too many married people or too many children? Probably both.) Everybody thinks this baby will be the … well the exact cat's meow. (*They* wouldn't put it that way, but that's the way *I* say it.) I can't imagine what they're thinking. Why can't this baby be mine and Hen's … just ours? And why is everybody making such a fuss about this *particular* baby? Is it because Hen's the baby brother and is special because of only having one hand? Like the baby's gone to war and come back armless? (I wish I hadn't thought about that. What if there's something wrong with it? What if it's born without something important?)

I want to go off somewhere and cry for a week, but I wonder if that will hurt the baby.

I can see, too, the things that bother Hen so much—all that hovering. I like it in a way. How many times have I ever been hovered over in all my life? And I like to be touched the way they do, but it's *all the time*. I'm not even safe in my bed. People pop right in with snacks and tea. Even to see if I'm asleep or not, and every now and then one of the little ones peeks in. If two or more do it, they giggle. It doesn't much help my throwing up. They call me Aunt Mary Catherine. I guess that means I *really* do have to grow up. (I never had an aunt. I don't know how to be one.)

I keep telling them I won't marry even if Hen comes home and asks me. They don't seem to hear me. I'm just getting lost in with all of them. I suppose Hen felt he was getting lost, too. Maybe just being the person from the war. Maybe they never see him, they just see his gone arm, even though he can do almost everything except cut his steak. In town I saw him tie his shoe.

But one good thing, since there's nothing much anybody wants me to do around here (everybody keeps telling me to go lie down or go eat or take a little walk, but not too far), Hen's mother sets me down with her treadle sewing machine making maternity clothes for myself. And she helps me plan dresses which can be easily fixed up for later when I'm not pregnant. Just about all my life I didn't have even one little piece of cloth to make something with, and here Hen's mother has a whole attic full of cloth she and Hen's sisters never got around to using.

The attic's full of baby clothes, too. Fancy things. And Hen's mother's already started knitting. Madelaine gave me a lacy nightgown. Odd for her to do that, as if it has a special meaning—a sexy meaning. As if Hen and I together is all right with her.

Finally it's Charlotte who decides I ought to go home. I don't have to say anything. She and Abel went back after one night here, but they come again a week later and Charlotte says I look pale and peaked and that I have circles under my eyes and I should go back with them. "For the baby's sake," she says. That convinces everybody I should go. Later she tells me Abel was all curled up again, just like after his mother died. Because of me! If I didn't feel so bad, that would make me feel good.

Hen's mother does an odd thing. As we're about to leave, she gives me a laundry box full of Hen's clean clothes as though I'm going to see him pretty soon. She also gives me two of his vests. How did she know I'd like to keep these when I didn't even know it myself?

She says, "You just give these to him," as if I'm the wife and am keeping track of his things, and as if she's sure I'll see him pretty soon.

I will never, never, never even think of stealing anything ever again.

"Mrs. Ledoyt …"

"Try to remember to call me Aunt Henriette like everybody does. Or you could call me Grandma—like everybody else does." She takes my hand again and holds it in both of hers. "Dear Mary Catherine."

(She's doing it, too—saying my name for no reason just like Hen does.)

"If you need me to come to your place" (she says, "*your* place"), "I want you to call on me. Honey, I really mean it. I want to be there."

So there's another "Honey." (Was it "Henny, honey" when Hen was around? I didn't notice. It sounds like something Abel would like to say.)

"I will. I promise … Aunt Henriette …" (I just can't face "Grandma" yet. I wonder if I'll ever be able to?) "Thank you for the picture. I know you want it just as much as I do."

"I'd rather you had it."

I throw up all the way home. Charlotte thinks we ought to turn around and go back before we're halfway. She doesn't think she can take care of me if I'm this bad.

"I'm *not* this bad. I'll be better as soon as we're back. It's just the bouncing of the wagon. I know I'll feel better at home. I promise." (I say "home" right to her. I never dared before.)

I take out the picture of Hen his mother gave me and put it beside me in the wagon. I look at it all the way home. And it helps that I'm leaning back against the box with Hen's clothes in it. There's no way he can avoid me now. But that's not true, he *can* avoid me, but at least someday he might want to get his things, especially his nice vests.

I was right. The minute I get into my own bed, I feel a lot better, physically, that is … the quiet, and people I know so well. But I'm just one big ache, and I'm afraid if I ever get three feet from Hen again, I'll grab him and not let go for dear life. He'll hate me if I do that. For sure, then, he'll never come around me again. But maybe he won't anyway. Maybe he could see that clingyness in me even before and that's why he's gone now. It's sort of for the same reason he doesn't like being with his family. I know how he feels. I mean even *I* got too much of it out at his place. I couldn't get away by myself for even a minute. Now Hen wants to get away from me. I'm not surprised.

I've taken to wearing his old black pants and his old army shirts. The pants won't fit me much longer. Charlotte and I dress alike now, in pants and loose shirts. Of course I don't have fancy boots.

I have a different daydream now, like, what if Hen comes for me secretly in the middle of the night. What if he takes me away just like in a fairy tale. Maybe comes in through the window. He wouldn't know about the baby, he would want me just because I'm me. We'd go to his shack and then climb our hill and that's where I'd tell him about the baby—up there at the top of Leaping Man's Hill.

Instead, who comes by is my mother.

She always comes when Charlotte is gone. I don't know how she keeps track of these things. Or maybe she's just lucky. I think she always has been—a lot luckier than me. Except she doesn't have anything to do with Hen, and I do.

Abel and I are in the big kitchen–sitting room making pancakes— yet again. Abel is doing all the work. He has pancakes down pat. He hears the carriage first. He still doesn't talk much, and only when it's just the two of us, but this morning he said, "Let's do round things." (He likes to talk in riddles. At first I didn't know what he meant.) Now he says "Kitty, Kitty, Katty, Kat. Hear that?" (He likes to rhyme, too. He likes all kinds of word games.)

My mother is with the same fat man, but this time he stays a safe distance away.

I'm beginning to show a little. My mother spots it right away. And after all, that's what she came here looking for—timed her coming for that, I suppose, so she'd be sure. She calls me "Little Whore." She thinks I must have lots of money by now.

I tell her, "I don't have one single penny more than I ever had. They don't think about money and neither do I." Right away, though, I'm thinking of that silver picture frame.

"Whore's get rich. Especially whore's with the T-Bone Ledoyt family—if they have any sense at all. They get clothes and houses and they look after their mothers."

I think of Hen's messy old rusty shack.

"I'm not scared to be a whore any more than you are."

I always knew I'd grow up like my mother and here I am, except it's *not* like my mother. Not really. I mean, it's Hen, and he's different from any of my paunchy, greasy old stepfathers. There's nothing greasy about Hen.

"If I had anything to give you, I wouldn't."

She goes right in my room and starts rummaging around. On my bed I have Hen's two vests laid out (I sleep with them beside me) and his picture is on the bedside table—beautiful Hen with two beautiful piano hands and that uniform.

Abel sticks right behind us the whole time. I wonder what he's dreaming up? I hope something, because I'll fight for the vests and the picture.

My mother says she'll go out to the T-Bone Ledoyt's and complain about how they're treating me. She says she'll say how Henny should either marry me or pay me for my services.

"If you go out there, I swear, I swear! I'll kill you. You'd better kill me right now so I won't be out to get you." I'm whispering. Usually I yell, but I'm saying this about the softest I can speak.

All of a sudden Abel is right next to me—and with a pistol! A little pearl-handled pistol. Where in the world?

"Abel!"

I said I wanted to kill her, but now I'm not so sure.

"Pay attention," he says. (I've told him that myself a hundred times.) "Mary Cat never says nothin' for nothin' for nothin'."

That gun looks dangerous in that little boy's hand and Abel has this really scary look about him. I don't trust him myself and my ma certainly doesn't. She used to think he was simple minded, but now she'll think he's crazy. That's how he looks, his face all screwed up and mean. My ma isn't taking any chances. She's really scared and leaves in a hurry, teetering away on her high heels, even before Abel says "Caw, caw, caw, caw" at her.

"Abel, where did you get that thing!"

"It's mine."

Here comes the typical nine-year-old for once.

"Of *course* it's not."

"*Is!*"

"Where was it?"

"Where I keep it. Under my pillow."

"But where did it come from?"

"Ma didn't want it anymore."

"Oh, Abel, what will I do with you!"

"I saved you. Like I always do."

"You're right. Goodness knows what I'd have done without you, but you shouldn't have that gun. Have you had it all this time?"

But he's back to Caw and won't say.

"Well, anyway, I guess it's worth another grape pie. Give me that thing before you kill somebody." But he's running off with it. I wonder if it's loaded? I wonder when it last was cleaned?

I shout after him, "You can't get off the hook saying caw all the time, you know." But I guess he can—for now. "You're dead daddy ..." Am I all the way back to that—to that good man who died saving Hen? (I know Hen thinks he shouldn't have bothered. He practically said that.) I warn myself not to ever say dead daddy again, at least not that way, as a threat.

He'll hide that pistol someplace where I'll never find it. Top of a tree most likely. I can climb almost as well as he can, or I could a couple of months ago, but which tree? What am I going to do with that child! Maybe I should go back to pinching, except he saved me twice now. And what if my mother's gone for good, all because of him? Wouldn't that be something? She looked pretty scared.

I can't wait for Charlotte to get back so I can tell her. I wonder what she'll do about that gun?

Children! What won't they think of next!

BUT WHEN CHARLOTTE comes, I forget about it. Because three people come with her, and a string of mules and an extra horse. At first I feel this big thrill. I think I'm going to faint again, but just in time I see each of them has two arms, so I don't, and I don't care who they are.

(We just never have guests so this is odd. I guess people have learned better than to come and visit here, what with Abel's mother wandering around all spilled-on down her front and not paying attention. Now that I'm here they'd get good food and welcome, too, and an outhouse without a lot of gone boards.)

Abel is running out to them (I hope without the pistol) and gets lifted right up with the fuzzy one.

But that's Fay! I can't believe it—coming back finally. I *think* it's Fay. But it *is*, all fuzzy and dirty. And riding that beautiful bay I lost. Fay's leading an extra horse and the other man leads the string of mules. (Is it a string if it's only two?)

Now that I'm showing (like my mother knew I would) I don't want anybody to see me. I look terrible and worse every day. I hope Hen doesn't come back. I *sort* of hope it. I'll hide if he ever does, but sometimes I just ache for him so bad. Not that I haven't ached for him ever since I first laid eyes on him.

I think to run inside, but I'd have to come out eventually, I can't hide forever, and I'm going to look a lot worse than this any minute now.

Charlotte, for a change, seems shy and nervous (I never thought she could look shy) so I guess who this other man is. It's the artist, the one she cares about, but never talks about, not in any real way. He's not one bit like anybody I thought Charlotte would like. He's plump and softish and pale, but he *is* smiley. He even has dimples. He looks too old for her, but he looks kind, and you can see he likes Charlotte. He helps her dismount. He's graceful even though he is fattish. I don't think he's quite as tall as she is. Being the kind of person she is, I thought she'd have to like a great big manly man, even more manly than she is.

Charlotte's dressed just as usual, so she looks all lumpy, but I notice she isn't stamping her boots around as she usually does. She's walking carefully, as if she didn't know how. I guess she's so used to clumping around she really doesn't know any other way. I know exactly how she feels. I mean about the shyness. I'm mostly only shy with Hen.

"This is L.D." (At first I thought Eldie.) She forgets her manners. She doesn't say my name, she just presents him to me, as if: Look, this is L.D. My artist.

He *is* nice. After I see him for half a minute, I don't even mind looking like I do in front of him. He takes my hand—not to shake it, but to hold it—and smiles at me. He's the kind of person who really looks at you and, like Henny's mother, he just likes you, almost no matter what. I haven't been doing my special cooking so much lately because I just know Hen isn't coming back here any time soon, and then I don't have the energy lately, but I want to now, for Fay and this man.

I tell Fay I'm sorry, but he waves me away and shakes his head. Says, "Don't be. Please don't be." As if me not being sorry would be doing him a big favor. He wants to help me. He's like he was—hardly looking at me, but he does talk a little now. He has a nice, deep voice. Completely different from what I thought he'd have, being so skinny and boylike. He does seem more grown-up than before, though. All over. Maybe even bigger. Or maybe it's all that hair and the beard. He looks at me funny when he thinks I won't notice. As if the idea of me having a baby is just too peculiar. Or maybe the idea of a baby inside a person is too fantastic (which it is). Or is it that it's me it's happening to? I feel the same way: How can it be me? It can't be me.

That night I'm so tired I almost don't sit on the porch with the rest of them after supper. I do anyway but every now and then I drop off to sleep. At one time I wake up and see that Fay has come over to sit beside me. He would *never* have done that before. It's dark by now but I can see he's looking at me. What is this all about? Why would anyone come at me when I'm fat and ugly with somebody else's baby? But Fay liked me even before. Of course who else was there around here for him to like? But I wonder if he's seen any other women ever, even while he's been gone? He's kind of like Abel, growing up here and never going anywhere, though I know he did read a lot. That's something. You can learn a lot that way. What should I do about him, now that I don't have Hen and I need somebody?

I go in to bed pretty soon. I suppose Fay will sleep in the barn. They've never used their ma's room all this time. I don't suppose they'll even put L.D. in there. Abel's fallen asleep on Fay's lap long before. Fay carries him in to bed and we leave Charlotte and L.D. out there by themselves. If I stayed in the kitchen, I could eavesdrop on them—except they're talking quietly—but I'm too tired. Besides, I don't do things like that anymore.

The next day Charlotte doesn't exactly dress up for L.D. She still wears her boots and black pants, but it's her best black pants, and instead of an old ragged man's shirt, she wears a women's blouse—pink, if you can believe it. You can see she's uncomfortable, even with just that.

It's so odd, just two days later Fay asks me to marry him. I mean we've hardly said two words to each other since I first came here. Of course we did see each other quite a bit before I scared him off. Doesn't he care about what I did to him? And can it be he doesn't see how pregnant I am? Sometimes men are so blind. Just to make sure, I say, "You know this is Henny's baby."

He says, "I figured that. But then Henny's ... God knows ..."

I'd belong to this ranch then, and I'd be able to live with Abel, and it would be quiet. And then Hen will never make a decent husband. He said so himself and I know that by now. I don't know if he'll make a good father or not. Probably good considering how sweet he is with Abel, except he'd never be there. But I want him anyway, husband or any other way. I'd keep on being his whore just like I really am. Except I should grow up and do what's best for the baby—not think about what *I* want all the time. If it was just me, I'd wait for Hen forever if it takes that long, or just wait while he goes off with somebody beautiful, but I'd still wait.

It isn't a complete surprise when Fay asks me. I had a feeling he might. I say, "You know, I'm in love with Henny," and he says he knows that but he thought maybe I needed somebody. Then I say, "Thank you. Thank you very, very much," and he ducks his head like he does. (He doesn't even look at me when he asks me.) We're on the porch again—Charlotte and L.D. are off for a ride by themselves. I think they're going out to paint mountains. (That's just about the first time I ever saw Charlotte going off *not* to work, just to go off.)

He says, "I have money."

"I know. Or I didn't know but I thought so. But I don't mind not having any. I'm used to it."

Fay just stares off at the mountains over where Hen's ranch is. I stare out there all the time myself (though if Hen was there, they'd let me know right away, so what's the sense in looking in that direction more than any other?). There's a big bank of clouds hovering over the mountains so they look dark purple and you can't see the ins and outs of them, but you can always see the ranch over there even when the green just looks like a darker patch. Every time I look at that ranch, I feel sad.

I say, "I guess I do ... I mean need somebody."

(If I married Fay, at least the baby's name would be *Ledoyt*. That would be one good thing.)

Fay reaches out to hold my hand. He *has* changed. I let him, but all of a sudden I feel so bad I don't know what to do, though there's nothing new in that. I tell myself: You're going to have a sad, sad baby if you don't watch out. It'll get born and then you'll both be sad together. I tell myself I should force myself to be happy. What baby would want *me* for a mother if I don't ever smile, and, after all, aren't I doing exactly what Hen is spending his whole life doing? Me and my child will both be just exactly like him if I don't watch out.

Shouldn't it be enough in my life to have Hen's baby that I have to have Hen, too? Can't I be happy with just that? Except what if it dies? Or what if the baby doesn't have all its parts? Or what if it doesn't speak? *Ever?* Or what if it ends up just like Hen? Or what if Hen dies!

So to make myself stop thinking about it, I tell Fay about the pistol. (I like how he looks now, with hair all over and a pretty good beard—a lot older, and even kind of wise.)

"That was Ma's," he says. "Pa gave it to her. She never liked it. I wonder if she really gave it to Abel? She was getting everybody all mixed up. She probably thought he was me. Or maybe even Pa." Then he looks as sad as I feel all the time lately. "I should have been here."

"It was my fault she died. You know that, don't you? You would have been here if not for me. I'm sorry." But he shakes his head, No. No matter what I say, he thinks it's all his fault. I don't want to hurt him anymore but I'm afraid I will no matter what I decide to do. I say, "Fay, I think … I have to think. I don't love you, you know that, but I suppose I ought to marry you. I guess you know that, too." It's so hard to talk about it. I just want to go away and curl up someplace. I suppose that's how Hen feels, like: Just everybody please go away. "Fay, I have to be by myself. I have to go out to Hen's shack and be alone."

"I could come with you and make sure you're safe. I wouldn't stay in the hut, just nearby … out of sight."

"No!"

Can't he see? But he's a nice boy, and he just wants to look after me. (Sometimes it even seemed Hen wanted to look after me, too, when he took me to town and watched me having a good time. He really did, but with Hen, it's off and on.)

When I tell Charlotte she doesn't like the idea at all.

"But I need to be alone for a while, and I need to be alone *there*. Just a few days is all."

"In your state you shouldn't be alone for half an hour anywhere. Anything could happen. Then what would you do? I can't let you go."

I have to laugh, the way she's taking charge of me. I used to feel like the hired help all the time, but this is different. Now I don't know what I am. We both laugh.

"I can't let you hurt yourself."

"I'm only talking about a couple of days."

L.D. is on my side. He tells her I should go. He's about the only person who could make her change her mind, though how can she stop me if I just take off? Hard as that will be in my state, but Fay would help me saddle up and pack up. He's on my side, too.

"Oh, all right, I'll ride you over and see that you're settled in."

Before we take off, Charlotte gives me that little pistol. She makes me take it. "That's the only way I could get it away from Abel, to tell him you needed it. He even had a box of bullets."

"But this won't be any good against a bear or cougar. Where was it, anyway? We've all looked everywhere."

"Back under his pillow. But it wasn't there when I looked this morning."

So Abel still has his hiding place. I'll get him a pocket knife to put under it instead.

We ride out talking, not like with Hen. Charlotte wants me to wait and marry Hen. She says, "Fay came back so Henny will, too."

"They're not at all the same!" I practically yell it.

"You're right," she says, "Fay has to grow up."

"He had a birthday. He's eighteen. Now I'm only one year older than he is."

"Eighteen! Nineteen!" The way she says it you can tell she doesn't think much of either of those ages.

"But how long should I wait around for heaven's sake! And even if he comes back, you know Henny won't marry. He just won't. He's told me that a hundred times. And I need to do what's best for the baby … Don't I? *Don't I?* What about L.D.?" I say. "Are you going to marry him?"

I don't know why I throw that out, but I'm sorry I did, because she says, "He hasn't ever asked me." But then she says, "I guess I'd say No, if I'd have to leave the ranch. I mean, it would be a whole new, dressed-up kind of life and I'm not sure I'm suited to it, and I wouldn't be in charge like I am here."

"But he's not that kind of pushy man at all."

"No, but his painting is so important. Really! *He's* so important. I'd feel I'd have to go where he goes and help him in his career. I would need to do that for his sake. I love this ranch and I don't want to leave it. If I leave it, it's a goner."

"You could have a baby, too, anyway."

"Oh, Mary Catherine!" She pauses such a long pause I think that's all she's going to answer about that, and then she says, "But *you're* having our baby."

So! So I'm beginning to understand things. I wanted to be part of a bundle, but the bundle is getting too many people in it, and they're all too strong for me. And I think the bundle is mostly for the baby, anyway. "Oh, Hen," (I say the "Oh, Hen" part out loud by mistake) if you'd come back maybe it could get to be just the two of us and our own private baby.

At first it's worse being out there and no Hen. Tears come the minute we ride up. I try to hide them, but I guess Charlotte can tell, because she brings in my food and blankets and Hen's old army shirts and his black pants that I wear all the time now, even though they won't button. She doesn't look at me, but before she goes she gives me a big hug. "I'll be checking in on you, say around the supper hour every day. You take a nap now, and don't wander so far that I can't find you. I mean it, Mary Cat. I don't know for sure why you came out here, but …"

I know what she's thinking. I look her in the eye and say I won't. (That's not what this is about—getting lost forever.) "I want this baby," I say, though I'm not even sure of that or of anything. I'm all mixed up. I don't know what I'm about to do. Maybe I will just get myself lost after all.

After she leaves, I flop myself down on Henny's cot, and there's that sketch of the naked girl, still there. *Of course* still there. *Of course* he won't marry me, he's madly in love with somebody else. That's always the way with things. It's hopeless.

I cry and cry, not even caring if it might hurt the baby. I fall asleep by mistake without any supper. I don't suppose that's so good for the baby either.

Towards morning a scattering of rain on the roof wakes me. I think how Hen would have leaned himself up on his stump and listened. How he'd say, "That sounds nice." I pull the pillow around so as to hug it and rest my head on it as if on Hen's chest. Maybe he'd say, "Poor little waif," like I heard him say once. That's what I feel like. And poor little fatherless baby—though of course I should be used to that, being fatherless myself. But this baby has a lot of friends and aunts and a grandmother. It won't be the same. People already love it and they haven't even seen who it is.

I sleep again (under Hen's army blankets) and the sun warms the hut so I don't need a fire in the morning.

First thing I open the door and there's a beautiful gray fox, black and white and gray, black stripe down her tail, and a red chest. (I've always wondered why they call them gray!) She has three kits with her. She looks right at me and doesn't run off scared. That's Hen's doing. It must be. He tames everything, and lets them be. The kits look more like they're in the cat family than anything doggish, pushed-in little cat faces and big cat ears. (They say those gray foxes climb trees, too. I've seen them *almost* do it so it might be true.) I come out softly and slowly and sit on the doorstep rock. The kits are curious. After I sit quietly for a few minutes they come closer. One, the smallest, the runt, doesn't know any better than to come a yard from me. The others come almost as close, but they stay off to the side and when I turn to look, they shy away. After a few minutes of this, the mother gives a funny bark-meow-cough and calls them back, like enough's enough, and then they leave, not scared at all.

"Thank you." I say it out loud. "And thank you, Henny."

(The past few days I've been saying more thank yous than I usually do in a year.)

Mornings I don't feel quite so sad. I make tea. (Ever since I got pregnant, I can't stand coffee.) I take a walk down the path by the creek. When it's cool in the evenings, I go up on our hill. Our Hill. That's what I keep calling it, though I don't think it's a good name. I talk to myself out loud, not anymore to the mountains, but to Hen. Sometimes I hardly know I'm doing it. Sometimes it's just saying his name like he used to say mine, for no reason. Sometimes I hear myself make little squeaky noises, can't-bear-it kind of noises. I'm glad nobody is around.

I take the pistol when I walk out. I promised Charlotte I would, but I don't know what earthly good it would be. I never shot a gun in my life. It probably would be safer in Abel's hands. I suppose I ought to shoot it just to see what it's like. I'd like to know. I always think learning something, almost no matter what, is better than not learning. My teacher used to say that all the time, even when bad things happened. She'd say, "Well, now you know."

But it's the nights that … Except I'm glad I'm out here by myself in nature … in *Henny's* nature. You can stay alive with nature. You can be in love. Like up on "Our Hill" the view is so nice I always think, I love you, I love you, I love you, the way I did up there before, with Abel. I just love. I don't know what. I hope it was like that for Hen, too, that that was maybe why he was always out here. I hope he can feel love for *something:* a view, or maybe a fox family, or that poor jay. I guess he does, the way he always looks at views and tames things.

Out in back the other night I heard the weirdest noises, so I do take the pistol out and practice. I shoot at one of the old tin cans from the peaches I brought Hen a long time ago. I can hear when I hit it, but I worry that the crack of the pistol will scare off my foxes. Hen's foxes. They're there almost every morning. Evenings, too, so I shoot in the afternoon.

I daydream a lot about how Hen might come for me. I think to turn around and there he'd be. (I do turn around.) He wouldn't say a single word. He'd slip off his horse the way he does, and I'd be coming down the path wearing his pants tied up with the soft old halter rope. He'd have heard I was here. He wouldn't have come because of the baby. He'd have come just for me.

I'm not sure I want him to see me though, what with me so fat looking and with nothing that fits. Since he might not know about the baby he'd just think I was getting too fat. I look fatter than my mother. And he might not want me if he knew about the baby anyway. He doesn't want children. He said that, too. No children and no marrying and no noise, and he said he'd never change his mind.

Oh, for heaven's sake I can't put up with myself! If I told Hen to stop all this nonsense—to pick a date and stop being crazy, then I'm going to have to do as I said to him, so I will. I'm going to set the date at dawn exactly two days from now.

I write to Charlotte that I'm coming back morning after next, so I won't be able to change my mind. I wonder if she's been trying to convince Fay not to marry me like she was trying to get me not to marry him? I don't think she can. I know he loves me. Maybe even enough to go against Charlotte.

But I'll have to hug Fay, and I'll have to let him … all the things Hen did. I'm not sure I can. Even for the baby's sake.

I tack the note on the door, except the next person to come, and all by himself, is Abel, and he comes in the morning. He just couldn't wait till afternoon to bring me the pile of cold pancakes he made for me—not my favorite thing, but I never told him and I never will. I get a real good hug. I need that. It almost makes me cry though I promised myself I wouldn't anymore. I've wasted enough time with that.

I must be another bit fatter because he looks at me funny. When I was there all the time, he probably didn't hardly notice how I changed. I wonder if anybody told him anything?

So I do. Being a farm boy, he knows it all, but maybe not so much about people. I tell him I'm not just getting fat but I'm having a baby, and he says, "Boy or girl?"

"How would I possibly know, I can't look inside? Well, what do you want it to be?"

He thinks and thinks and shuts his eyes and goes, "Hmm, hmm, hmm, hmm, hmm." Oh, I *do* love this child!

"You'll be the honorary big brother, you know. Kneel down," I say. I tap him on the shoulder with a little stick. (He knows about knights now.) "Henceforth, and forever onwards, to be known as the honorary big brother, Abel Ledoyt." He ducks his head the way Fay always does, pleased and shy.

We have a real nice day. Abel eats so many pancakes I think he'll burst. We feed some to the new jay that's now about as tame as the first one was. It doesn't take long.

I just leave the note on the nail for Charlotte. Whatever day she comes, I'll go back with her morning after next one. I'll hate to leave the foxes. She's such a good fox-mother, the way she'll stand and watch out for them. Warn them. And she looks like a happy mother, the way a mother should be.

So I go "home," we, me and "their" baby. I don't really want to leave, but do I want to have a baby all by myself? I guess I sort of do, but I know better.

We get back in to our waiting-for-something-to-happen ways— our usual. What happens, of course, is I get bigger and bigger. What happens is Charlotte, all of a sudden, sewing. Beautiful things for the baby. (L.D. has gone into the mountains to paint, but he'll be back.) And she keeps suggesting names. She says, "It'll be born and you won't have thought a thing about names. How about Bill or Betsy. I always liked Betsy."

"But Hen should name it, too."

"Oh, Henny! He doesn't deserve to name anything. He has no right even to want to. Haven't you got any favorites?"

But hard as I try, I can't imagine the baby in any real way. Names would make it too real. They're the ones who believe in it. I don't think boy or girl. I just think baby in general. I don't think how it might look like Hen or like me or like his sisters and mother. I don't even think how it's going to be half-French (well, I thought it right now), though its other half is God-knows-what.

Hen's mother comes over. Aunt Henriette. (I should practice saying Grandma.) And they finally do clean out their ma's room for her. Aunt Henriette helps them. Without her, they'd never have gotten around to it. I didn't dare do it or even suggest it, though I thought about it, but I can only guess at how they feel, losing their mother. Aunt Henriette changes it all around and then she stays in it herself. Her being in there starts to get everybody's idea of it changed. I help her. After all, their mother wasn't my mother and I never saw her being the real person they say she used to be, so I don't have all those feelings about her. Aunt Henriette says they used to be best friends but afterwards … "Well," she says, "you saw it for yourself."

She wants me to wait and marry Henny. If I love him, that is. She says he needs me more than he knows. She thinks he'll like the baby when he finds out about it. She says he always did like children in spite of what he told me. She says all the things I keep hoping. Is hers the reality of it or just a lot of wishing like mine is? I tell her I'd like the baby to have a father. I say, "Sometimes I think I'd marry just about anybody, not for the baby sake, but just to have somebody for myself."

That gets me a nice wad of sympathy. She hugs me a big Abel kind of hug. She says, "You have me. You have us. We'll stick by you."

I have to get out by myself—or sometimes with Abel. We go to the pond and work on the dam or just sit. Everybody probably knows where we ran off to, but they let us be.

Henny

I ache … my back <u>always.</u> The arm I don't have. My head. I shouldn't try to sleep on a park bench.

I'll write things down, I'll burn it. I'll be empty. All sounds will be far off. I'll not hear sounds any louder than that woodpecker. I'll stay away. Not take part. Not again. I promise myself. So at least that comfort.

I can't. I don't. I <u>won't</u> think. I hear explosions that aren't there and I <u>know</u> … I can <u>hear</u> they're not there. Mary Catherine, you're wrong, there <u>is</u> no next year. But … <u>you</u> … Why can't I care? But I appreciate. I should be doing for you … I like to see you smile … giggle. The way she clasps her hands over her mouth. Then I see her smile in her eyes. She looks at me … such a look! Always! That's love. She <u>did</u> have a good time.

She had a good time. That was the point. She liked it all, even the lovemaking. (For once—for that time—it <u>was</u> real.) But she will be thinking … even though I <u>told</u> her. Maman, nothing was secret. Not like lots of men. In the army, nothing but lies and all the time. Did anybody tell the truth? I never lied, but what good does it do not to lie? People get ideas anyway. Back there, then … I wanted to marry. You never knew. Now not possible. Not possible back then either though that time it wasn't my fault.

Surely she is thinking things. I have to show her she mustn't. I <u>told</u> her I would hurt her. I <u>told</u> you I hurt everybody. How did all this get started even so—even with no lies? She was always <u>there</u>. If you just hadn't <u>always been there</u>!

He sits and stares at the sky—the dawn. Clouds are different over here. Billowy. It smells green. Everything is watered. Last night the cop told him to move, but then he said if he went over to the bench behind the trees, he could spend the night if he had to. He's looking like a tramp. It's the old army shirt that saves him, and, of course, the lost arm. That gets to them.

It's early. Nobody's here but the starved stray dog that spent the night with him, he curled up on the bench and the pooch under. They're both hungry. He wishes he had something to give it. Nice little mutt, the exact right size for Abel. And ugly—all three of them—all four, himself, Fay and Abel, and this scrawny white dog with both ears torn. Tail doesn't look so good either. The ugly Ledoyts. At least the men. Those bushy eyebrows, the starved look. Could he take the dog all the way back to Abel? It has a bad case of mange but that can be fixed. He got mange from a dog once. He'd itched all over his stomach where the dog had been sleeping on him. Papa said, "The moral is, don't take mangy dogs to bed with you." Warn Abel. The look in its eyes reminds him of her. Of course, it's a little-waif-dog. Or maybe more a lost Henny dog. He ought to straighten himself up and go on back. "Go home, little mutt." Not necessarily back to Mary Catherine, but back.

She probably is <u>exactly</u> the right sort of person for the way I am now— the perfect wife for a one-armed rancher. Who could ask for more than a loyal whore? A virgin whore though not anymore, not after what he did to her.

Women always get the worst of it. It's my fault this whole thing began. Or is it? Why didn't she go away?

"Damn it! Damn it!"

That scares the dog.

"Come on back, boy. I didn't mean you. Come on back."

And it comes. Trusting creature. He should name it Mary Catherine.

"You little whore-dog, you haven't got a place to go back to either, do you, Ol' Buddy?"

But even Charlotte is a lost soul. (Make a list of all the lost souls: Me, Aunt Oriana, Uncle Bill, Mary Catherine …) Charlotte's more a sister to him than any other sister. What will become of her? But she loves her life. At least that. Is it because she tries harder than he does? She calls him "Lazy, good-for-nothing, yellow-belly, asshole." (<u>I know it</u>! I <u>know it</u>! You don't need to say it anymore.) "Get on home and stop this nonsense." I know it.

Go home?

But nobody needs me back there. I can stay away as long as …
Necessary.

At least this time nobody will read this garbage because it's written on a brown paper bag greasy from his fried fish supper. The perfect thing for a secret diary. It goes in the trash can next move. Then he and Mutt will go eat.

"Come on, Mutt, Ol' Buddy."

For now he'll just call him Mutt and let Abel name him.

Mary Catherine

CHARLOTTE TELLS ME he's been seen in town, but he hasn't gone home to the ranch. She says he'll get in another fight for sure. She tells me to go out to the hut, stop wearing his old clothes, bring lots of good food. They're planning a whole drama. They are—the setting and all. I suppose they think to plan the weather. Even Hen's mother is in on it. I might as well let them, but I'm a wreck. I'm tired all the time. I look terrible. I'll cry. And who's to say he'll even come out there? You never know what he's going to do next. What if, instead, he comes here to the ranch to find me? Besides, there are other old line-riding huts.

His mother gets his clothes all washed and ironed, which they were already (except for the ones I wore), but she does it over again. I can't breathe just thinking about going out there, but I'm so big and fat I can't breathe anyway. I can hardly get up out of a chair, let alone up or down from a horse, but I'll have to. I'm not sure I want to do this. It would have been different even a little while ago when I wasn't quite so huge and so exhausted. Besides, isn't it dangerous by now—for me to be alone way out there? They kept warning me about that before, but now not a single word.

I can't believe how his mother is in on it, too. It doesn't seem like something she'd be part of, being so straightforward and all. (I finally do call her Grandma. I guess I need a grandma of my own, and she's a lot nicer than any real grandma *I* might have.)

So they get me all set up out there. They put me to bed on the cot. But this just doesn't feel right. It's so *planned.* Hen wouldn't like it a bit if he knew. He's always as honest about things as his mother.

They don't say so, but nobody has any idea when he might come, or even *if.* If he's busy getting in fights, goodness knows where he'll end up. I hope he isn't fighting, because I'm in no mood to nurse somebody's cuts and bruises. I've done enough of that to last a while.

There's nothing for me to do out here but feel scared: of Hen coming, or of Hen *not* coming, and daydream (though I don't think about what the future might be like anymore, it's too scary), and sleep and get kicked by the baby.

How could they leave me here alone? I never was afraid to be here by myself before, but I am now. I sit out on Hen's stone (I don't want to lie in bed *quite* all day looking at that sketch of the naked girl) and feed jays. I'm going to nail a towel up on top of that sketch first time I find nails and a hammer and a towel and have the energy to do it. The energy will have to come first. (I try not to think about that girl now that there's even more of a contrast between us, me so fat and all.) There's two jays now, the dad jay and the mom jay. I promised myself I wouldn't cry anymore, but the jays … Everything is all linked up into moms and dads.

Of course nobody comes all evening long. Well, at least I have some important, uplifting books, Wordsworth for one, and Kipling, and the food is good. Aunt Henriette's—Grandma's—French vegetable pie, the same kind she made for Hen and me on our trip to town, though I don't particularly want to be reminded of that trip right now. I put on one of Hen's vests, the velvet one. I hope I don't mess it up, wearing it for lying around.

But they didn't leave me here alone. I get all tucked in, ready for the night, when I hear funny noises. At first I'm scared. Something is out there. It sounds big, like a bear. I put the pistol in my pocket—though I know that won't do much good—and I go to the door with Hen's pan and a big spoon. I whoop my crazy yell and beat on the pan. (It already looks like it was used for this purpose lots of times, so I'm not spoiling it any more than it is.) After that everything is quiet just as you'd think it would be. Then I hear somebody say, "Mary Cat?" It's Fay. *Of course.* "I said I'd stay nearby and look after you."

"I could have shot you."

"Mary Cat?" His voice sounds funny this time. He comes out from the stream side. Just a shadow shape in the dark. He must be camped in that grassy patch where I like to sit and watch the minnows in the stream sometimes. "Mary Cat, if Henny doesn't come?" It's a question. He's even asking after he heard my witchy hollering.

Maybe it's because I was just now scared by what I thought was a bear, and I'm so glad it turned out to be Fay instead, or maybe I'm scared in general about my whole life which I am, but I say, "Yes. The answer is yes. You're a good person. Do you want to come in?"

"No, and I'll be gone tomorrow morning. I'll just be here at night."

"Come on. Have some of Aunt Henriette's pie."

I can practically hear in the scuffling noise that he's tempted, and then he comes. We hug but my stomach is in the way. Then he kisses me, so lightly, so shyly, on the cheek, as if a moth flew by.

Good Fay. Wonderful Fay.

Two days later and I've given up (though I already gave up a long time ago, before I even came out here). It's morning. I go to the icy creek to wash a little except, in my condition, it's hard to lean over enough to really do it, and the water's too cold. I like to watch it streaming by, though. Usually I see trout.

I'm on my way back to the shack when I hear a horse, already nearby. I stand still, shivering, wondering … wondering *everything*. Have they come for me or could it finally be?…

I stand. I just stand there. I couldn't move if I wanted to.

He stares.

All rumpled and ragged and pitiful and beat up and with the most ragged, pitiful, beat-up little dog in a pannier basket behind him. My daydream man … my poor prince on his big gray horse, come to sweep me off my feet.

He slides off his horse still staring at me. He steps back, away from me. And again, steps away. And away.

He didn't know! Exactly like Charlotte said, it never occurred to him that such a thing could happen.

He makes a couple of funny noises that make me think of the squeaks I kept making when I was out here alone before. I never thought *he'd* squeak.

But … And now … For a moment it's just like that other time, his eyes flickering all around, and then he can't look at me any more. He gets back on his horse—grabs the pommel and leaps up the way he does, right over the dog—and gallops off. Nobody ever does that—gallops off at full tilt in the middle of all these stones and brush. And I'm just left here. He can't stand it ... Me. Can't face me. I'm so ... I know I'm a painful sight. I'm a painful sight even to myself. This is the end for sure.

I try to call out "Please," and "Wait," but my voice is hooked up some way and doesn't sound out. "Henny. I *can't!*"

And I *can't*. I *won't*. Like he said himself. I can't bear it. I'm on my knees and then I'm all the way down (I have to go down sideways, I'm too big to go straight down), my head in the dust.

This is how it's going to be forever.

I don't know how long I lie there. I may have passed out. And then somebody is lifting me. I think: Of course, Fay, good Fay ... But it's Hen! He's holding me up. He's carrying me into his hut—to his cot. He's kneeling by me and has his arm around me. (His stump around me, I'm on his wrong side.)

"My God, Mary Catherine. I didn't know. I should have thought ... And I left you ... to do it all alone."

"It's all right. I'm going to marry Fay."

I know that's not the right thing to say now, when we've just met again after so long. I guess I want to shake him up—or *see* if I can shake him, but I shouldn't, he's already shaken up enough. It should be just one thing at a time.

"Don't do that." Then he's hugging me so tight it hurts and I wonder if he's hurting the baby. "Please don't marry Fay. Don't worry, I'll love you. I *will* love you. I really will."

What a strange way to put it, as if he's trying to convince himself more than me. Which I guess he is. Or it's like the first time he made love to me and he isn't inside himself at all and has to tell himself what he ought to do.

"Stay with me." And then he says, "Some of the time."

I suppose he's trying to tell me he still won't marry. And I don't care. I never did care. I don't even care what's best for the baby anymore.

"Except," ... He says, "You'd be right to marry Fay. It's the right thing."

"All I want is to be with you. You know that. I was with you in town and not married. I just want to be where you are."

"I have to be by myself. You'd have to take me as I am."

"I always have."

"Fay would be a damn good husband, and I … You used to have this smile. I used to love your smile and I … and I …" Then nothing but sputtering and stuttering and the way his eyes look around all over the place. Is he going to cry at last? But he isn't. *Of course* he isn't. Instead he gets up and walks away. That's because he *was* going to cry. Poor Hen.

But just as I'm thinking, Poor Hen, he says, "Poor waif," and comes and kneels beside the cot again. "Poor waif. I'll never make you happy."

"But I *am* happy."

Can't he see that? I've hardly ever been this happy. We'll be doing all those things I haven't done. We'll make plans. We'll think of names. With Henny here … or *someplace* … nearby, I don't care how many people at our ranch or over at Henny's think the baby belongs to them.

Things are never solved. I know that. But as long as I *sort of* have him, I'll take that.

"I'm happy. You make me so happy."

Henny

THIS ISN'T HAPPY!

He wants to shout it. Why is she always so happy at nothing? *Always* that way: a view from a hill, a ragged bunch of wildflowers, and himself, only around when *he* feels like it … Why couldn't she ask for what's her due? In her state her due? Too ignorant to know she isn't happy. You have no right to be so happy. Accepting so little. Accepting crumbs. He doesn't say any of that, what he says is, "You're a pretty girl. You deserve more than just this—more than just me."

She looks so tired. Even her hair looks tired. Hands as usual, worn and scratched and ragged fingernails. Her eyes, red rimmed. She used to light up all over. She used to have the most remarkable smile. She'd get pretty in half a minute. Wriggle like a puppy. She's not so pretty now. He does these things to people. All the time. Always.

Always.

And now he gasps. It's blood all over. Again. But it's Uncle Bill this time. That had never been one of his visions before, but here it is, bloody Uncle Bill, blood all over the place and Uncle Bill holding himself together, gasping, gasping as he's gasping now himself, and the pasture, lush and green and full … full of iris. Same color as the violets back in France. And Papa yelling. "Help him. Get my horse. Gallop. Get the wagon." And he did, but it was too late. Everything is always too late.

"It's too late."

He's on the floor again. "Hen! Henny! It's not too late."

She's gotten up from the cot, forgetting all about herself—for his sake as always, holds him. And here's the dog, jumped out of the basket and come to him. He's getting licked all over, held, loved …

Like before, he wants to knock her down and take her. Anything to get rid of the vision. *Anything!* But there's a baby—here between them. He can feel it against him. He can't do things like that now. He has to wait it through, until he can breathe.

214

Licked all over. Held. Loved.

He leans his head against the baby. His baby. Oh, my God!

And when he can breathe: "I see things ... Mary Catherine. I see things that aren't there. Blood, blood and body parts. Pieces of people. Shoes, wrists with wristwatches. Shredded clothes, shredded skin, hanging. Like off a clothes line. I hear explosions that aren't there. Things bursting inside my head—inside my ears. I'm half-deaf from it. And we don't know each other. Not in any real way. You don't know how I have a sore back all the time."

She says, "Oh Henny."

"Don't stick with me because of sympathy. That's a bad reason. It doesn't last. Listen, you have to face it. It's as if you don't even know I'm crippled. *I was left-handed for heaven's sake.*"

"I don't think you're crippled, and I don't love Fay. It's you I love."

"Can't you ... *Won't* you ever see what's real! Look at me." He tears at his shirt, rips it down over his stump. "*Look* at me!"

But she doesn't care.

"I won't marry."

"You've told me that a thousand times."

"But I won't leave you. I'll never leave you. Not *really.*"

Mary Catherine

Hen's mother—Grandma—stays here all the time now. (She brought over a rocking chair, brand-new, bought just for me, but she and Abel sit in it as much as I do. She says after the baby comes it'll be just for me alone.) Hen doesn't stay here, except sometimes. He seems embarrassed in front of everybody, but then he always *has* felt that way ever since I first knew him. His mother doesn't make quite so much of a fuss over him as all the others do, but he's uncomfortable with everybody but Fay and Abel.

(That poor little dog! … But Abel is happy with it. He whispers in Henny's ear, something long, and when I ask Hen afterwards, what he said was, "Thank you, thank you, thank you, thank you," about fifteen times.)

Hen's father comes over to talk to Hen alone. They're all trying to convince him to marry me. They've even gone to talk to a preacher. I think they've even set a date, and the place is supposed to be Hen's family's ranch of course. Hen's mother tells me, again and again, she doesn't understand why I don't care if I'm married or not. I think to tell her: it's because I love him and I want him to do what he needs to do, but *she* loves him, too, just as much as I do, so instead I say, "I guess it's because that's the way I grew up myself. I really don't know any better. I'm a … you know what I am."

But she hugs me like she does and says, "Nonsense." (She always says things right out like that. I like it.) "And you care as much as I do." She's right, I care, but I care more that Hen should do what he needs to do.

"Maybe he'll change," I say. "Maybe he'll get less crazy one of these days. Grandma, he told me … He said he sees and hears things that aren't there—*dreadful* things, blood all over."

But I've made her sad. She looks away, off into nothing just as Hen did when he didn't want to let himself cry. I say, "Grandma!" real loud. That reminds her of the baby and makes her feel better right away. It always does.

She says, "Well what *do* you do if your son gets a nice girl in trouble and won't marry?"

"I'm not in trouble. I'm here with all of you helping me and I do have Henny in a sort of a way."

"But what if you wanted that grandchild to have every chance in the world? What would you do in my place? And you might be one of these days."

"Grandma, why is this baby so special to everybody? You have eight grandchildren, why do you care so much about this one, and why does Charlotte care so much?"

"I don't suppose Charlotte will ever have any children of her own, and you know how close she and Henny are. For me, maybe it's because … my poor youngest—my only son, and I've hoped so many hopes for him. First I was so glad he wasn't killed, and now … He's having such a hard time. I had all these hopes, and then you came and I hoped again. It may not seem like it to you, but you're two of a kind in some ways."

I don't see that at all: I haven't been in a war or anything, and I've had a pretty good life all along, what with my teacher standing up for me and then taking me in, and then all my prizes, but I don't ask how come because she's looking so thoughtful and so sad again.

But all the time everybody *still* keeps trying to talk Hen into marrying, even Charlotte. They just don't stop. I tell them they should be talking to me because I won't let him anyway, so nothing can come of all this talk. I tell them *I'm* the one they have to convince, and I refuse to marry unless Hen wants me to.

I know he would never be able to stand a really big wedding like everybody wants, especially his sisters. They've been planning it even though Hen won't ever let it happen. He just won't be there, but they don't pay attention. Those sisters are like little girls. It's as if they've had it on their minds since he was born, and I'll bet they have. Baby brother's wedding. I'll bet they played that game lots of times.

They want to have me in a white dress. I can picture that, me, big as the barn, let alone the barn door.

Well, at least they're having fun. Maybe even *they* know it really isn't going to happen.

Hen lies with his head on my stomach. He likes to feel the baby moving. He's calm here. Even seems happy. So am I. I can keep my hand on the back of his head. I can hold my hand on top of his when he holds my stomach. He'd like me out at the hut with him some, but nobody will let me go there now, so he comes here—more and more as it gets closer and closer. We spend a lot of time alone—or they're letting us be alone a lot. I suppose they want to give Hen plenty of chances to ask me to marry him. He did give me a ring, but didn't say a word about what for, and it's not a wedding kind of ring, anyway. (He ordered away for it. I'd have liked to go someplace with him to buy it, but I like it a lot anyway. It's delicate and kind of French-looking.) He brought the carriage here so I can go places without too much bouncing. He's so careful and gentle and generous, but when he brought the carriage over, he'd been in another fight. And of course he still trembles all the time. (Except when he listens to my stomach.) Sometimes he can't hardly light his cigarette. Not everything has changed.

I ask Hen about the little scars all over his front, and he says he doesn't know what happened. He says he woke up with people picking little metal splinters out of him. "I love the scars," I say. That makes him laugh.

Then he asks me about that arrow on the back of my hand. He says, "You don't have to tell me if you don't want to."

I say, "That was back when I was young and foolish—when I was nineteen."

"I thought you were nineteen now."

"I am."

He hugs me then. He says, "That hug is because you had to grow up so fast and sudden."

I have names picked out. He wanted me to pick them all by myself, so I did. After a long time thinking I thought, Fayette. Fay would like that, and I owe him a lot. And then everybody would know this baby is half-French. And I want Charlotte for if it's a girl. I tell Hen I'd name a girl Henriette because I love his mother so much, but I don't care for that name, not in English. I like it in French, though.

"Two hands," he says, when he first sees the baby, as if: how did that happen?—as if a miracle, and it is, all of it is. "He's all there," I say. I was glad of that, too. Hen opens each soft tiny curled-up hand and kisses the palms. I'm thinking: maybe piano hands—I hope piano hands, ragtime hands, but I wouldn't say that in front of Hen.

I don't want to do anything but look at the baby. Grandma says I shouldn't spend every single minute of my life (and the baby's) rocking him and holding him, but I can't help it, he smells so good and his skin is so silky. In some ways I even want to show him off to my mother, as if: Look what I did—this absolutely perfect being! But another part of me hopes I'm rid of her for good. I feel like keeping that pistol in my pocket all the time and pulling it out the moment she comes. I'd say, "This is one thing you'll never take from me in a million years." Except I don't want that pistol anywhere near the baby.

I will never call *my* mother Grandma. Never!

I don't think I'm ever going to be sad in my life again. I just know it. I can feel it. Of course I worry something will happen to the baby, but he's got a lot of protectors here. If he's not supposed to be held and picked up and cooed at all the time, well, he's just out of luck. Even Grandma keeps doing it herself.

Hen brought his cot from the hut (Charlotte's old bed is so little) and sleeps beside me and helps with the baby. Grandma was going to do that, but he wanted to. She said it was a good thing for him to be doing. And it was, because later, on one of those nights when the baby wakes us (which he does at least twice a night), Hen brings him to me to nurse, and then he cuddles up behind me on Charlotte's narrow bed, holding both of us; we're both half-sitting up against the pillows, and he gives me two big hugs, like signals—signals that I don't need to wonder anymore what he means by them ...

"Marry me," he says. "Marry me secretly, just the two of us ... just the three of us. We'll go to town as soon as you're able to get around. Don't tell anybody."

So I don't.

Abel

THE RANCH IS DOING fine and finer. That's because they've got me. I do everything. I picked currants and after I cooked currant pancakes. I moved three new bulls all by myself—prize bulls—big ones. I went to the village and got hay all by myself. I needed a little help with the bails, but Henny said it won't be long before I'll be able to do it by myself. I can saddle up if I stand on a stone or a fence railing. I helped Charlotte dig a new ditch. Things are freshly painted and I did a lot of that. We have flowers all over the place. I do the vegetables because I know how from before when I had my pumpkins. Our new ditch waters everything nice as could be.

Aunt Henriette says she's glad the baby looks exactly like Cocky-Hen. She says maybe he won't be thinking about himself so much now. She says when Cocky-Hen was a baby, he had a full head of black hair just like this baby. To me she said, "Not like you, Pumpkin Top, all you had was red fuzz. Nice fuzz, though." Aunt Henriette says she hasn't seen a man so all wound up with a tiny baby like Cocky-Hen since my father with my big brother, the big Fayette. She thinks the baby is the best thing that ever happened to Henny since the war ended, and that now maybe there's more hope.

I'm going to teach the little bitty Fayette to climb. Last time I climbed the barn roof Mary Cat had to come up after me, but I'll come down any time she says "Pancakes." Any time she says "Come on down and pinch me."

One of these days I'm supposed to go to school. I might. Mary Cat and Charlotte say I need to be with other children but I don't know why. Why? My great big brother, Fay, ran away from the school so much they couldn't make him go. I might do that.

I'm just about exactly the same amount older than the little Fayette as the big Fayette is older than me. That's a lucky thing.

Aunt Henriette thinks Mary Cat is happier than she ought to be. She thinks she should be sad because she's not married to anybody. She has a nice ring, though, with little blue stones all along the sides.

Maybe Mary Cat will marry me when I grow up. I'll ask her now so she'll know to wait. Then I'd be the father of the baby instead of the big brother. I know how to be a big brother because of Fay, but since I never had a dad, I don't know how to be one. Fay knows, he had one. Mary Cat doesn't know. Charlotte knows except she never knew her *real* dad.

One good thing, Mary Cat will be living here all the time for sure now: me and her and Charlotte and the little bitty Fayette and sometimes Cousin Henny-Cock and Cat-the-Pig and Bird-the-Dog. (Dogs are better than pigs for having fun, and every time I yell, "Come on, Birdie," I get to laugh like anything. "Come on Cow Pat. Come on Road Apple. Road Apple Dumpling." We run like anything. If a person heard me yelling "Come on Apple Dumpling," they wouldn't even know enough to know it was funny.)

Fay was here, but we don't need him so he's gone again. He said he'd be back in the spring. He talks a lot now, so I guess maybe I will, too. Pretty soon, but not yet. I like Caw. It fools them. They have to try and guess. I talk real talk to Mary Cat's baby. I whisper him things. Anyway, caw is real talk, too. If you're a crow it is.

I'm the one-and-only honorary big brother, and there won't ever be another.

Mary Cat and Catty-Pig and Birdie-Dog and Cocky-Henny … That makes a really good song. Cocky-Henny's here most of the time now, but never when there's lots of folks around. He doesn't like hardly more than two people at a time. He says that doesn't count me. He'll be with me any time.

Cocky-Henny put in a lot of hay so we'll need extra help come summer, but now we don't. We have me.

CAROL EMSHWILLER has been widely published in literary, feminist, and science fiction magazines. She is the author of the short story collections *The Start of the End of It All, Joy in Our Cause,* and *Verging on the Pertinent* and the novels *Carmen Dog* and *Ledoyt.* Her work has been anthologized in *Intersections, Roger Caras's New Treasury of Cat Stories, Insights: Creating & Performing, The Penguin Book of Erotic Stories by Women,* and *Dangerous Visions,* among other publications. She lives in New York City, where she teaches fiction writing at New York University. She spends her summers in Bishop, California, near the setting for *Ledoyt* and *Leaping Man Hill.*

"First and foremost, Emshwiller is a poet—
with a poet's sensibility, precision, and magic. She revels in the
sheer taste of words, she infuses them with an
extraordinary vitality and sense of life."
—*Newsday*

*Designed and typeset
in Adobe Caslon and Eastwood by Kirsten Janene-Nelson
after the design by David Peattie for* Ledoyt. *Editorial and production
work by K. Janene-Nelson and Justin Edgar at Mercury House,
San Francisco, and printed on 55" Glatfelter Natural paper
by Bang Printing, Brainerd, Minnesota.*